The Year
of the Rat

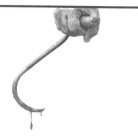

Robin McFarland

Published by Plot Press Limited
P O Box 38,
Christchurch 7546,
Canterbury,
NEW ZEALAND.

First Published 2014

First Edition

The author has asserted his moral rights in the work.

The Year of the Rat is a work of fiction. Any similarities to persons living or dead are entirely coincidental.

Cover Design & Photography by Chris Winstanley.

ISBN 978-0-473-30695-3
ePub ISBN 978-0-473-30696-0
Kindle ISBN 978-0-473-30697-7

All things truly wicked start from an innocence...

Ernest Hemingway – *A Moveable Feast*

Also By Robin McFarland

Salt of the Earth

A Novel of Short Stories

Some readers' comments on *Salt of the Earth*:

"… these stories are superb…and need recognition nationally" – Kaite Hansen, Canterbury.

"'The Incredible Melting Woman' nearly killed me, that's how hard I laughed. – Bernie, Te Puke.

"I so very much enjoyed the wonderful stories..." – Eleanor, Auckland.

"...absolutely fantastic...a pleasure to read..." – Chris, Auckland.

"Thanks...very much enjoyed it, and will spread the word". – Tim, Auckland.

"Like your book, had to get it on Kindle in UK." – Steve, ex UK, now Christchurch.

"...don't usually feel inspired to write to a (fellow) author but want to congratulate you..." – Janet, New Plymouth.

Salt of the Earth has also been adapted as a ten-part series by Radio New Zealand.

The Rime of the Venal Insurer

The Rime of the Venal Insurer is a recently published work. It is a narrative poem based on Coleridge's *Rime of the Ancient Mariner*, and is a satirical take on the insurance industry in the wake of the Canterbury earthquakes of 2010 and 2011.

Preamble

One naturally hesitates when writing about a personality like Bruce Campbell, even if he is fictional. Will the reader think that you, the writer, are approving of, or even advocating, the sort of behaviour indulged in by the character? Worse, will they think that you *are* that character, or that the story is in some way thinly disguised autobiography? In fact, should you just write happy stories about fields and flowers and a world where lambs snuggle up to lions, and where no evil exists?

But of course, most fiction depends upon the tension created between what we commonly accept as good and evil. Without the murders, Macbeth might have been just another Scottish king. Without the goading of his father's ghost to avenge his death, Hamlet would have been no more than another mildly troubled young man with a few oedipal problems. Take away the folly of adultery and Anna Karenina might have been just another bored Russian aristocrat. In fact, until the serpent crept into the garden we had not become human – that is how important evil is to us.

And so Bruce Campbell sets off down life's path as a bullied schoolboy. His Road to Damascus experience occurs when he is fifteen, and it will drive the course of his life as he evolves from victim to simple obsessive, to brutal martinet, to psychopath.

I imagine most people wonder what could drive a person to kill another person. Is killing in fact a sane and normal thing to do? As a society we reject killing, unless it is sanctioned by the state. That is, we are not permitted, as individuals, to decide on motives for killing. But if we're asked to go and kill people in a foreign country because its inhabitants think differently from us, we're expected to do it without question.

So it is frowned upon to kill another human being whom we intuitively feel may threaten us in some way, but it's okay to kill that same human being if we are told that he or she threatens our nation.

And yet, I imagine that in Palaeolithic or Neolithic times there may have been great survival value in knocking the odd person off. It might have given you access to more food, a better partner, or more valuable real estate. Or it might simply have removed a threat to your own continued existence. Therefore, selective killing gave you a better chance of survival and of passing on your DNA.

Enter the psychopath, a personality for whom things are quite clear cut. Whereas most people will dither around if they feel what they're about to do will adversely affect someone else, the psychopath is not so constrained. These people act boldly, without recrimination, and without fear of consequence. They apparently lack what we call empathy, so can therefore inflict suffering on others without becoming bogged down in some moral miasma.

The definition of a psychopath was once quite explicit, and "deviations", which we now consider quite normal, such as homosexuality, used to come within its ambit, presumably because they were considered immoral. Therefore, psychopathy was a moral dilemma rather than a psychological one – a matter of choice rather than compulsion.

These days psychopathy is considered to exist along a continuum, with simple doesn't-quite fit-in sociopathy at one end and the ruthless serial killer at the other.

In fact, it now seems that many psychopaths can subsume what may be their baser instincts, and survive quite well, embedded in "normal" society. Imagine the advantages, for example, of not being constrained by social convention. Imagine how you could soar to the heights of giant corporations, leaving others trampled behind in your wake. Imagine earning a multi-million dollar salary, while half of the world's children starve, and feeling not a pang of guilt. Imagine how you could bring the world's economy to its knees through questionable business practices, and still happily walk away with a fat bonus. What stood us in good stead in the jungle can equally stand us in good stead in the jungles of politics or business.

But what you cannot do in civilised society is to simply go out and maim or kill someone. Society draws the line there. Society can sort of understand killing if it is fuelled by testosterone, perhaps assisted by alcohol. And in sort of understanding it, society is prepared to grant a bit of leeway, particularly if the killer is immediately remorseful. Indeed, things become even more blurred when motive is taken into account. What if one were being attacked? What if one were defending one's loved ones, or property? Such excuses may not get you off scot free, but they'll inevitably attract a less weighty sentence.

But the simple cold-blooded killer? No; we cannot accept that. We cannot, we say, even comprehend it. And yet that simple cold-blooded killer may be doing no more than responding to genetic data that was coded into his ancestor – a man who jealously guarded his cave, who didn't wait to be knocked on the head by some upstart, but who took matters into his own hands and resolved such problems before they arose.

So, *The Year of the Rat* is the result of my own musings on how a personality might disintegrate when it is not governed by social norms, and when it becomes obsessed with another person.

Certainly, in writing it, I am indebted to the long history of killing in fiction. The ritualistic dance that surrounded love and life and death in Malory's *Morte d'Arthur* is always fascinating, with its confusion of perfection and imperfection and its clearly defined social morays to which all knights must aspire, but to which only one will ever succeed.

Equally, the types of personality that are drawn in more recent fiction: Lafcadio in Andre Gide's *Les Caves du Vatican*, Humbert Humbert in Nabokov's *Lolita*, and Patrick Bateman in Bret East Ellis's *American Psycho* all seem to push the Nietzschean boundary of individual freedom to its natural and logical conclusion. That is, in a world without meaning, any act is as sensible as any other. Therefore, if you simply shrug off social convention and respond to whatever instinct stirs you, then you are ultimately free.

And yet, somehow that freedom comes at a price. Because while evil might have made us human, exercising the right to indulge that evil again makes us inhuman.

Rob McFarland
Banks Peninsula
November 2014

Chapter 1

I raised Christ to my lips, and saw my reflection: goggle-eyed Caliban. Beyond the rim, you, restless, toe-kicking, fingers trailing on burnished rimu. Nothing in that place – neither marble font, nor gilded chalice, nor even God Himself could dim your beauty.

You shrugged at the patched white shawl until it fell, and hung insolently from one shoulder.

Rags! You were thirteen, and yet with that one shrug you defined two lives.

Chapter 2

Fifty years scoot past, and I find myself in a small squat up a blind alley in Aranui, no more than a beer bottle's throw from what is generally considered to be the worst street in Christchurch. By "worst" I mean sociologically, economically, although the street itself is no oil painting. Here we struggle, and to emphasise the seriousness of our struggle we maim and kill each other. We join; we affiliate, and we patch ourselves to demonstrate our discontent. Money is short. Many of us would find it hard to put a decent pinot gris on the table. That is how bad it is.

How I ended up here is as much a mystery to me as it is to my neighbours, or would be if they cared enough to think about it. Look at me: a lily-white, male professional – the three tickets, I'm given to understand, to a cushy seat at life's banquet. I've even been called "reasonably good-looking" and "quite well-built", although, admittedly, much of my musculature seemed to evaporate during the time I was in prison, and has refused to return. I'm tertiary educated, I have (make that "had") a reputable profession, with a solid work record behind me. I should have been a contender for, Christ's sake! I don't know what for, but something! Like a respectable habit that I could at least maintain without worry; or failing that, a nice comfy retirement would have sufficed. But it hasn't worked out that way.

Come February 22nd 2011 I'd been tolerating these less-than-desirable circumstances for a few days shy of a month, believing that things could get no worse, when they did. The earthquake that knocked *me* arse over tip also knocked the shack arse over tip, so that it then sat askew on its foundations, its windows cracked and its bricks crumbling. Holes gaped in its buckled roof, and buckets of used paint tins pilfered from the local rubbish dump now collected rain water. Walk in the front door and you'd find yourself accelerating to a canter by the time you'd covered the few metres to the back. The rats came and went as they pleased, scampering through holes in the walls, from which plasterboard now hung in ragged garlands. Birds tweeted in the ceiling space. A thing I came to know as "liquefaction" had sprung up in the small wilderness that passed for my back yard.

For weeks I had to share a temporary public toilet, provided courtesy of Christchurch City Council, and in so doing came to know my neighbours and their bowel movements much better. I was given bottled water to drink. I complained to the landlord, mentioning the fact that I was paying good money. He immediately countered with the fact that I was paying probably the lowest rental in the city, seemingly on an as-I-pleased basis, and that I was, by his reckoning, almost a thousand dollars in arrears. And anyway, he said. Think of the rest of Christchurch. I should consider myself lucky.

Bugger the rest of Christchurch! If living in a leaking, sloping, rat-infested pig pen in some mean little back street is lucky, then the rest of Christchurch is welcome to my luck. So I did what I usually do: calmed myself with a couple of drinks and told myself, well, at least it couldn't get any worse. That argument, by the way, is connected to the fallacy that there's always someone worse off than you. Well, think about it. That logic can't be applied to the person who is the worst off in the world so, like my roof, it just doesn't hold water. I'm not trying to say that I *was* that worst off person; in fact, right then I can't have been, because things were about to get even worse.

Until recently I owned a car. It was my one possession of any real worth – a twenty-one year old white Honda City, leopard-spotted with rust. Some things at twenty-one are undeniably past their prime, women and cars amongst them. This thing belched and farted and rattled, and as a visual reminder of its distress, emitted vast clouds of what seemed like smoky steam. I steered it clear of mechanics, fearing a negative diagnosis. I had resigned myself to the fact that it was not long for this world, and used it sparingly. But it went. It went until one night it went into a bridge abutment in Avonside Drive, with me at the helm, a little the worse for wear.

It was, I don't know – late. It was dark, and I tend to lose track of time once the sun goes down. I don't like the nights much. In this case the darkness had been exacerbated, apparently, by the fact that I'd forgotten to flick on the Honda's lights. I sat there, stunned, as you do, hoping it was a dream. I think I may have been rubbing at my chest, where it had collided with the steering wheel, because I hadn't been wearing a seat belt. If I'd been wearing a seat belt I'd have been rubbing my chest where it had been bruised by the seat belt. I'd once calculated, in an idle moment no doubt, that the average person, entering and exiting a car twenty times a week, and taking ten seconds to fasten a seat belt, and then another ten seconds to unfasten it, would waste more than 666 hours over the course of an eighty year life just buckling and unbuckling seat belts. That's almost a month! If you were down to your last month, wouldn't you rather spend it in some better way than mucking around with a seat belt? Anyway, it was my life, and it wasn't up to much at the time, so I decided to forgo the seat belt in favour of the extra few hours. I acknowledge it's a gamble, but at present I'm still ahead.

But there I was, rubbing at my chest, when I heard this braying woman's voice. It was a young voice; I could see glimpses of a young face through the shattered windscreen. I seemed to be wandering, not physically, but mentally, and I briefly had the impression that I was floating under cracked ice, and that she was calling to me from above.

"Shaun! Shaun!" she was saying.

"No, Bruce," I felt myself whimpering, my voice eerie and dream-like.

She had one of those new phones that do anything, and right then this phone was being a torch, and she was shining it through the cracked windscreen of my Honda City.

"Oh my God! Oh my God!" Her voice came, muted by the windscreen and semi-consciousness. "Shaun! Quick! There's, like, an old guy in there! Call the cops!"

Consciousness surged back in. Wrong call, lady! There were dozens of things I needed before I needed a cop. A tow truck would have been the obvious one; an ambulance, that might have been nice. A drink – I could really have gone a drink! In actual fact, I was about to get everything, except the drink. Soon Shaun was on the scene with *his* phone, and it was also being a torch. Together they had me pinned in beams of light as bright as the midday sun.

"Y'oright, mate?"

This was my new mate, Shaun. He'd poked his mouth through the small gap that existed at the top of my driver's door window, because the winder doesn't work. I could feel his breath steaming over my face, and remember thinking vaguely that it smelled of cannabis. I remember thinking, too, that "all right" was a relative term, and that I was "all right" relative to, say, a starving, one-legged, leprous pauper in a war-ravaged banana republic, but not "all right" relative to, say, Bill Gates. My condition lay somewhere in that middle ground. Nodding seemed to be the best option, so I tried, but there was something wrong with my neck. It hesitated when I asked it to go backwards and forwards. It went from side to side a bit, and I don't know quite what Shaun made of that. So then I tried to speak, to reassure him that all was well, in a relative sense, and a kind of gurgle came out. That, I think, was because of the blood I was swallowing from the nose that had been broken when it had come into rapid contact with the windscreen.

It was at this point that Shaun came over all butch and took matters in hand. I heard him talking to someone on his phone, snatched phrases of "old guy"; "blood"; "dying". Dying? *Dying!* Bugger off! I felt like saying to him. I'm not dying! I just need a bloody drink! He must have dialled 111, because after that there was only blackness, and when I awoke it was to find myself in a hospital bed wearing a neck brace.

A couple of fractured ribs, the broken shnoz, of course, a problem in my neck that *might* be a dislocated vertebra, or *might* just be a strain, the x-rays had been pretty inconclusive, and well, this *was* a pretty well-used neck, anyway. My knees were pretty well buggered, but they'd been pretty well buggered before they met the underside of my dashboard at great speed. But on the whole I was considered to have been "pretty lucky". There seemed to be a lot of prettiness in my situation.

"I should buy a lottery ticket with all the luck I'm having," I joked to the doctor who was pottering about my bed, and who had just delivered the good news to me.

She was Asian, and looked very young – too young to be making life and death decisions. But spoke impeccable English, and bustled about as if she knew what she was doing. She looked me over with what I could only interpret as disdain. Admittedly, I could have prepared myself better, and would have done so had I known my night out would end in such disarray. It goes to show that your mother's advice about always wearing clean underwear, in case you get hit by a bus, is not without foundation. I could have said, with one hundred per cent certainty, that my underwear was not clean. My free hand, the one that was not attached to a drip, wandered over my unshaven chin, up into my matted hair. Now that I thought about it, even *I* could detect the sour odour of alcohol working its way out of my pores, and infecting the small room I was sharing with Doctor Sung. So pungent was it that it was trumping the smell of cleanliness and disinfectant.

"We were obliged to take an evidential blood test," said Doctor Sung, and I believe I detected a trace of smugness.

So the upshot was that I now have neither a car, nor a driver's licence. I do, however, have an invoice from the St John's Ambulance people. I don't know which St John they commemorate in their name. St John the Baptist is the patron saint of, obviously, baptism, but also bird dealers, tailors, hail and hailstorms, religious converts, printers, lambs, motorways, farriers, cutters and Dodge City. He also keeps an eye on epileptics, convulsive children and generally people with any sort of disorder involving spasms. He's a busy bloke; but so is St John the Apostle, who looks after bookbinders and printers (who are so easily seduced by evil that they need two saints to hold it at bay), booksellers and authors, tanners, theologians and typesetters, painters, papermakers and engravers, lithographers, compositors and editors. And in his spare time he deals with poisoning and burns and Milwaukee, Wisconsin. Neither John puts his hand up for ambulance drivers.

But my point is, I can't see either of these Johns firing off a bill to some poor unfortunate they'd picked up by the wayside. The ambulance people seemed immune to this argument, and the matter eventually went to a debt collector, where it will no doubt be filed along with the many others they have collected on my behalf. That, for me, has become the meaning of a debt collector – someone who collects these outstanding debts, and manages them on my behalf.

After some quite heated debate, the tow truck chap decided to accept the remnants of the Honda, and to sell it off for scrap, given my stated inability to pay; but there is now a court fine to contend with, and talk that I may be charged for cosmetic repairs to the bridge abutment. Cosmetic repairs? Have you seen Christchurch recently? I drew the analogy of applying a coat of paint to one rivet on the submerged Titanic, but again it fell on deaf ears.

So that's me, as of a few weeks ago. Sounds bad, doesn't it? But, believe it or not, my life was poised to continue its downward spiral.

I hadn't always been dogged by bad luck, though. Ho, no! There had once been a time when old Bruce Campbell BA had set his sights firmly on a meteoric rise. To mediocrity and beyond! For generations, that had been the Campbell motto!

Chapter 3

I was born in the year of the Rat, 1948, which makes me clever and wealthy and hard-working. I'm also sanguine, popular and very adaptable. If I have a damning weakness, it is that I'm stubborn and selfish, and guided solely by my own interests.

I was also born under the auspices of Sagittarius, which makes me intelligent, philosophical and inclined to call a spade a spade. But then, I'm known to be tactless, ruthless, inconsistent and overconfident. It seems we can't have everything.

Of course, I believe none of this. Rat? For God's sake, get a grip! And I've yet to hear a satisfactory explanation as to how a group of randomly dispersed stars can influence the character of someone born hundreds or thousands of light years away. They don't look much like a centaur even now, those stars, but give them another couple of million years of galactic evolution, and they could just as easily look like a frog; and how would that affect my character?

I'm more than happy to go with the old nature/nurture argument when it comes to character, and I tend to come down more heavily in the nature camp. If your father was a useless piece of shit, there's a reasonable chance you'll follow in his footsteps. Try to break the genetic mould at your own peril!

Take us Campbells, for instance. The name itself is a synthesis of two old Gaelic words, "Cam" and "Béal", which translates roughly as meaning "crooked mouthed", or more kindly, "wry mouthed". My mouth is not crooked, although I have a dryness about me that can induce wryness, when, I am told, I have a lop-sided smile. But stubborn? Ruthless? Well, we have only go back a little more than four hundred years, to Glencoe, to see how the Campbells dealt to the Macdonalds, and it doesn't get much more stubborn and ruthless than that!

"Memory is strong," wrote Eliot, of Glencoe, "Beyond the bone. Pride snapped/Shadow of pride is long..."

Pride. A silly human failing. But I doubt there's a Campbell or a Macdonald in all of creation who has not been steeped in the hatred that trickled down from that single slip of the sword. Although, perhaps I credit my ancestors with too much conviction. They were, after all, descended from some sort of crofter underclass, bullied from pillar to post by landlords, by the English, and probably by vengeful Macdonalds.

They sailed, these ancestors, assisted into Port Chalmers in the early 1870's, having heard that the land was awash with gold. They fossicked briefly, failed, and then settled for a life of sweat and toil in the West Coast mines. Good, solid work that no doubt at least put porridge on the table. Here, as in their native land, they became drudges for those with more money, more aptitude, more skill and more sense. My branch of the Campbells peeled off and settled in Auckland around the time of the Great Depression.

When I appeared, in the Year of the Rat, I can say with almost absolute certainty that my appearance would not have been welcome. I believe my parents' marriage had been a shaky alliance from day one. My father performed some sort of manual work down on the waterfront, we lived in a rented flat in Freeman's Bay, which was not the upwardly mobile area it is now, and my father pre-spent ninety percent of his weekly wage at Gleeson's pub, which was but a short stagger from where he worked. Make what you will of that, Mr Micawber! Result: misery.

One of my earliest memories is of good old Dad lying like a cast sheep in our front garden, being berated by my mother. He made some vain attempt to defend himself, but then pissed his pants and went to sleep. It says something about my mother, I suppose, that she covered him with a blanket before we went inside and ate whatever she'd been able to cobble together – offal, or an oxtail if we'd been lucky. Often it was no more than a heel of bread with a smear of butter or pan drippings. The upside has been that, whereas most people cannot confront a cow's entrails without turning as green as tripe, and would retch at the thought of a liver or a kidney, I have no problems. Sweetbreads, trotters, testicles, udders and ears, probably; whatever the butcher had on offer that no one else wanted, I've eaten.

My parents stayed together in this yin-yang of a relationship for nine years after I was born. But whereas the opposing forces of yin and yang are intended to complement each other, my parents didn't. I could see, even as a child, that they tore each other apart. My father's drunken rants, and my mother's weeping: those are the iconic memories of my early childhood.

It was the birth of my sister that seemed to galvanise my mother into action. Somehow she'd avoided conception over the intervening nine years. Perhaps it came down to brewer's droop – a sometimes efficient, although unreliable form of contraception amongst the drinking poor. It always strikes me as rather harsh, though, when the poor are berated for being drunkards, and for giving birth to droves of children. What else do they have in life? The phrase often attributed to Marx, that religion is the opiate of the people, is equally applicable to drink or sex. Church on Sunday can mask only so much pain; there's six more days of the week that need dumbing!

So there came a day when my mother packed a small suitcase, dressed me in my best, which differed little from my worst, wrapped my sister in a shawl, and via a series of buses and a harbour ferry, we were at last delivered to my grandparent's home in Takapuna. There an abode of sorts had been prepared for us. The woodshed had proved surplus to the old couple's requirements, now that they'd "gone electric". It was a rough, timber building of no more than seven or eight square metres, and in our honour this tiny space had been lined with hardboard. Some simple, rough-sawn wooden shutters had been installed for aeration, along with a door, and there we lived for the next four years. My mother and I had single beds with matching sagging wirewoves, one against each wall, and between them squeezed the battered cot that contained my sister, Colleen. Later it would be replaced by a third bed, so that each of us would have to enter the bed from the foot. There was no additional floor space, and our clothes dangled from hangers, suspended from nails driven into the ceiling joists, and bent into hooks.

No domestic purposes then, of course. A woman foolish enough to leave the support of a perfectly good husband could expect little charity. Is there a patron saint of divorced or separated women? As unlikely, I would think, as there being a patron saint of contraception. Certainly none stepped forward to ease my mother's passage through life, and she eventually teed up a job at the local hardware store, where I later learned that she spent much of each day repelling the owner's advances.

There was the odd man in her life. She would creak the door open when she thought Colleen and I were asleep, and I would see the shadowy figures crawl onto her bed, perhaps suppressing a giggle, hear the bed protesting under the added weight, and then listen to the stifled breathing as it rose in crescendo. I cannot begrudge her this little pleasure now. Even when I was ten, although I was unsure what it was, I sensed that she needed it.

In daylight, these men would pass through my life as "uncles", sometimes showering me with sweets, occasionally delivering me a clout, and when I was twelve, after a highly publicised divorce, a divorce based on her own admitted adultery, my mother married Uncle Bill. Not in the Catholic Church, of course, but at the registry office.

Uncle Bill was a dour sort of bloke. "Practical" was how he described himself, meaning perhaps that he wasn't a thinker. He was built along the lines of Orson Welles in his declining years, had a constant butt-end dangling from his lip, but hardly drank. That, I imagine, was his major selling point. Even at twelve I recognised him as possibly the most boring man I was ever likely to meet, but he'd got us out of the woodshed. And from the woodshed we went to a compact three-bedroom home in Glenfield.

I was in Heaven. For the first time there was a semblance of normality about my life. I didn't have a father rolling around drunk amongst the petunias. I didn't have to try to explain to people why we lived in a woodshed in my grandparents' back yard, or how I'd misplaced my father. There was only Bill to explain, and that was easily enough done. I told people my father had died, and indeed, he might as well have. I told them I hated Bill, when in fact I was indifferent to him.

And then, the following year, somehow I was in a quite good secondary school.

But still I remained innocent to the fact of Lena.

Chapter 4

Non, rien de rien,
Non, je ne regrette rien...

Edith Piaf, wasn't it? Music's not my strong suit, but I do like showing off my language skills. My education may have been ultimately pointless, but at least I can now say "pointless" in four different languages – five if you count English. Don't believe me? Here:

Άσκοπος

Inutile

Sinnlos

Frustra

See? Easy as falling into disrepute! But really, kids, if you're thinking of taking up languages, take the advice of old Bruce Campbell MA (hons). Stick with Te Reo, or Chinese or something that's actually useful. Believe me, when in Rome you may very well do as the Romans do, but you won't be doing it in Latin. Better still, learn binary language; learn Parseltongue. Learn something that is of some use in this god forsaken shit hole of a world!

But *rien de rien*? Listen, Edith, if you're short on regrets, you're welcome to some of mine, because *moi, je regrette tout*. Well, if not *tout*, then certainly *beaucoup*. I've got regrets coming out my ears, Edith! Some days I start out by just regretting the fact that I've woken up, and then I move on from there.

You get these annoying people who say they wouldn't change a thing about their lives. It astonishes me! You'll have this squat, ugly toad of a bloke with a voice like fingernails on a blackboard. He's been stuck in some dead end job for the last half century, he's got five failed marriages behind him, and his kids loathe him. You're at a party, and here he is boring the tits off anyone who'll listen to him. "Ho, no!" he'll be saying. "Wouldn't change a thing!" Bullshit! If you could turn him into Russell Crowe tomorrow, you can't tell me he wouldn't jump at the chance. Okay – perhaps not Russell Crow; but you get my meaning.

So what would *I* change? Well, parents, for one. On the whole, I think I'd go for a privileged background. It opens up more opportunities to you than a father who rolls around in the petunias and a mother who struggles daily to keep a roof over your head, and to put a bit of gristle and sinew on the table.

I'd like to be taller, and I'd like to have a fuller head of hair. I started thinning in my early twenties. Looks? Well, since I ditched the glasses and got the contacts, looks haven't been too much of an issue, but twenty-twenty vision would be on my bucket list. I have had to resort back to the glasses, though, on special occasions, and the reasons for that will soon become clear.

I'd probably go in for sciences rather than the arts, because then you can do something meaningful. I could have done it. I dabbled in science quite profitably until I foolishly decided my future lay in languages. I dwell on it sometimes – it could have been me who came up with this idea of the Higgs boson particle, in which case it would be called the Campbell boson particle. Campbell's Uncertainty Principle? Well, I'm not certain if I could have made that particular quantum leap, and theoretical physics has always rather Bohr'd me, ha ha.

But you do get remembered if you do something interesting in science. Who remembers that seminal work of mine, *I Ching Influences in Mallory's Morte d'Arthur*? No one. Never mind; I've long since resigned myself to the fact that the only thing I'll ever have named after me is a brick in the wall at the crematorium. Or do you have to pay for those?

Personality aside, I think the glasses had a lot to do with my early unpopularity. I got them when I was six, and they were those thick ones that look like a back street optician has just taken the bottom out of an old glass Coke bottle. The lenses were so thick that, in the right light, they generated a prismatic effect. Under favourable circumstances, I could cast rainbows on walls just by looking at them. Even worse, due to my parents' pecuniary circumstances, a fashion statement was not possible. The frames were what you got, and they were heavy, black things, probably made from Bakelite, or even painted wood. They sat on my face like scaffolding. And it was at this time that the nickname "Goggles" was coined. Thank you Kenneth Grig!

From my side they were great. I was at first bewildered, and then amazed, to discover that the world was not, as I had thought, veiled by an unbroken haze. But when I looked in what remained of our bathroom mirror, it told me the story from the other side. The lenses were so thick as to be almost opaque. Behind them my eyes looked like a series of concentric circles –a target.

And a target I became, for every ruffian who daily dragged himself up from the slime of the slums of lower Freemans Bay, so that he could fritter away a few hours of some unfortunate teacher's time. Because no teacher would have taught at Napier Street from choice, surely. But the slums were where I came from, too – round behind the "Destructor", the giant furnace that fumed twenty-four hours a day, as it burned the city's rubbish. Its smoke and ash and toxins spewed over our cottages, as they stood shoulder to shoulder, in various states of rotting disrepair. Because we, the drinking working classes, lived where no one else would. A few Island families had even started to colour the uniform whiteness of the area.

The journey to and from school was, for me, like running a gauntlet. I'd edge out from the front door, cast a furtive eye up and down the street, and if there was no looming bully in sight, off I'd go. I had an old leather school satchel that I wore, unfashionably, as a shoulder bag. Other boys wore theirs on their backs, but that would have made me easier to grab hold of. Inside the bag, wrapped in newsprint, was my bread and dripping, or, if it had been a good week, butter. If it had been a vey good week, a scraping of Marmite. And from the front gate to the school, I would run. The more I could shorten that journey, the less chance I had of being accosted and taunted, or jostled, or pushed to the ground, or punched.

The camphor bag didn't help things. My mother had great faith in the prophylactic properties of camphor. She would buy camphor in preference to food, believing that to ward off disease was her primary function, and providing sustenance was secondary to that. The camphor bag became an issue in Standard One, when I was paired at my desk with a boy of questionable intelligence, called Graham Duncan. We were doing O's, forming series after series of this boring letter, as a precursor to cursive writing, and Duncan was not doing well. I'd been aware of him eying me, and sniffing ostentatiously, and then he started waving his arm around.

"Yes, Graham, what is it?" asked Miss Morgan.

"Please Miss; Campbell stinks!"

And thus began a second nickname: Stinkpot. Ironically, I discovered years later that a stinkpot was an incendiary weapon used in naval warfare by the Chinese – a sort of earthenware jar that would be filled with sulphur and other offensive materials, and then launched from the masthead of a junk onto the deck of an enemy ship.

I, however, was not an incendiary weapon, and I bore this second nickname with no fortitude whatsoever, being often reduced to tears. As winter moved on into spring, as the threat of disease receded, and the camphor bag was removed from around my neck, so the nickname would fade, to become nothing more than an unpleasant memory. But autumn would herald the return of the bag, and with it the return of the name.

These children were like pack animals, their nostrils flared, their senses honed to detect weakness. And once that weakness had been identified, they would home in on it, and attack. Given free reign, I believe these tormentors would have ripped me to shreds on the playing fields, or in the back streets and alleyways. But there was always some saviour – a teacher, or a passerby who would drag them off, and I could make good my escape.

It's still there, this pack instinct, and I believe it to be concealed in adults only beneath the thinnest of veneers, and sometimes not at all.

Is there anyone who regards a 1950's primary school education as a serious learning experience? Well, for me it wasn't. My learning was more by a process of accretion, than by anyone actually teaching me anything. I was too concerned with protecting my hide to worry about listening to what teachers had to say, but things stuck to me, and I suppose in that way I learned more in those first eight or ten years of life than I have in all those years that followed. I suppose everyone does. Like learning to walk, and to name things, and if you happen to be on society's underbelly, to know that those things can never be yours. You learn to recognise your mother and your father, and to recognise their absence. You learn what to like and what to fear. You learn that life is unjust, and you learn that one day you will die. You try to piece things together, and to make sense of it.

Apophenia is the name given to the human tendency, or need, even, to see a pattern in otherwise meaningless events or circumstances. Our need to see a man in the moon; our fervent wish to see the face of the mother of God in a piece of toast, or some dirty underwear; our undying belief that there *is* a God, and that He moves in mysterious ways, and that the world therefore has order and purpose.

I think much of my early life was dominated by apophenia. Hours, days, weeks were given over to trying to apply meaning to what was happening around me. I wanted connection in my life. I wanted smoothness and elegance and refinement and perfection. I wanted Grace! Instead I got my father in a bed of petunias. I got bull's testicles. Later I got my mother's laboured breathing beneath the humping shadow of a stranger. I got the taunts of strange children. The pattern I had deduced from this, by the age of twelve, was that there was no pattern.

But primary school had not been *entirely* unkind to me. There had been the occasional teacher, who had made the occasional connection, but to me it was as inexplicable as the sparking of a synapse. And then, when I reached out, I was just as often beaten. I was beaten for stealing marbles from the marble bags that hung like temptations from hooks in the cloak room, because I had no marbles. I was beaten for stealing food from brown paper lunch bags because that food, with meat and jam and cakes, was better than the bread spread with dripping that stained my newsprint with grease. I was beaten for exposing myself to Deirdre Thompson in the damp, shadowy rift between two prefabricated classrooms, albeit Deirdre Thompson was not beaten for flashing her tiny, pre-pubescent cleft at me.

In my final year of primary school, if I'd been called upon to write a thesis paper, I would have called it *The General Incomprehensibility of Other People*. Unbeknown to me, Jean-Paul Sartre had already covered much of this ground some years earlier, in *Huis Clos*: Hell is that which is not ourselves, he'd grandly proposed.

My hell was those large, physical boys who chased, caught and humiliated me. My hell was the Delphic pronouncements of Kate Largo, whose mystery promised so much, but delivered so little. My hell was the teachers and their rules and their straps.

In that apophenic tendency I found the desire to see a father in every man I met. In the uncles who trailed their odours of musk through our wood shed; in the male teachers who strapped me; in the shopkeepers and street cleaners and truck drivers who inhabited our immediate world. And what I got, eventually, was Bill.

Bill, with his perennial burned-out butt end, with his gut that hung leaden over a tightly cinched belt, with his grunts and his monosyllabic approach to conversation, was like a prosthetic father. He had been designed and made to look and act like the real thing, but would always fall short.

Because I had *known* the real thing, and he inhabited a bed of Petunias. But beyond that, I had known more; I had known his head nodding over a special meal of sausages. Even now, I can recall the laughter of that night of nights, when he wove himself into the very fabric of my life, as he draped his arm about my shoulder and said, "Y're a good boy, Bruce!" If I could have captured that vapour of alcoholic rhetoric and bottled it, my life would have had all the meaning it ever needed. But now? Now sometimes I can doubt that it ever happened.

Bill was a grocer. Society was in the process of deciding that it no longer needed grocers, and by the time I arrived in secondary school it was deciding it didn't need Bill. At least not Bill the purveyor of dour humour and dried goods. He'd had his own little Self Help shop. I can still summon up its smell of spices and the fat, salty odour of ham as he turned the handle, and wound it through the slicer. Biscuit tins lined the walls, Griffin's Aulsebrook's, a boy running, a tin of biscuits under his arm, his scarf floating behind him, happy, as if flying. You could be happy with biscuits, and here, in Uncle Bill's shop you could buy those biscuits by weight. "Half a pound of ginger nuts, please, Mr Roberts!" And he'd weigh them out on big scales, applying counterweights to one side, then tipping the biscuits into the shiny silver dish, until the balance needle hung honestly, just to the customer's side of zero. All gone. All gone, like Bill.

In nineteen sixty-two, after a period of soul-searching and despondency, Bill took a job with one of the new supermarkets. He managed the section that stretched five aisles, from toilet cleaners to potato chips. He stacked shelves with pre-packaged biscuits and rice and sago. He could even get you wheat for your chooks if you needed it, because that was how much he cared. But ham was now beyond his ambit. Ham was in butchery. His old customers would stroll through, and he'd still greet them by name, as if that mattered anymore.

"Oh! Mr Roberts, isn't it?" And they'd bustle past with their trundlers, on their way to the next Special of the Week. Until the day he died, he wore his white grocer's apron with pride.

From nineteen sixty-six, my mother and I were on our own again. But now she had a home to call her own. Now she had money from the five hundred pound life insurance policy that Bill had taken out. Now she had a widow's pension. This time, there was no procession of uncles. My mother was by now in her late forties. Her average looks had faded; she was probably menopausal, and feeling perhaps that she was beyond men. It didn't matter to me. The following year, my first year at university, I would leave home.

Chapter 5

Lena! Beautiful Lena!

Lena Rags came into my life when I was fifteen – almost sixteen, and in the manner described at the beginning of this confession. I was smitten! Nothing less! Perched there on my narrow pew, goggling like a frog through my thick lenses, she wrenched the heart from my chest and wrung it out before the altar. And yet, she didn't even know I was alive.

More prosaically, her name was Lena Kaplikas, but because she was always dressed in other peoples' hand-me-downs, clothes that for most other people would have long since become dusters, and because her surname seemed to be beyond the range of most New Zealand tongues, she had earned the queenly title, "Lena Rags."

She lived no more than a short, infatuated walk from our three-bedroom weatherboard, and had done so for the entire time I'd been there. Yet, tragically, I'd been unaware of it. We inhabited slightly misaligned worlds, you see. When she was at primary school, I was at intermediate; when she graduated to intermediate, I had moved on to a boys-only secondary school. Her friends were younger and girls, whereas my friends, the couple I had, were older and boys. It was as if our worlds might have never collided had it not been for her brief journey past that baptismal font.

And yet, we breathed the same Glenfield air, redolent of hay and pollen in the summer, heavy and damp in winter! That self-same breeze that romped in her hair, that hair the colour of moonlight, might very well be the next breath I took! Inhaling Lena! The winter rains that made me tired and languid and sometimes boorish, must surely also pluck at her energy. We were twin strands in a braided rope!

Rags's father had been exported from Lithuania sometime around the onset of the Second World War, and through a series of misfortunes had wound up in Scotland. There he met Rags's mother and, each no doubt being unable to understand a word the other said, they employed a universal language, and set about producing two offspring. And then, in the mid nineteen fifties, they joined the rush of immigrants to New Zealand looking for that elusive "better life" and, incredibly, found it in Glenfield. The result was that Rags, the older of the two children, retained a charmingly engrained burr to her speech. She has never lost it.

"Och!" she would say, when surprised, which seemed often, the "Och!" degenerating into a phlegmy cough in winter. And neither was she hesitant about delivering a solid, although good-natured wallop to the shoulder of anyone whom she thought might be teasing her. My one bruise from Rags, I nursed for weeks, palpating it to draw it out and make it last.

Mr Kaplikas was a hulking creature who surveyed the world with suspicion from beneath a beetled brow. His arms hung ape-like from his sides, seeming too long for him, and yet supporting a vast battery of muscles. It was as if the sheer bulk of the muscle made his arms too heavy to lift, so there they hung, like clubs. He was seldom heard to attempt English, leaving the communications side of things to his Scottish wife, whose Glaswegian was sufficiently thick that it often required translating by Rags. Whatever Mr Kaplikas did speak, whenever he spoke it, sounded as if it would have been more at home in the mouth of an ogre.

They lived, not in the palatial clapboard grandeur that was now our lot, but in a run-down fibrolite dwelling on the less sought-after, shady side of the valley. It was known as "the old Gunson place", although a Gunson had never occupied it within living memory, and until the Kaplikas family moved in, had been vacant for years. A patchwork of holes, from thrown stones, permeated its outside, some of which I could claim as my own. It had long been a favourite local sport to hurl stones at the Kaplikas house, and to scamper, heart racing, up the road and into the bush, before the giant emerged to bellow unrecognisable obscenities, and to shake a fist the size of a pineapple. It would have been unmanly to have declined a dare to stone the Kaplikas house. That, of course, was before I'd known that this rough shell contained the pearl of Rags.

The sister, Ona, by the time I first saw her, had become a miniature Rags. She had Rags's pale and slightly Slavic features, the same platinum blond hair, as fine as freshly spun web, a nose that was neither too snub, nor too straight, nor huge, nor bent. It sat on a face as innocent as a newly born lamb's, square between two perfectly spaced eyes of the clearest, periwinkle blue. The chin was broad, in that Slavic way, but not too broad, on a neck that was almost swan-like in its fineness. It would be churlish to say that her body still bore its small burden of baby fat, because it only served to plump out her skin, with its smoothness of cream. And her limbs! Her limbs had the natural grace of a dancer! Ona was like a spare Lena. But then, no. Nothing could best Lena. Nothing could compare to Lena. Nothing! Creation reached beyond itself when it formed Lena.

I was soon to discover that neither Rags nor her sister was attainable, being guarded night and day by the behemoth. His two roles in life were to glower and to guard his daughters, and to that end he hovered over them like a bell jar. He would walk them to the bus for school, and be waiting there for them when they returned. Where, by the age of ten or eleven, other children had bikes, Rags didn't, and therefore no independence. And once she was home, the door was closed behind her, and she was a prisoner in her sieve-like fortress. My Rapunzel!

It was explained to me later, that they were made to study, so that they would do well "in their new land". I assume the behemoth would rather have had male heirs, but the throw of the genetic dice had landed him with girls. And if he had girls, then he'd at least make them as successful as boys.

Later, when I'd got to know Rags a little, she was bright enough, her interests being of a practical more than an artistic nature. Whereas other girls were interested in music or boys or makeup, Rags was always going to "do" or "be" or "become", and she eventually "became" a radiographer. But Rags, you never needed to become anything! You didn't, because you already were!

As she grew, and started secondary school, a girls' school, she seemed to attain a little more freedom. I'd see her in the street, and try, in my stuttering, Caliban way to speak to her. She never rejected me. Her replies were polite, and then she would move on, and I was left with the feeling that she'd just stepped around a pile of excrement on the pavement, thanking it for not attaching itself to her shoe.

She never knew, I hope she never knew, but I would watch her secretly, learn her habits, so that we could meet as if by chance. I would be at the bus stop in the mornings when she was there, although we took different buses at different times. I would try to arrange to look as if I'd just arrived back on a bus when she arrived. I suppose, in hindsight, it was obvious. I suppose she thought of me as some pitiful creature lurking in her background, lusting hungrily after her through my Coke bottle glasses – something to politely avoid.

I was in my second year at university when I got my first contact lenses, and the world began to see me differently. It was also the year that Rags appeared at university. She'd always seemed to be ahead of others at school, and then she left straight from the sixth form, without going through the ritual of the final year. It meant she had to pay her own way for the first year, but presumably the behemoth had found sufficient cash to fund his daughter's education.

Because I was now living in a Grafton flat, I'd seen little of her over the previous year. I'd kept my eye in, of course. Every time I'd visit my mother, which evolved into every Saturday, when she'd cook "meat" for me, I'd make a point of surveying the horizon for Rags. What she had set beating inside me years before persisted with a metronomic doggedness. It has never stilled.

Without my glasses she failed to recognise me at first.

"Bruce!" I said. "Bruce Campbell!" As if selling something.

"Och!" The same dear, idiosyncratic, lovable yawp.

"So, what are you studying?"

It was arts. I'd thought it would be sciences, but the behemoth had her pegged for a teacher. Primary, of course, but he wanted her to have the backing of a university degree as a kind of ultimate weapon. Nothing would be left to chance with the Kaplikas sisters. The fact that Ona later went mad, and has spent her life in an institution may, in part, be attributable to this. But in fact, our courses were not dissimilar, with Rags a year behind where I was. It gave us something to talk about, while I could slaver over her beauty, and dream that I may one day become the frog she would kiss.

She'd changed, of course; matured, as one does. The buds of breasts had filled out into creamy, rounded orbs, although I imagined their creaminess and orbishness, because they were always shielded in layer upon layer, decreed proper, no doubt, by the behemoth. Her waist had narrowed, not waspishly, but to merely emphasise the roll of her hips as she walked, and the swell of her breasts. And her legs! The calves that peeked from beneath the behemoth-designed calf-length skirts were flawless!

I asked her out once, in an act of immense courage. I found her one day... No, I didn't find her. I'd been shadowing her, flitting from column to column so as to remain unseen. But there she was, sitting alone in the cafeteria, reading, with only an apple for company. I'd paced a little first, warming myself to the task, plucking courage out of the air, before I walked up to her with what I took to be a swagger. I swaggered too far, and one of my great, swinging, clumsy feet kicked the table leg, knocked the apple onto the floor and startled her into another heart-melting "Och!"

I was chasing the apple around the floor, while she was laughing the last of that season's phlegmy laughs, it now being well into spring.

"Listen!" I said, standing and holding the fruit aloft. She appeared to cock an ear, glance around, listening for something to listen to. "No!" I said. "What I mean," I said, "is that the University Players are conducting a performance of 'A Midsummer Night's Dream', and I wondered, that is, if you want to, if you might like to go."

That is pretty much verbatim what I said, as clumsy and stupid as it may now appear. Albeit I said it holding a green apple aloft, and quickly added "with me" as an afterthought.

Her face had become serious; almost pained. She reached up for the apple, as if I might hold it as a ransom against her acceptance. She looked down at her book, brushed some imaginary crumbs from her breast.

"I can't," she said, and she said it so beautifully that her one rejection was worth a thousand acceptances from others. "My father..."

"I see!" I said, trying to sound brusque and businesslike about it, a man of the world. "Well!" I said. "Thank you!"

And I backed away before turning and marching out of the cafeteria, my swaggering gait forgotten. From outside I glanced back through the fog-fringed windows, and she had gone back to reading her book, the apple untouched on the table beside her. And I knew in that moment that even if she'd had no father, possibly even if we'd been the only two people on the planet, she would not have gone to that play with me.

<u>Chapter 6</u>

It was in the winter of 1965 that Colleen had her accident. We'd both seen the car, but I just couldn't seem to hold her back. I've thought back on that moment over the intervening years – how I could feel the pressure of the seat beneath my hand, but my fingers just refused to close on it.

I must admit, I'd never taken much to the idea of a sister; it just seemed to complicate an already confused situation. And to make matters worse, she was one of those doll-like creatures that, apparently, everyone found it difficult not to like. I, however, was prepared to make a supreme effort.

Then, when Bill came along, well Colleen had taken to Bill in a way that made me wonder if there was more to it than met the eye. She was all over him, and in turn he lavished her with gifts and treats and seemed to spend every waking hour that he was not being a grocer with Colleen.

Around the middle of each December a Christmas tree now sprouted up in our living room – a real pine one that Bill had himself hacked from the bush with an axe that each year was produced, honed for the occasion with its own whetstone, and after use was moth-balled for another year. We, the women and children, were expected to tinsel and bauble the tree, and to do so with a level of relish that showed our appreciation. Colleen enjoyed the procedure; I didn't.

Presents would then accumulate on or under the tree, and a sense of unbearable excitement would mount until Christmas morning, when the presents could be opened, and recriminations could begin.

Colleen had not been old enough to remember our former life, when Christmases came and went almost unnoticed, treeless, when the highlight was six o'clock mass, and when, if it had been a good year, I might be presented with a pair of someone's hand-me-down socks, or a handkerchief that my mother had found in the street, and washed. The prevailing sentiment that had ruled our Christmases back then had been, "It's the thought that counts".

The Christmas of 1964 saw an awkwardly wrapped gift appear under our tree, whose general aspect shouted, "Bike!" Bill smirked around it, nodded ostentatiously at it and, as much as his spherical shape permitted, made bike-riding gestures. Colleen became breathless in anticipation, counting down the days, sleepless through the nights, until finally, on Christmas morning, she was able to tear away the wrapping to reveal the candy-pink every girl's dream beneath.

She was seven. The bike was too big for her, but Bill produced his tool kit, fitted blocks to the pedals, and spent days following her around the back lawn, holding the seat, until Colleen eventually learned to ride the thing in that semi-standing way: the handlebars at around shoulder height, the seat un-sat on, as she bobbed up and down astride the low-slung crossbar with each pedal stroke. It was a disaster in the making.

Now declared reasonably competent, she was allowed to venture further afield, but "Not on the road!" my mother had declared, and "Always with someone else present". This chilly August morning that someone else was me.

The screech of the car's tyres attracted attention. People rushed from their front doors, and sensing entertainment, began to gather at the crash site. The driver of the car, a grey-haired veteran of sixty or seventy, was making a considerable show of being distraught, pacing back and forth lamenting, "What have I done? What have I done?" when it was really quite apparent what he'd done.

The keening and general hubbub soon reached my mother's ears, and she came sprinting across the street, her arms outstretched like one half of a pair of lovers about to hurl themselves into each others' arms. She would have known it was Colleen. The twisted wreck of the candy pink bike that lay some distance from the scene was a dead give-away.

Her hands shot to her face, one each side, framing it. Understanding that the principal actor in this drama had now arrived, the gathered crowd took a step back, allowing her the space to deliver her lines. She knelt dramatically at her daughter's side; took her hand.

"What's wrong with her?" she whispered, and the gathered crowd craned forward, the better to hear. "What's wrong with her?" she asked again, this time a little louder. Then over, and over, "What's wrong with her? What's wrong with her? WHAT'S WRONG WITH HER?" each time louder than the last, until she was shouting, screaming her question to the heavens.

And yet it was obvious what was wrong with her. It was obvious from the fact that her face had been half-ripped away, and now hung to the side of her head; it was obvious from the imprint of the tyre tread, whose signature remained on the flesh beneath, and from the fact that what remained of Colleen's head was ballooning into a giant, misshapen purple thing as we watched.

She was obviously dead.

And as I say, I've replayed that scene in my mind over the years, felt the pressure of the bike seat under my hand, felt my hand propelling the bike forward, and wondered at the inability of my fingers to grasp that seat, to pull it back.

Chapter 7

I used to take drugs when I was younger. To be honest, I've taken quite a variety of them until fairly recently. Non-prescription, or recreational drugs is what I mean here, and that can include drugs that would normally be obtained under prescription, but that I've managed to get in some other way. Illicitly, in other words. And when I say "a variety", I don't mean in some cocktail form. Generally it's individually, although some drugs are like bacon and eggs – you wouldn't consider having one without the other.

But recently I've been pretty much down to alcohol. Yes, it's a drug! I'm not one of those people who try to downplay it, or wriggle out of it by classifying it as a beverage. A beverage? Of course it's a bloody drug! And a pretty damned efficient one, too! Certainly its served me well over the years, always there as a faithful companion when others have deserted me.

The only reason I haven't experimented more widely with other drugs of late is availability. If I'm being honest, I'd have to say I look every day of my sixty-five years, and probably a bit dodgy besides. That's more to do with the way I dress now, and the fact that I can look a bit unkempt. So no-one's going to sidle up to me in the street, and say, "Hey, old timer! Fancy a hit of crack cocaine? No? How 'bout a spot of Pseudoephedrine, then? Nice and pure! Some good old-fashioned acid more up your alley? Weed? Or, hey! Hang on! I've got some legal highs, if it's the law you're worried about!"

I'd probably say yes to the lot of them, if given the opportunity. I've always been quite open to experimentation, and also fairly keen on giving reality's nipple a bit of a tweak. They'd have to be free, of course, and unless dealers have changed over the years, they're not in the habit of handing out free samples.

I was introduced to cannabis by "Chump" Charnley when I was seventeen. Chump was having his third crack at School Certificate, while I was in what was then called the Upper Sixth Form. Basically it was a final year at school where you pissed about, perhaps got a bursary that was worth bugger all, perhaps got a scholarship that was worth slightly more, or as in my case, applied for Division U at Training College, where they paid you about a third of the average wage to go to university. A great scheme, considering education was essentially free! The only drawback was you had to be a teacher afterwards; well, for at least as long as they'd paid you to go to university. The out for that was, if you could find a psychiatrist prepared to say you'd gone crackers, they'd let you off. You could get your education and a good dollop of cash besides, courtesy of the taxpayer, and then walk away scot free. Didn't worry me, though; I was quite happy to teach. You've got to do something, after all, and as the excruciatingly boring George Bernard Shaw said, "He who can does. He who cannot teaches." Which goes to show how much he knew, because I both could and did.

So having committed to becoming a teacher, the Upper Sixth year for me was in every respect a social experiment. I came out of it with what was known as "Higher School Certificate", a meaningless scrap of paper, and after having a go at Bursary exams, on the grounds that I had to be seen to be doing something, a second meaningless piece of paper saying I'd failed in all subjects except English. Well, you don't have to actually study for English, do you? You speak it and you read it every day, and even a well-oiled parrot could have passed the sorts of exams you got back then.

Comprehension, essay, bit of grammar, Julius Caesar and perhaps a Graham Greene novel. My Latin and French weren't bad, either.

But back to Chump and drugs. I'd had very little to do with Chump over the years. He'd started off in the same year as me, but in a much lower class. Three F or something, I think it was. Three F predestined you for a life of sweat and toil, possibly involving other peoples' excrement. But his parents must have believed he had some talent tucked away somewhere, because they held his nose to the educational grindstone until the bitter end.

Most boys, having failed the School Certificate exam once, went off, and if they were lucky got a trade, or they might become labourers, or van drivers. In other words, the Peter Principle was allowed to operate freely. A few, like Chump, were determined enough to give it a second crack, and most succeeded this time around. Not Chump, though, and here he was, back for a third attempt. English was mandatory for School Certificate, and you had to get at least 30% in it. Chump had failed to achieve that in either of his tries, scoring 19%, and then 27%. So he was getting better. But a second stumbling block was, he failed all his other subjects as well. Both times.

The simple fact of the matter was that Chump was never going to be able to append the letters SC to his name. But word began to circulate that he was doing a roaring trade in what was then quaintly called "pot". Unbeknown to we inmates of the Upper Sixth, the Age of Aquarius was dawning. Groovy was on the way out, and words like "cool" were starting to be used by those cool enough to use them. We were vaguely aware that something was happening on Haight-Ashbury, but we didn't know quite what it was, or even where it was. The Beatles were going *sort* of psychedelic, but we didn't know quite what that was, either, and anyway, weren't the Rolling Stones just that tad more edgy? Did we really want to be identified with four blokes who seemed vaguely androgynous, and didn't hesitate to identify themselves with flowers, when we could be painting it black, or getting no satisfaction?

But Chump seemed to have got the jump on all of us on the coolness front. It was as if he'd leapfrogged the mainstream, and had dived straight into Ken Kesey, the Merry Pranksters, and the Grateful Dead. He seemed to be conducting his own Electric Kool-Aid Acid Test from his school locker. Where he got the stuff from, God knows. Perhaps his father was in the Mr Asia syndicate. Perhaps he grew it in his wardrobe and told his mother it was bean sprouts, or a school science experiment. He used to deal it quite brazenly from his locker, which was always devoid of books anyway. I sidled up to him one day as the little swarm of boys around him began to dissipate.

"Chump!" I said to him, nodding.

He always had that look about him as if his ancestors had buggered off up some evolutionary blind alley and got lost. He looked as if he should be drooling. His mouth hung permanently open in a pimple-infested face, and his eyes had the appearance of dead meat. He turned those eyes on me now.

"Uh!" he grunted.

I peered over his shoulder into the open locker, and there was a stack of Bryant and May matchboxes.

"Selling matches?" I said.

An aeon seemed to pass, while understanding gradually dawned on Chump's face, and slowly, with what seemed to be monumental effort, it rearranged itself into a sneer. A little sound came out of the mouth, which gave me to understand that the sneer was in fact a laugh.

"Air!" he said, meaning "Yeah!"

"How much?" I asked him. "For a box of matches."

"Quid!" he said.

This was a year prior to us going decimal. A quid was a pound, and a pound was about to become two dollars. A decent weekly wage then might have been around twenty-five pounds, so a quid was no small sum.

"Give y' ten bob for one," I said, thinking this was a negotiable situation.

The smile now firmed to an unequivocal sneer.

"Quid!" he said.

That night I helped myself to a pound note out of Bill's wallet while he tossed and farted beside my mother, and the next day I went back, slapped it into Chump's hand, and walked away with a matchbox full of a sandy, greenish substance I had every reason to believe was marijuana. He could have given me ground-up dogs' droppings, and I wouldn't have known the difference. But here I was, on the highway to hell, and loving every minute of it! Oddly, in our several months of dealings, the only words I ever heard Chump utter were "Air" and "Quid". It may be that he knew others, but if he did, I never got to find out. And neither did the School Certificate examiner, because Chump was rumbled later in the year when a passing teacher demanded to know what was in the dozens of matchboxes in his locker. Folklore has it that Chump was heard to utter another word on this occasion: "Nuffin'".

"Nuffin" didn't wash with Mr Biggs, though, and he marched Chump and his matchboxes down to the headmaster's office. It was getting on towards the tail end of the sixties, and rather than involve the law and tarnish the reputation of the school, it was quietly agreed that Chump should just forget his educational aspirations and simply fade away. I heard later that he'd run afoul of a dealer in Australia, and disappeared. What was left of him was dug up by dingos on the fringes of some desert, and later discovered by a jackaroo during an annual roundup. There wasn't *much* left of him – maybe no more than a sneer. It was one of those dental record situations, and I remember it surprised me that Chump had ever been to a dentist. He just hadn't seemed the type.

The weed Chump was peddling was pretty mild by today's standards. No buds – just a whole lot of leaf ground up, for some reason, to the consistency of sand. You'd get the odd seed that would detonate like a small hand grenade if you happened to roll it up, so it suggested the plant had actually flowered, but where the heads went is anyone's guess. Perhaps there was some elite of dope smokers who got all the good stuff, and we were just getting the crumbs from the rich man's table. Good starter material, though. You could do a whole matchbox, and hardly notice the effects at all.

The first time I got a hit of anything good was more than a year later. It was at one of those university parties, where it was almost competitive to see who could become the most tanked. A Sunday afternoon. We'd chipped in and bought a keg, and I'd downed a couple of Tuinal as well, just to be on the safe side. Suddenly there was the whiff of hemp on the wind, and a family-sized joint appeared in my peripheral vision.

"Good shit, man! Acapulco gold!" an anorexic-looking bloke in a dirty singlet wheezed around a lungful of the stuff, as he passed the thing to me.

Was it? I don't know. What I do know is that I spent the next two hours paralytic in the cordon of weeds that passed for an herbaceous border. I could think, but I couldn't move. Eventually the vast quantity of beer I'd consumed decided it could wait no longer, and I lay there and pissed myself and thought of my father, and of how the apple had not fallen far from the tree.

Fortunately, my experiences with drugs have been mostly happy ones. I wasn't predisposed towards paranoia, so I could take acid with relative impunity, which I did, frequently. Bummers happened all around me, but not to me. I mean, you don't want to go silly, and I didn't. A four way trip was a four way trip, or perhaps a two, if you really wanted a decree absolute between yourself and reality. But there were people who *did* go silly. There were people who would down oodles of the stuff and disappear for days; sometimes weeks. When they came back they'd converted to Christianity, or were now following the latest guru that had just sprung out of India. Or they'd just become strange, and may then have to be carted off down to Ward 10 in an old rug, for a few hundred volts between the ears. It was a well-worn path between Grafton and Ward 10 in the psychedelic era.

Jimbo Dakin was one such person. He'd buried his acid in the back garden in a matchbox, but failed to ensure it was contained in something waterproof. Simple oversight. When he dug it up he found that the dozen or so tabs it contained were gone. Simply vanished. So he ate the box, and then *he* vanished. He was gone for several months, and reports kept coming in that he'd been sighted from points as diverse as Cape Reinga and Bluff. When he did come back he was married, he was a staunch advocate against drugs, he was an equally staunch Baptist, and he had with him a staunch and pregnant wife. I'd quite liked Jimbo, but we didn't mix much after that. We seemed to have little in common. I heard they later bought a dairy.

Despite the drugs, university was a breeze for me. If that sounds arrogant, it's not intended that way. I just have a good memory, which has remained strangely resilient to the ravages of substance abuse and time. So I could apportion my days and nights, spending equal amounts investigating issues of a social nature, alcohol, drugs and women mostly, and then the balance on work and sleep.

I must admit, women have always had a fascination for me: their otherness. And I say that in complete deference to Rags, because for me, there'll never be another woman.

Then Eve dropped in on me.

Chapter 8

You haven't met my Eve yet, have you? Let me introduce you.

We're going back to the late sixties again, and I'm sorry, because I know that seems to be a period in history that bores the flares off of most people. But honestly; think what it gave to the world! Valium! Acrylic paint! Hippies! Kevlar! Moon landings! A huge upsurge in the global demand for cannabis product! A huge upsurge in LSD consumption! A huge upsurge in mental illness! Richard Nixon! Henry Kissinger! Free love! Sit ins! Love ins! Vietnam! Frank Zappa! I could go on! You may very well find the late sixties boring in retrospect, but believe me, it was a maelstrom living through them!

Eve Ruigen! A Dutch name, meaning something. She was one of those peripheral beauties that milled around the campus with the air of a self-styled goddess. By "peripheral" I mean that she was not the main event, but on occasions came close to it. Quite small, but with a presence that belied her size. I was making absolutely no progress on the Rags front, and one night at a party, Eve just fell into my lap. No, I mean quite literally – she fell into my lap while under the influence of a combination of unknown substances, and there she stayed.

This was about as close to actual intercourse as I was likely to get with a woman back then, so there I stayed, too. Grafton parties tended to degenerate into messy scenes, and the mornings would normally find people in varying states of decomposed consciousness, lying throughout the house, garden, and occasionally roadway. It was mid morning before I detected a stirring from Eve. I could see her moving, but I was unable to feel her moving, because my entire lower half had gone numb. She opened her eyes, and said, "Who are you?"

"I'm Bruce," I said.

"Oh." She seemed to think about this, and then said, "Well, hello, Bruce," snuggled down as if I were a bed, and went back to sleep.

Mid afternoon brought on another awakening, and this time I expressed to her my urgent need to visit the toilet. To be honest, due to the numbness, I was unsure what I might find once my lap became vacant, but fortunately all was well. She assisted me in restoring feeling to my legs, and we just seemed to fall into a natural relationship after that.

It was in the late sixties that girls became women. I don't mean that there was a sudden global maturing, but up until that stage, it had been acceptable to call a woman a girl. A woman of eighty could be called a girl, and would have been unlikely to take offence. She may even have been flattered. Now women of ten or twelve found it demeaning to be called girls. They were women! There were "Women's Issues!" There were "Women's Rights!" There was "Women's Lib!" I was doing my best to liberate as many women as possible from chastity, but mostly I'd been liberating my hand; but now here was Eve.

To call it love at first sight would be an exaggeration of fact. Looking back on it, looking back over all those years, I now wonder whether it was ever love. Like magnets, whose opposing poles attract each other, we perhaps no more than collided there on that overstuffed, smelly old armchair, and stuck. You couldn't help but admire her beauty. She was elfin. In bare feet she would hardly have reached my shoulder, and she looked years less than her nineteen. She had a crepuscular complexion that made you think of either dawn or dusk. It alluded to something exotic; something golden. Something Polynesian, perhaps, or even Spanish or Southern Italian. She looked young.

But she was the antithesis of Rags: black and white; night and day; troubled and calm; finite and infinite. We could talk, though, and I know it sounds odd, but that's what we did. In the midst of all that carnal activity that was going on, throughout much of the Summer of Love, we talked. We talked for six months, not continuously, obviously, but most days would see us in the coffee shop, talking, and I gradually found a little piece of my heart being eroded by her. Our ideas often seemed at loggerheads, but we each held them passionately. And then, at the end of those six months, as if on cue, we had sex, and that was equally ferocious. So we were passionate. I'll concede that. But love? I still don't know. I do know that she wasn't Rags. Could I have loved her? I don't know that either, but I suspect I was not capable of it. I don't know if she was.

We married after she became pregnant in late 1972, almost for want of something better to do. I assume the child was mine, although in the end it didn't matter, because she lost it long before full term. I've wondered over the years if she somehow aborted it. She was not particularly maternal. But then, I could never imagine myself as a father, either. So none of it mattered, and throughout our years together, we never tried for another child.

Rather, we drifted through our lives, separate corks bobbing along on the same aimless current. She was an artist, or at least, that was how she styled herself. She'd been at Elam when we met, but left before she completed her bachelor's. The bohemian aspect of art is what appealed to her then, more than the actual doing of it. She was slightly at odds with her time. I could have imagined her on the fringe of the Ginsberg and Cassidy and Kerouac set – part of that New York beat scene of the fifties. She was too violent for the seventies. She didn't fit in. Strange how we can be born out of time.

Her early paintings were dark and savage things, suggestive of inner conflict. If you could paint a storm of the soul, that was what Eve was painting. It scared me to think of the mind that had conceived those paintings, and of course, nobody bought them.

Later though, as she neared middle age, she would have liked to have been taken seriously. She would have liked to have done commissions, grand works that the public saw and admired. Instead she did small things, which she sold at markets – little more than paint-by-numbers, really. I don't think she was ever really happy during the time she was with me. Certainly, from what I can tell, she's not happy now. She is one of those people who sees her life as a mishap; a great catastrophe, but is unsure as to where it all went wrong.

As I said, the passion in our sexual relationship was such that you could call it brutal. There were times when we would each come away bruised, bloodied and torn. It wasn't especially vicious. It wasn't as if we pummelled each other. But it was *intensely* passionate – we each put our all into it. But the passion in our workaday lives wilted, and then died. We stopped talking. We began to watch television when we ate together. We'd see films, or go to the theatre, and then afterwards we didn't talk about what we'd seen. We'd read books, and not discuss them. We'd eat out at those restaurants where they have multiple television screens, so couples don't need to communicate. We'd have been ideal candidates for that modern style of eating out, where each party has some kind of digital device. Otherwise we'd try to persuade other couples to go with us, but that seldom worked, either. By this stage, Eve was coming to be regarded as dangerously volatile, and I think I was regarded as a bit of a loose cannon, too, although in a different way – an oddball, perhaps. I'd got to that age. By now we'd be going home to separate beds in separate rooms, and in the last few years we were together, neither of us moved to invade the other's bed in a fit of sexual frenzy. It was a question of energy. There seemed no point. There was no longer any passion in it; no pleasure.

By the end, we were having "trial separations". These were Eve's idea, although how we were intended to gauge the success of each trial was never discussed. She would go off and stay with one of her woman friends. Possibly these were lesbian relationships. I never asked, and she never said. Not that it would have worried me. I was just beyond caring by then. After a week, or maybe a month, she'd come back, and slot in as if she'd never left.

After I'd been arrested and charged, she hardly spoke to me. The words she did use attached mainly to her, and how she felt about it. She said she was ashamed. She was humiliated. She was revolted. She was disgusted. She never visited me in prison, and what little money we'd saved together, she spent.

I can hardly blame her.

Chapter 9

But Eve had not been my first dalliance. No; that had happened some years before.

My eighteenth birthday had just rolled by, which my mother had helped me celebrate with a stringy lamb roast. Cooking had never been an art form for her, and once she'd graduated from tripe and testicles she always seemed to struggle. I did use to appreciate the effort she put in, though, and always thanked her extravagantly. I had become a caring son, if only to try to ease the pathos of her existence. Nevertheless, there was inevitably something desperately depressing about the two of us sitting there celebrating *any* occasion. And, remember, it was our first year without old Bill's dour manner to leaven proceedings by injecting into them the odd cough, or grunt or fart. Meals were never the same without his "Very nice! Very Nice!" to round them off. I think, to my mother, his presence lingered like a phantom limb, and I would see her glance occasionally at his empty chair, and the ghost of a smile would light her face. Some of his best shirts still hung, gleaming white, with sweat stains fresh at the armpits, in her wardrobe. A gentle reminder of when her life had reached its apogee.

But let's not shilly-shally in that make-believe land of musings and regrets. It was spring, I was young, and I was still a good few years away from being declared insane. It was late December back in, well not '63, as was the case with Frankie Valli, but rather in '66. The Auckland evenings had begun to edge out, and were dusky and often warm. The sand could lay stalled at body temperature on the beaches long after dark, and the slight scent of early pohutukawa blossom hung in the thick night air. It was a time of year that leaves a tingling in a young man's loins long after the sun has gone down; an itching that begs to be scratched; a lethal string drawn back on a hair-triggered bow.

I'd been associating with the roguish Lionel and Luke for some time. Obviously these are not their real names, but to confound any legal proceedings, that is what I am calling them, because both are now prominent in litigation in prominent law firms. We have not seen each other in almost forty years, but I have no desire to tangle with prominence.

I think it fair to say that I had, by now, begun to part company with the rails. I don't mean to overstate my condition; you wouldn't have described me as completely *off* the rails, but I was definitely teetering. A good shove and I'd have been off. There had been the marijuana, and a few episodes of illicit drinking; I'd become a little light-fingered, in part to sustain my developing taste for the two afore-mentioned. But I wasn't out of control, in the sense that Lionel and Luke might have been considered by right-thinking society of the nineteen-sixties to be out of control, had right-thinking society known what Lionel and Luke got up to. Fortunately right-thinking society of the sixties sustained itself on a diet of anaemic television and urban myth, so Lionel and Luke flew well under the radar.

Luke was the owner of a 1946 Morris Eight, which he'd inherited from his grandfather. My grandfather had left a stained mattress, but Luke's grandfather had left him a car. That was the sort of inequity I was up against. It was a two-door little thing, in grubby condition, and with barely enough power to get itself away from the kerbside. Its rusted doors opened from the front to the rear, so you opened them whilst still moving at your peril, and yet the sheer risk of doing so encouraged you to do it. It shuddered vigorously on the clutch, and in wet weather admitted torrents of water. Once coaxed into life, normally with the aid of the auxiliary crank handle, it emitted noxious vapours, which would seep up through what remained of the floor, and that must surely have been injurious to the health of its occupants.

Nevertheless, the Morris Eight had been the venue for several "shindigs", as Luke liked to call them. "Shindig", I know, has connotations of a large, uproarious social gathering, but in Luke's mind it meant an occasion when a few (usually just the three of us) seventeen or eighteen year old young men gathered together, consumed as much alcohol as they could hold, puffed half-heartedly on cigarettes that had been stolen from a smoking parent or lifted from a careless dairy owner, and, whenever possible, smoked weak marijuana. The Morris served as the nerve centre for these operations, and a successful shindig would end with all participants either comatose or being violently ill, and on a particularly good night, both.

Lionel's contribution, apart from a wit that was drier than the rustle of a breeze through a hayfield in February (his metaphor, not mine), was alcohol. He seemed to have access to unlimited quantities of it. It wasn't as if he ran a bar; we couldn't always choose what we had. One shindig might be powered by beer, the next by whisky or vodka, and a third by a combination of those sickly-sweet liqueurs that one particularly memorable night has forever killed my taste for. The important thing, though, was quantity. My contribution, sterling conversation aside, was Chump Charnley's beginner's grade cannabis.

The December night began innocently enough, with the three of us sharing a small bottle of vodka. There was no pretence towards refinement; this wasn't a cocktail party; we simply swigged the stuff from the bottle. Over the course of perhaps half an hour, and as the contents of the small bottle evaporated, and as a manly glow began to overtake us, talk veered, as it often did, towards girls; or more accurately, in our case, the lack thereof. Lionel, apparently,

had a stupendous amount of sexual experie⌐
own admission, was only marginally behir
library of knowledge on the subject, but
discretion, and busied myself rolling a j
called "Charnley's Cheer".

The small narcotic effect of Chump's dope mingleᴅ ⸱⸱
vodka, and soon inspired a greater depth of insight into the matter of
girls, or lack thereof. Finally, as if the confines of the Morris had
become a confessional, Lionel admitted to knowing of one.

"What? A *girl*?" asked Luke, seeming floored by the idea.

"Yeah!" said Lionel, affecting an air of nonchalance.
"Friend of a sister of that mate o' mine, you don't know him, Allen."
He seemed to be reaching for something, clicking his fingers, and
then plucked the name from the air. "Elaine!" He ruminated on it,
and you could see him imagining her in his mind. "That's it!
Elaine! Elaine Someone."

"Mmmmm!" Luke was nodding enthusiastically around a
mouthful of smoke. "Elaine Saltato! Heard about her – some
fatherless little whore. Boom boom!" This was the kind of
pejorative language we used when it came to discussing girls.
Whores, harlots, wenches, pro's, strumpets. We did it to put them in
their place. All tarred with the one brush. All there just for our
picking. Boom boom? I'm not sure. "Mother's some sort of
druggie," said Luke. "Easy pickings, eh!"

And so, there, in the Morris Eight, on the foreshore of
Milford Beach, drunk and slightly stoned, a plan was hatched.
Lionel, being vastly experienced, was of the opinion that a "leg
opener" would be required.

"I've heard she'll go off for anyone! said Luke. "Knock, and
it shall be opened unto you," he intoned, adopting a Biblical
baritone.

"Yeah, but it pays to be on the safe side," cautioned Lionel,
and both Luke and I could see the logic in that. "Atchly," he went
on, "I got just the thing here!" And he fished about in his bag of

...d pulled out an interestingly shaped bottle and waved it "Rochdale Cider!" he announced. "It's sweet! Gets 'em ...ed! Chicks love it! Still," he said, after giving the matter a bit ...ore thought, "pays to be on the safe side."

And so he uncorked the cider, swigged a quarter of its contents, opened a second bottle of vodka and from that replenished the quantity of cider he had swigged.

"There!" he said, having re-corked the cider. "Put a bit more octane in it!"

A little after eight the Morris was puttering about some backstreets of Northcote where unloved cars perched on wooden blocks on unloved lawns in front of unloved houses. In one of these, unloved Elaine lived with her unloved mother. Two windows glowed dull buff behind webbed and ragged curtains, bothered only by the blue flicker of a television. Lionel now assumed control, and was soon picking his way amongst debris on his quest to the front door.

His virile knock was answered by the silhouette of a tiny, slender girl, her hair parted in the middle, and swishing in the backlight as she swayed shyly from side to side, hands clasped in front of her; a cheap, plastic Alice in Wonderland. There was a brief amount of talking, mostly on Lionel's part, after which he produced the bottle from behind his back, brandished it, and the silhouette nodded. Then Lionel came back.

"She says her Mum's nearly blotto. Give her ten minutes, and she'll sneak out."

There was a nervous period of waiting. Dogs barked. A cat stricken with some disease or injury slunk by, its belly dragging on the pavement. An objectionable group of youths slouched past uttering cocky, animal challenges that we could barely hear behind the Morris's tightly wound windows and locked doors. They rocked the Morris violently, then bored, moved on, and were soon replaced by the sight of Elaine tripping up the pathway, childlike, a small skip to her step.

With Luke driving, she sat between Lionel and me on the narrow back seat – bare springs mostly, with its leather and padding now largely gone. I'd pocketed my glasses, preferring partial blindness to ridicule, so in the slow strobe of passing street lamps I could distinguish only a hint of Elaine. The voice and stature of a child of ten; looks unknown; breast development uncertain, although apparently minimal. But I could feel her female warmth hard against my thigh, and a hopeful erection crushed itself against its denim confines.

A full moon was snooping over the shoulder of Rangitoto, and beginning to cast an alloyed light on golden sand. We sat at one end of the beach, the last, solitary bather or walker having now departed for home. We – Lionel, Luke and I swigged manfully at vodka. Elaine clutched her bottle of Rochdale as if it were her lifeline to the world of oblivion, that world where mothers were not addicts and she was not meat.

Slowly Lionel's arm crept out to encircle her, and slowly she leaned into his shoulder. Slowly the level in the cider bottle dropped. Slowly Lionel began to undress her amidst only a pitiful show of resistance. Slowly he pushed her back onto the sand. Slowly he mounted her and quickly came.

Luke was next, according to an unspoken seniority, and I followed. *Sans* glasses I could see little. What I did see, though, through closed eyes, was Rags. Rags smiling radiantly. Rags yielding herself up to me in a cacophony of ecstasy. And as I crashed down on her in one, final, euphoric thrust, as I lavished Rags's face with kisses, licked its sweetness, I did, however, taste tears. And I have no reason to believe that those tears belonged to anyone but Elaine.

And so we sat and smoked and drank and quietly celebrated our achievement, while Elaine lay naked, and vomit oozed from her side-turned, gaping mouth, and the moon crept up to gaze full on her. Until Lionel thought to create a monument to the occasion, and with the glowing tip of his cigarette dotted an L in the ivory skin of her belly; and as we laughed, she barely flinched. The law of unspoken seniority again decreed that Luke was next, and then it was my turn. Without my glasses, and in dim light, I'm still unsure how my B turned out. But I've sometimes wondered since about Elaine, and if she ever lived up to that promise burned into her belly.

She was thirteen. So perhaps I have her to blame for that predilection for young and tender flesh which came to haunt me in later life!

Chapter 10

You might have thought it odd that I play fast and loose with the rules of grammar and syntax. For example, you will no doubt have picked up on the fact that I earlier referred to "us Campbells", when of course any year three student knows it should be "we Campbells". The reason for this is that I no longer give a shit about grammar and syntax. In fact, I deliberately thumb my nose at them. I flout them to the extent that there are occasions where I will intentionally use "who" instead of "whom", and sometimes even vice versa, so read on at your peril!

My punctuation's a mess, which means, like George Bush, I can turn a compound sentence into something utterly incomprehensible. I laugh in the face of subjunctives, and split infinitives can go to hell in a handcart. And you will also have noticed that I'm fearless when it comes to beginning a sentence with a conjunction. I just don't care! Let the last man alive turn out the lights and deal with the civilisation's final dangling participle!

For twenty-seven years I taught English to young people who didn't want to learn it. I led thousands of horses to water, but those I could make drink I could count on the fingers of both hands. Perhaps that is why I appreciated people like Vivien. They at least showed an interest!

But *I* learned something. I learned that, even if English, as a language, is not subsumed into Cantonese or Hindi or Urdu, its future is not as the language of Shakespeare or Chaucer or Milton. Its future is as kind of strangled text speak. A squawk! Its future is as a neutered pidgin of five hundred words that can be strung onto the barest of bones of something you could not even begin to call a grammatical structure, and tapped into a hand-held digital device! And if that is the future, why should Campbell stand as a bulwark in its way?

When you emerge from teacher's training college, it is into the real world – or at least as real as the world gets for a teacher. Because I'm not sure how real it is to spend the first twenty-two years of your life in one school or another, and then go and work in one for another forty years.

I'd had a holiday job briefly over one Christmas break. Most students worked as much as they could, whereas I was able to get by quite nicely on my studentship money. So it was more out of interest, really, that I pried myself out of bed at five one December morning and followed the ants' trail of students down to the waterfront.

Casual work loading or unloading ships was one way in which students, or those too indolent or incompetent to hold down a regular job, could earn money. You have to understand that social welfare was not quite the organised rort it is now.

The sun was barely breasting Rangitoto when I arrived in some butt-strewn, waterfront shelter at five forty-five. A queue was already snaking its way from a small window, behind which a single incandescent bulb of inferior wattage lit a small room dull yellow. This queue had grown to perhaps seventy or eighty men, and it would soon swell to more than a couple of hundred. I noticed that almost all of them had a sort of weapon tucked into his belt.

At around seven, an authoritative-looking man with a clipboard began at the head of the queue, and after a short interrogation sent each man off in some direction, presumably to work. When he got to me, he looked me up and down, seemed to study my glasses for some time, and then said:

"Godawoolook."

"Pardon?"

And he moved on to the next man, looked him up and down, made some notes, and said, "King's Wharf, Star O' Ceylon." That man moved off purposefully.

I looked about in confusion, thinking perhaps I should be heading in the direction of Godawoolook, but not knowing where it was. After a minute or two a bloke who looked like he hadn't seen a meal in a couple of days, and a bath in even longer, came up to me and said:

"Needawoolook!"

"Pardon?"

"One o' these!" he said, and he disengaged the weapon he had at his belt, and flailed it about purposefully.

"What is it?" I asked.

"Woolook," he said. "Use it fer loadin' bales o' wool!"

"Oh. Well, where can I get one?"

"John Burns 'as 'em! Ten bob!"

So as the early morning sun began to glimmer across the harbour, and the cranes began to nod their heads over the couple of dozen ships that lay alongside the wharves, I wound my way along Quay Street, up Anzac Avenue, down Alten Road, until I arrived at John Burns, which then stood on the corner of Stanley Street. I handed over one dollar seventeen, and came away with a wool hook.

The excitement of owning a wool hook had me up even earlier the next morning, and I was even higher up in the queue, with only twenty or so men in front of me. Around seven, the same bloke came out with his clipboard, and when he got to me, he again eyed me closely, and again focussed on my glasses.

"Can y' see with them things?" he asked.

"Yes, perfectly," I said.

He glanced down at my belt, and nodded.

"See y' got y'self a woolook," he said.

I was surprised he'd remembered me from the day before, but I nodded, and gave him what I thought might be an engaging smile. The glasses tended to make me stand out for people. I became less memorable once I'd got contacts.

"Freyberg!" he said. "Maria Janska!"

I tried to thank him, but he'd already moved on to interrogating the next man, so I found my way down to the Freyberg Wharf, found the Maria Janska, where I also found another man with a clipboard.

"Y're in't 'old!" he told me in some obscure British dialect, and gestured to a ramp leading up on to the ship.

I followed the few other men plodding soullessly up the gangplank, and we then made our way down a steel ladder into the bowels of the ship, where, despite the relatively early hour, it had already heated to an almost intolerable temperature. There was the continual throb of some sort of motor going through the body of the ship, and I could imagine that hold cover sliding back over us, and the vessel setting sail at any moment, with us as unwilling stowaways. The smell of everything the Maria Janska had ever carried filled the air with a scent that was almost exotic. We all stood, or sat around; played with our wool hooks; a couple of the more experienced hands stretched out and slept; one sauntered over and pissed in a corner, and when an hour had elapsed and nothing had happened, I said to one of the men:

"Um, what are we supposed to be doing?"

"Casein!" he said.

"Casein?"

"Yeah! Be 'ere soon!"

A few minutes later there were excited shouts from above, there was a whirring, and looking up I could see the derrick on the deck of the ship idly pivoting its boom across the patch of sky above. A large pallet swung into view, slowly descended, and as it neared floor level, a couple of the men who were still awake wrestled it to a gentle landing. It was stacked with bags marked "casein". Our job, it turned out, was to take the bags of casein from the pallet and manhandle them into the corners of the hold. The empty pallet would be hauled back up, and perhaps ten minutes later another pallet would appear, and we would again spring into action. I gathered that we were to continue doing that until the hold was full, after which we'd move onto another hold, or another ship.

I looked at the men around me, and wondered what drove people to such lengths of desperation to make a living. I wondered if this had been what my father did for work. Perhaps he had worked right here, in this very hold, loading casein on board the Maria Janska. I glanced about me again, studying faces; perhaps he *was* one of these men! But he wasn't. These men seemed sober, or at least relatively so, and none paired readily with a bed of petunias.

After an hour there was a kind of change of shift. Some new men came down, and our crew began to make a move to leave.

"What's happening?" I asked the bloke who'd filled me in on the casein.

"Ups!" he said.

"Pardon?"

"Ups! Two hours on, two hours off!"

"Oh."

I walked off the Maria Janska, off the Freyberg Wharf, and I never went back. I kept my wool hook as a sort of memento of my two hours in the real world. I used to hang it on the wall of our living area, as a work of art; but when Eve seized it one day, in a fit of rage, and threatened me with it, I decided it was better kept hidden. And then, as hidden things do, one day it simply disappeared. I couldn't tell you where it is now, if my life depended on it.

My first teaching job was at a school slightly to the south of the city, and to protect the innocent, it shall remain nameless. Was I young and dewy-eyed and brimming with optimism? Perhaps. But, let's be honest, the English language is hard to get that excited about. I mean, the average bloke who knocks out a living loading casein into the bowels of the Maria Janska may speak English, or some bastardised form of it, but he wouldn't know a haiku from a hole in the ground. And why should he? It's not going to improve his ability to load casein into the bowels of a ship, is it?

And the sorts of young people I had in my charge were just the sorts of people who, in a few years, would be loading casein onto the Maria Janska. There were their female counterparts, of course, but in a few years they would be at home raising the next generation of casein loaders and stuffing diazepam into themselves, or punching a cash register at a supermarket checkout.

It was about this time that I began to realise that English literature existed of and for itself. Ninety-nine point nine nine percent of the English speaking world didn't care about English literature, and at least half of that ninety-nine point nine nine percent had never heard of it. We graduates who pedantically cared about how things were written were like a lot of crusty old men standing around, eruditely wanking themselves off in some bookish corner.

My thinking on this was crystallised by Boyle, a young fellow who was aptly named, because he might as well have been one. It was Form 5D. If you were in Form 5D, your future was already mapped out for you, and it would not involve an appreciation of the sonnet form. It would more likely involve loading casein into the belly of the Maria Janska.

Last period on a Friday is never good. Nowadays, I'm sure, young people's thoughts are already flying off ahead to a weekend of substance abuse and violence, but even then it was hard to get any level of cohesion, let alone enthusiasm. It was a winter's afternoon, when the closed windows and the old steam-fed radiators had induced a listlessness in the room. There was an unspoken degree of unhappiness, and continual ructions were springing up around the class, and in the midst of this I had embarked on Sonnet 116...

"Let me not to the marriage of true minds
Admit impediments!" I had begun. *"Love is not love*
Which alters when it alteration finds..."

...when I became aware of a stifled sound beside me. It was Boyle, and he had his arms folded on his desk, and he had his head stuffed into his arms, and he was guffawing.

"Is there a problem, Boyle?" I asked.

He raised his stupid head up, looked about him as if garnering support, and said:

"Well, i's bullshit, innit, sir?"

The word "sir" was said as you might say "slur". It didn't sound pleasant.

"I beg your pardon, Boyle!"

"Well, wossit mean, sir? It dun't mean nuffin." And he began to guffaw again.

"Well, if it 'dun't mean nuffin', as you say, then why are you chortling?"

But the idea of chortling inspired in Boyle a further round of half-stifled laughter. I felt a slight anger rising inside me. Uttering the word "bullshit" had already made Boyle a candidate for a beating with a cane, but I'd always been resilient to the idea. Hurting people like Boyle was an attractive enough propostion, but it seemed somehow primeval to publicly inflict pain as a means of coercion. I felt it said as much about the inflicter as the inflictee. So I opened up Boyle's hypothesis on the meaning of Sonnet 116 for general discussion.

"Does anyone agree with Boyle that Sonnet 116 'dun't mean nuffin'?"

Brows furrowed as some of the best minds of 5D applied themselves to the problem, and the final consensus was, "Dunno".

"What? You agree that it 'don't mean nuffin', or you just don't know anything?" By now I was becoming quite worked up.

They didn't know anything was what they decided, and so *I* decided that they would spend the balance of the period writing a two page essay on Sonnet 116 as 'meaning nuffin'. Alternatively, if they were unable to do that, then they could write a two page essay on knowing nothing. If the two pages were incomplete at the end of the period, it would form part of their homework.

A few days later I got a note from the headmaster, a Mr Twill, inviting me to see him in his office.

"Mr Campbell!" he greeted me. "Please! Sit down!"

Twill's room was a dusty, musty space, where papers and books roamed like wild animals over shelves and tables, and spilled onto the floor. In the anteroom, Mrs Peveril clacketty-clacked on her old manual typewriter, and at regular intervals her bell would ring, she would swat her carriage back to begin a new line, and the clatter would begin anew. There was a prevalent rumour that Mr Twill and Mrs Peveril were dabbling in a physical alliance of sorts. Students theorised about it on toilet walls.

"Mr Campbell! It's come to my attention that you have asked your students to write an essay on knowing nothing."

"Yes," I said. "Well, not entirely. They could also have written an essay on why Sonnet 116 means nuffin'."

"I'm sorry Mr Campbell. I don't quite follow you."

"One of my students advanced the original hypothesis that Sonnet 116 meant 'nuffin'. As we could not reach any general agreement on this hypothesis, I suggested that they may like to write an essay on the subject, enabling us to explore it further. But then, as most of the class agreed that they didn't know anything, I gave them the option of writing an essay on knowing nothing."

"But, surely, Mr Campbell, that is a paradox! I mean, how can someone who knows nothing write an essay on what they don't know?"

This was a fair point, and one I hadn't thought of. But an even more interesting point, and one we were not addressing, was, how could any child arrive at this point in their education and know nothing?

"Well, my feeling, Mr Twill, was that they must know something to know that they know nothing." Twill stared at me uncomprehendingly. "What I mean to say is, even someone who knows nothing knows something, even if it's only the very fact that he knows nothing."

"But, Mr Campbell! To expect them to write an essay on it!" He ducked his head back and forth as if mystified by the idea. "And anyway, is it in the syllabus!? That's the question!"

We decided that it in all likelihood it was not in the syllabus, and given that there had been several anonymous complaints from sources that described themselves variously as "angry pairent", or "reel wild", we decided that I should withdraw my requirement for the essay.

"We don't want a rebellion on our hands, do we, Mr Campbell?"

And so it was that Boyle was able to illustrate for me why my chosen field of endeavour meant "nuffin". And I began to wonder, if Chaucer had had a Boyle of his own to contend with, and if that Boyle had explained to him that his efforts amounted to "nuffin", if the anonymous creator of Beowulf had been bothered from his labours by some scruffy lout who declared that it all meant "nuffin", would we have had English literature at all?

But there was a small part of me that was allied with Boyle. A small part that had begun to say, this means nothing. Absolutely nothing!

Chapter 11

So I stopped caring about trying to convert the Boyles of the world, although that little Boylish part of me now nagged at regular intervals from some psychic cranny that I chose not to explore. I would still read books, and on the whole I still enjoyed them. But I now doubted the worth of what I did. I now wondered whether the loaders of casein performed a more valuable function in society than I did.

While this was happening, Eve was becoming an Artist. Well, I suppose she *was* an artist, if splashing paint on a canvas makes you one, but she was now trying to earn a living as one. She'd been trying to get together a sufficient number of canvases for an exhibition, from which she imagined her musings on the dark side of being a woman would sell like hot cakes. Bear in mind that these works had titles such as "Abortion!", "Foetal Position", "Suicide", and my personal favourite, "Death of a Virgin Bride". It showed a naked, bloodied woman prone on a bed, while over her loomed a man, a large bowie knife where his penis might otherwise have been.

I came from school one day to discover Eve distraught in our small living room, "Foetal Position" on an easel in front of her, now slashed to shreds. She also had the makings of a black eye.

"What happened?" I asked.

"Fucking gallery!" she said.

I should explain that Eve had now started to swear. I think this may have been to do with feminism – the idea that if it was good enough for men to swear, then women could do it too! I'd never been that keen on swearing, mostly because I felt it demonstrated a poverty of vocabulary.

What had happened, it seemed, was that Eve had been hawking her paintings around various galleries, trying to persuade one of them to mount an exhibition. She'd met with little success, but most of the managers of these galleries had been discreet enough to palm her off with excuses, such as being booked up for the next twenty years.

She struck one manager, though, some apparently feisty woman, who took it upon herself to provide an honest critique. They were "rubbish" she said, referring in particular to "Foetal Position". This work was especially dear to Eve, who felt it embodied all that was evil about male domination of women. It depicted a woman in, as you might imagine, a foetal position, surrounded by men in various physically threatening poses. The background was what looked like gathering storm clouds. It illustrated, said Eve, the male desires for dominance, and for a woman to remain childlike – even embryonic.

The gallery owner had appeared to be unable to see that level of depth in the painting, and, naturally, Eve had become outraged. Things eventually descended into fisticuffs, at which the gallery owner must have been more proficient than Eve. "Foetal Position" was damaged in the fracas, when the canvas had met with Eve's head, and in a fit of despondency she had then performed some sort of ritual slashing of it once she had got home. The police may or may not now be involved.

We sat there and looked at what was left of "Foetal Position". It was beyond repair. Other works of a similar bleak nature leaned against the walls glaring back at us from the depths of their collective despair.

"I might as well just do shit like Jackson Fucking Pollock!"
she said, dabbing at her eye. It was coming along quite nicely, I
noticed, and showing more colour than most of her paintings.

"Would that be in his action painting, or drip period," I
asked. She curled a lip at me by way of answer.

"Fucking Kandinsky!" she said. "Matisse! Fucking men!"

Eve never connected readily with the abstract movement.
Again, I suppose, born out of her time, she was more a realist.
Perhaps a neo-realist. She believed she could express more *meaning*
through realism, and *meaning* was what she believed art was all
about. This view was at odds with most of the art-buying public,
who believed that art was about having something pretty to hang on
your wall. But she might have gelled with, say, Gilman and Ginner
and the Camden Town Group, although I feel they may have been a
bit tepid for her. There would have been problems. Eve made her
own crosses, although once built she loathed them, and was never
happy to bear them.

"There's more to life than noughts and fucking crosses!" she
once said, referring to McCahon, whose chief crime, I think was that
he was Another Man.

I believe this was a kind of jealousy, though. While there
was a huge originality of thought about Eve, and her intellect
roamed over a terrain of continental proportions, she could not
translate it into art. Between the idea and the reality fell the shadow,
as Eliot put it, and for Eve that shadow remained insurmountable.

Nonetheless, as you will have gathered, I am a sympathetic
person, and it was distressing for me to see her like this. Unlike me,
she had not completed a worthless degree, and so could not earn a
crust by teaching something pointless to young people who didn't
want to learn it. Short of having some sort of casein-loading job, she
was condemned to continue trying to earn her living as an Artist,
although I believe that was now toned back to artist.

These paintings that were redolent of meaning had been
large, and time-consuming and expensive to execute. "Death of a

Virgin Bride", for example, was life-sized, and I could imagine few people who would want a life sized bloodied woman, loomed over by a man with a bowie knife for a penis, hanging on their lounge wall. In other words, short of being snapped up by the Louvre, it was unsaleable.

We discussed it, and once Eve had settled down, once her eye had healed and she'd reconciled things with the woman constable who came round to enquire about "the incident", she decided to redirect her talents into smaller pieces which, although still quite gloomy, had just sufficient public appeal to sell. Well, there are always miserable people out there, aren't there? And they were sufficiently obscure that the buyers thought they just might be getting something that had hidden depth. Perhaps they were getting in on the ground floor of a movement. After all, why paint an apple black? Why paint Parnell with a nuclear cloud hanging over it? Why? They could hang these paintings on their walls, and they could muse over their meaning during dinner parties.

"Oh! That's a Ruigen!" they might say. "Yes! Such depth! Such talent! She's the next big thing!"

Eve displayed these works at outdoor markets and the flea markets that had suddenly become popular, and with an amount of haggling, she would get a few dollars for each one. There must now be literally thousands of original Eve's gathering dust in people's attics, or being re-cycled through garage sales. Or more likely, infesting rubbish dumps.

By the mid eighties Eve had decided that her future lay in ceramic art. It didn't, but it would take us two years to find that out. We would spend hours at the museum, where she would moon over its collection of East Asian ceramic pottery and figurines. Finally, I acquired a small kiln for her, the astonishing thing being that the school art room took more than a month to notice its absence. Thus equipped, Eve embarked on a series of projects that, again, had a feminist edge to them. The Venus of Grafton, for example, whose face could have been torn from Munch's "The Scream". A set of three women whose limbs had been distorted, so that they resembled characters from a Tim Burton film. These women may have been suffering, but again, did people really want suffering on their coffee tables?

It seemed not. The ceramic phase ended in 1988, and then the kiln lay unused. Eve went back to painting small pieces, selling them for a pittance at markets, and became more and more angry and introverted; and this is when our first "trial separation" occurred. I remained unaware that we'd separated for the first two weeks. I just came home one night to a note, saying, "Gone to stay with Gemma!!!"

I did puzzle over the exclamation marks. Three of them!!! As a footnote to this, I'd like to declare my position. I'm coming to think the exclamation mark is overused in modern writing. Well, not so much in modern writing, perhaps, as in daily written intercourse. Some people litter their writing with them. There are other things I'm against: omg, lol, wtf, and all that other drivel that evolved from text speak; emoticons; the demise of the question mark. I could go on, but my point is that people use these forms of communication because they can't communicate. If you've failed to communicate humour in what you've said, I can't see that hanging an lol or a smiley face on the end of it is going to make a blind bit of difference. I mean, is your hitherto po-faced reader, thus prompted, now going to be mirth-stricken? Emoticons the same. I got an emoticon from the social welfare office the other day. Could I come and see them in connection with my unemployment benefit ☺. Love to, but no car, no money and a dodgy knee ☹.

Anyway, Eve had gone to stay with Gemma. No cell phones in 1988, and if there were, Eve did not have one. I knew of Gemma's existence, but did not know where she existed, so I opened a can of baked beans, and continued doing that for two weeks – not the same can, of course. After two weeks, Eve came home and asked me how I thought the trial separation worked out.

"I'm sorry?" The concept of a trial separation was relatively new, and I was not familiar with it.

"Our trial separation. How do you think it went?"

"I'm sorry, but I was unaware we were having a trial separation."

"Well, why did you think I'd gone to stay with Gemma?"

"I – I thought you were having a holiday."

"A holiday!" Eve now began to look as dark as one of her paintings. "If I'd wanted to go on a fucking holiday, I'd have gone to fucking Club Med Tahiti!"

Well, she wouldn't have, because she wouldn't have been able to have afforded it, but I could see her looking about for something with which to arm herself. She was apt, when overly excited, to pick things up and throw them.

"Oh," I said. "Okay." I couldn't think of anything else to say.

"Okay!!!" And yes. She did actually speak with exclamation marks, too. "Is that all you've got to say? O-fucking-kay!"

"Well..."

I felt at a serious disadvantage. I was being asked to comment on something I'd only just discovered had happened, and that I'd up until now thought was something else.

"Do you mean the trial separation was okay? Is that what you mean?" She was looking particularly edgy.

"Well, yes, I suppose..."

"So you'd like it to become permanent?"

"Um, well..."

"That's fine by me then!"

And she stormed from the room.

Chapter 12

I never used to drink like this; not this heavily. Yes I did. Well, no, not when I was young. Not when I was pre-teen. There are times now when the bottle between my lips feels so natural, it's as if I'd been born with it there. But it's not the drinking that worries me. It's the gaps. Lapses in time. What happens in them?

I think Eve may have had some mental illness; you know, like schizophrenia, or what's that new one? Borderline personality disorder. She had all the hallmarks. Her delusions of adequacy. Anxiety. Depression. The stated sense that she was no one. Well, everyone's someone, I said to her. Not her. She felt like a vacuum, she said; she felt nothing; she even acknowledged at one point that she felt I was controlling her! Christ!

Did I tell you she attacked me once? With my wool hook? I'd hung it on the wall above the mantel. Taken down some stygian piece of *SHITE* that she'd hung there. She wanted real? There was more reality in that ten inches of whetted steel than in all the fatuous *BULLSHIT* she'd daubed onto canvas over the years! How many cotton bolls had to die, for Christ's sake, to satisfy her witless belief that she could paint!

But my wool hook? Such a simple thing, almost artless in its beauty. And the conversations it kick-started, just hanging there! My two hours in the real world. Everyone likes a laugh, don't they?

What set her off that night? The sour tincture of whiskey on my breath, was it? Or that wild musk of another woman that I'd leave smeared on me, just to taunt her? Some trifle – I can't recall what it was. I was starting to have little time lapses even then. Nothing serious. I'd wake as if into a dream, and I'd be somewhere. Or had I been somewhere? I couldn't tell. Dream, sleep, wakefulness – there was a creative blurring between them. Sometimes I'd come into a new consciousness, and I'd have in my possession some item I didn't recognise – a bracelet; a lock of hair. Once there was blood that didn't seem to be mine. And then, in a quiet moment, it might come back to me, and I'd think, "Ahhhh!" and feel puzzled that I'd done that particular thing.

I think I'd slammed the door when I'd come in that night. I think that was it. I did that to get her attention, because otherwise she was likely to ignore me. Quite rude. I'd come in after a hard day's drinking, and there she'd be, beavering away at her easel, creating some rubbish that no one cared about, and she'd just ignore me. I didn't *always* slam the door. Sometimes I'd walk around the outside of the house, and conceal myself in the small shrubbery (well, weeddery – neither of us was a gardener). And then, through the window of the living room, where she invariably left the curtains undrawn, I'd watch her. Sometimes I could watch her for hours – the small gestures and tics that people make when they believe they're alone. The odd things they do. Once, I remember, she slid her hand down inside her blouse, cupping and weighing each breast in an odd gesture, and then affecting the most forlorn gaze you could imagine, staring into the darkness that hid me, tears streaming from her eyes. There was definitely something wrong with her.

But, yes, this night, I *must* have slammed the door, because I remember, she started from where she'd been working at a canvas – some trivial little thing. Some nonsense. She turned. She looked like a mime, the streaks where mascara had run emphasising the passage of the tears. And of course, I immediately wanted her. To rasp my face on hers, feel her tears, taste them, her sadness, to become one with her.

There was a struggle. As I've said, our lovemaking was always passionate. We fell against the wall, and I heard a huff as the wind was expelled from her lungs. I forced her to the wall a second time, to emphasise my desire, and heard her head crack against the plasterboard. Then, somehow, she had the wool hook. I grabbed her hand, and it was as if we were dancing. She held the handle above her head, but I held her hand, my other arm around her waist. As we danced our polka, our foxtrot, our tango, as we spun around the room, I slowly forced her hand down, until we collapsed over the back of the old sofa.

I could see in her eyes that she understood the necessity of what I was doing, and yet, such is the desire of the animal not to be hurt, that she resisted me. Her eyes, though streaming tears, were fierce and hateful; and yet accepting. I forced the hook until its tip touched her breast, then forced it further until the blood appeared, and then down, down, watching with a detached fascination as the skin stretched and slowly ripped, and I heard her scream.

We made love then. As I've said, our lovemaking was always intense. Always passionate.

Chapter 13

So where, you will be thinking, was Rags during all of those years? Forgotten? Cast aside without a thought? Consigned to the scrap heap of oblivion?

Never!

I'd realised early on – about the time that I decided Rags would never have me as a lover – that she needed me as a protector. Surely that was love in its purest form. Our lives may not be shared, but they could at least run parallel.

We'd never stopped speaking. She never really avoided me. During our student days we'd meet on campus, and chat briefly, and each time my heart would ache and then wither as she walked away. I would still follow her. I'll admit that. I got to be quite good at it, only being caught out two or three times, and then being able to pass it off as coincidence.

Then, in my final year, just before I left to go to Teacher's College, she disappeared. I'd still watch out for her on my visits to my mother for our weekly "meating". And then once, I saw her passing, and rushed out, almost accosting her, I suppose. She looked flustered. She'd had the opportunity to train as a radiographer, she said. She'd accepted. The behemoth, apparently, had been amenable to the idea of this daughter working in health.

So at least I knew where she was, and I would make my occasional visits up to the hospital grounds to check on her, where she worked in a little ramshackle building, just up from the equally ramshackle building of Ward 10, where, as I've said, in the halcyon days of psychedelia, we would dump people for high voltage corrective therapy.

This went on for some years, and it wasn't until the winter of 1974 that events took a turn for the worse. I noticed that she was being picked up by some parasite in a tidy looking Cortina. He looked much older than her, and of course, it was then incumbent on me to follow him, to establish his credentials. Obviously I was no private eye, and I got no further than establishing that he disappeared into a city high-rise each day, went to the eleventh floor, which contained a law firm, a freight forwarding company, and an accountancy firm.

This pattern, of her being picked up by him, persisted through until 1977. I would still make a point of putting myself in Lena's path. For a while I pretended to be having treatment at the hospital for a non-existent back injury. Funny she hadn't seen me in X-Ray, she said. Yes, well. Otherwise it would have to be in the street, or to construct events so that I could see her when I visited my mother. It was never easy. Conversation was always stilted, banal, always a little strained, as if she'd rather not have to talk to me. But I understood that.

Then, it was coming into the summer of 1978, I happened to be passing when she exited the bus outside the hospital. A quick hello; she was on her way to work, and so was I. It was then she told me she was engaged; showed me the tawdry ring he'd bought her. She seemed buoyant and happy, but I could have told her then that he was not the man for her, because I was that man. They were to be married in late February.

I was not invited to the wedding, and I assumed it was because she didn't want me to meet him; afraid, possibly, of comparisons. But I watched it. I watched from a distance, and heroically wept as she swept into the church, gleaming in white on the ogre's arm, and wept again as she exited with the scrawny accountant. Yes, she'd confirmed it to me, in one of our later chance encounters. He was an accountant. An accountant, for God's sake!

I'll be honest with you. You cannot match the thrill that courses through you, that first time you have another human being completely in your thrall, and you know that human being is about to surrender its pulsing, brutish, ugly existence to you. Such power! With it comes the dawning awareness that your whole life has been lived for this moment! Of course, it's natural to be a bit squeamish about it, but then most people are conditioned into this idea of empathy, when quite obviously it is not a natural human emotion. Heavens above! We would not have evolved to be the most efficient killers on the planet, had we been hamstrung by empathy!

In fact, empathy is one of those words that are bandied around as if it's something real; as if we can just tap into it. Or worse, as if we just can't *help* being empathetic. In fact, a hundred years ago, there was no empathy, because the word didn't exist. At the birth of the twentieth century, it seems, no one felt empathy. It's a made up emotion! In fact, it's made up from the ancient Greek word, "ἐμπάθεια", which hints at passion and physicality and suffering. And ironically, the same word in modern Greek means hatred and loathing.

And as I began to follow this wretched little accountant around, that was the sort of empathy that drove me: hatred and loathing. I'd realised some weeks earlier that the situation with Lena was intolerable. Here she was, forced to live with this twerp, this skeletal little weasel of a puffed-up excuse for an accountant! I could sense her unhappiness – it radiated from her. Well! That was bad enough! I'd endured that for more than three years! But now, somehow, he'd managed to impregnate her! Here she was, swelling with his issue!

I had suspected as much for some time. When the vile thing was probably nothing more than a free-tumbling blastula, I could tell, even then, from the glow that began to inhabit her; from the way her unconscious hand wandered across the tautness of her skirt; I could tell then that something was amiss. But now this malign little intruder had latched onto her, and was feeding off her, and was beginning to erupt beneath that tender, furry pampas of her perfect belly!

It was August, and I had a three week break from school. I began to follow the accountant, always at a distance, always unobservable. Now that I had my contact lenses, I was able to blend, you see. The bulging lenses apart, I am not a particularly hideous, nor in fact especially attractive, example of humanity. I am neither short nor tall, nor thin nor fat, and therefore not particularly memorable.

Because I trailed him at a distance, sometimes I would lose him. His size made him inconspicuous, and his new car conformed to formulaic ordinariness, and seemed a bit zippier than the old Anglia I drove then. Sometimes he just got away on me, as I struggled to coax the Anglia up to the legal speed limit. His pattern was:

- 8:32 A.M. Exit front door with brief case (turning to peck pristine cheek of Lena, causing the bile to rise within me).
- 8:33 A.M. Insert key in lock of newish faun brown Toyota Corolla, parked in front of house, enter car, start motor and engage seat belt.
- 8:34 – 8:37 A.M. Sit, rapidly idling motor, to apparently "warm it up". This time may also be taken up by checking on personal appearance in rear view mirror, or otherwise fidgeting.
- 8:38 A.M. Engage first gear, and move away from kerb, at first shifting slowly through the gears, apparently ensuring that all the vehicle's internal fluids are flowing as they should, before accelerating

to a speed of between forty-nine and fifty-two kilometres per hour.

- 8:44 A.M. Move onto motorway on-ramp, and accelerate to merge with traffic moving north into the city.
- 8:44 A.M. – 8:53 A.M. Drive in a conservative manner in the slow lane, endeavouring to remain anonymous, and not annoy fellow commuters.
- 8:54 A.M. Leave motorway at Nelson Street off-ramp, and follow bumper-to-bumper traffic into the city.
- 8:58 A.M. Pull into ramp of underground car park in multi story building, and disappear.
- 5:08 P.M. Emerge from car park ramp, working slowly though the gears to disperse lubricating fluids.
- 5:13 P.M. Board motorway on-ramp, and accelerate to smoothly merge with traffic.
- 5:14 P.M. – 5:23 P.M. Travel south in the slow lane, driving in a conservative manner, endeavouring to remain anonymous so as not to annoy fellow commuters.
- 5:24 P.M. Leave motorway, and decelerate to merge with slower moving traffic on local road. Wave and nod at motorist who slows to allow merging to occur, and then follow line of traffic, although never exceeding fifty-two kilometres per hour.
- 5:30 P.M. Indicate intention, then pull to the left and stop on opposite side of street from house. Check ostentatiously for traffic approaching from any direction, before performing classic U turn.
- 5:31 P.M. Pull up outside house, engage handbrake, turn off ignition, shift car into first gear as a safety precaution, even though terrain is as level as a pond, disengage seat belt, collect brief case, exit car, lock

door, check that door is locked, walk to front door and knock.

- 5:33 P.M. Lena opens door, and another gut-wrenching peck is delivered to the beloved cheek. Door closes, scene ends.

Now were you as bored by this as I was? Good God! The man was a tiny automaton, and I could only imagine the sheer wretchedness of poor Lena's life. What must they talk about at home? The colour of the wallpaper? How he'd managed to cut seventeen seconds off his journey that morning by being a little more forceful as he merged with motorway traffic, even earning an unmerited toot, after which he'd slumped down into his seat and cringed for the remaining journey?

The only variation to occur to this routine was on Wednesdays. Well, I say variation, but because it occurred *every* Wednesday, it must be considered part of the routine. On Wednesdays this fly-speck of a human being would emerge from his subterranean car park, and rather than turn towards the motorway, he would head further into the bowels of the city. There he would stop outside another high-rise building, open the boot of his car and produce a small canvas bag. He and the bag would disappear into the high-rise, and would emerge almost exactly an hour and seven minutes later, he looking a little more flushed, the bag looking a little more dishevelled, after which the normal homeward routine would ensue.

I puzzled over this when it occurred the first time, and then, on the second Wednesday of my vigil, after he'd entered the building with his stabbing little steps, his small canvas bag slapping at his thigh, I followed as far as the lobby. I'd worn my glasses as a disguise, and an old cloth cap I'd bought at a Salvation Army shop. I was quite enjoying myself, to be honest, and had even allowed my beard to grow out a little, so as to be even less recognisable.

He even favoured me with a deferential half-smile, as the doors to the elevator slipped shut, which I didn't return. I noted that it stopped at the fourth floor, and checking the tenants' directory, I was informed that the fourth floor was occupied by Stearn, Dumbleton & Feary, Barristers, Solicitors and Notaries Public, and by Ex-Gym, the Fitness Centre for the Busy Executive. I can't comment on how Stearn, Dumbleton and Feary felt about the reek of sweat and the thump of dumbbells permeating their floor, but what was obvious was that this little ninny was trying to make something of his scrawny physique!

And if you think you were bored reading about his life, imagine how I felt having to live it with him! It was the most excruciating two weeks of my life!

Certainly there were minor deviations to the routine – occasions when the intrepid bean counter would become entangled in a snarl of traffic and his schedule would be disrupted. Then I would see him hopping about his seat in an agitated state, running his hand through his hair, glancing at his wrist watch, and then breathing an obvious sigh of relief as the traffic again began to flow. But none of this was sufficient to break the stultifying sameness of his life. And I could see that it would go on like this without end! This intervention I was planning would be doing him a favour!

The problem I was confronted with was that the very sameness of his life provided little opportunity for intervention. I could hardly run him off the road, or burst into his home (Lena's home) and hijack him. And then it occurred to me. His vulnerable point was very likely in his subterranean car park.

And so, I began to plan.

Chapter 14

You know how people collect matchboxes? No? Well they do, it seems. People collect all sorts of unusual things. Stamps are bad enough. Then there are the coin and medal fanatics. You can see how those might have some value, but when you get down to old chewing gum wrappers, or cards that might have come out of a Weetbix packet in 1903, then you've got to wonder. There are also the ones you'd have to ask some even more serious questions about – collectors of bottled foetuses, for example, or the phallological museum in Reykjavik. Yes, that's right – phallological, not philological. It's all about penises, not languages. I suppose the ambient temperature in Iceland may very well make a respectable phallus an issue of some importance.

In my declining years, I'd begun collecting whiskey bottles. It wasn't an organised collection. I don't catalogue them. In fact it was no more than a pile outside my door, which prompted complaints from the busy body next door, and an eventual letter from my landlord, requesting their removal. I stood my ground on the basis that every man was entitled to a hobby, but it all fell on deaf ears.

I was particularly disappointed in the busy body next door, here, in Camelot Place: a Mrs. Thrag. The name has a sort of Vulcan ring to it, doesn't it? I pressed her on it once, as a matter of interest, but she appears to have no idea where it came from beyond Mr Thrag, and he is no longer of this world. She herself has only a tenuous hold on it, hobbling on sticks and grizzling interminably. Her complaint in this instance came less than two weeks after I'd helped her out of a spot of bother. Never let it be said that Campbell was a man to turn his back on a damsel in distress. Admittedly, it had not gone well, and if there were any failings on my account they may, in part, have been attributable to the amber nectar.

She arrived one morning while the blear was still in my eyes, and began pounding on my door with the knob of one of her sticks.

"Mr Campbell! Mr Campbell! I know you're in there!"

As if I'd denied it! The sun was well short of the yard arm, and I'd been snoozing off a little excess from the night before. Mrs Thrag's first rapping had got me bolt upright, and then, once upright, my waste system declared that it needed urgent attention.

"Yes, Mrs Thrag!" I was still tucking myself in, and realising that my fly remained unzipped.

But I do try to be patient with her. After all, we'll all be infirm one day, and in need of a little care and attention. Her face was looking up at me like a piece of washing fresh from the machine. I'm no oil painting myself these days, but this was a face that urgently needed folding and ironing.

"I have a big rat, Mr Campbell!"

"Do you, Mrs Thrag?"

"Can you come and have a look at it?"

I was running my hand through what was left of my hair, feeling, I'm sure, even worse than I looked.

"All right, Mrs Thrag. Give me a minute. I'll be right over."

The hair of the dog theory is an old Scottish remedy. Get a few hairs from the dog that bit you, place them on the bite wound, and it will heal more quickly, goes the received wisdom. Silly, really: here you have an open, weeping and possibly infected wound, and you're chasing a dog round trying to pluck a few hairs out of it. Think how many people would have been bitten a second time.

As applied to alcohol, of course, it means consuming more alcohol to ameliorate the evil effects of what has already been consumed. There is some scientific backing for this idea, although it can at times be difficult to convince your stomach to accept more of what has just stripped it of its mucous lining.

Nonetheless, I searched out the bottle from the previous evening, found that it had a modicum of something in its bottom, and knocked it back. There was a brief moment when it threatened to return, another moment when my head revolved like a showground merry go round, and then everything settled back to normal.

I strolled over to Mrs Thrag's house (she later said "staggered"), and presented myself as present and fit for duty. She sniffed at the air and wrinkled her nose. Well, re-arranged the existing wrinkles would be a better way of describing it.

"Well, Mrs Thrag!" I said, rubbing my hands and attempting to exude cheer. "Where is the beast?"

"I've poisoned him!" she said.

"Good!"

"But he won't die!"

"Oh. Well where is he?"

"There!"

And she pointed to a cupboard whose door hung from one hinge. Mrs. Thrag's accommodation is but one step up the habitable accommodation scale from mine. As my eyes adjusted to the gloom of the Thrag kitchen I could see, extending from the cupboard, what looked like the business end of a bull whip. There was no way, I concluded, that the other end of that thing could be connected to any member of the genus *rattus*. There must have been some mistake.

"Oh!" I said.

Gingerly I crossed the patchy linoleum, picking my way amongst mysterious items that Trevor, her small, indeterminate terrier, had dragged inside. Some had feathers. Some still showed signs of life. But Trevor had decided to effect disinterest in proceedings, and was now feigning sleep in his basket. Gingerly I eased the cupboard door open.

Do you remember that first *Alien* movie, where you've been lulled into an early sense of security? The inside of Mrs Thrag's cupboard resembled a remote niche of the *Nostromo*, and I was Ripley. There was a large store of canned goods in there, several of which were quietly erupting from their cans. Chewed packets half-heartedly spilled their contents. I followed the bull whip, and on closer inspection, it did indeed seem to be connected to something. I peered even more closely, and as I did so, the something that it was connected to turned, reared up, and began hissing. I hadn't known that rats hissed. Hissing is the demesne of cats, in my experience, but this monstrosity was hissing in my face. I lurched back into the arms of Mrs Thrag, while *rattus* scuttled up the wall, and through one of the several holes in the pinex ceiling.

"He's up there!" said Mrs Thrag, jabbing one of her sticks skyward.

"I know, Mrs Thrag," I said. "I'm sure he'll just quietly die!"

"He'll smell!" she said.

Any smell generated by a decaying rodent would have been lost in the general malodour of the Thrag household.

"I have a ladder," said Mrs Thrag.

"Do you?"

"Yes. It was Alphonse's."

The hair of the dog remedy was kicking in quite nicely, and I was starting to feel pretty jolly about things again. The world was taking on a more rosy hue. I was ready for a bit of an adventure.

"Right ho, Mrs Thrag. Let's take a look, shall we?"

So, equipped with Alphonse's ladder and Mrs Thrag's bedside torch, I set off in pursuit of my foe, up through the manhole and into the ceiling. The sun was now beating down on the iron roof, and the small cavity of the ceiling was unbearably hot. Within a minute, a blend of perspiration and used alcohol was dripping from me.

"I can't see him, Mrs. Thrag," I announced.

"He's up there!" she shouted. "I can hear him scratching."

Now, above my own panting, I could hear it, too – a hideous, rasping sound. I advanced towards it, crouched, stepping from timber to timber, and holding the torch at arm's length before me, its feeble beam lighting a small cone. I moved it this way and that, trying to detect the source of noise, when suddenly the light dulled to ochre, flickered and died. A wave of panic surged through me. I glanced back, and could see a faint rectangle of light, outlining the manhole access.

"Mrs Thrag! Do you have another torch?"

"All right!"

I waited, immobile, as the seconds ticked by, and the intensity of the scratching rose, and seemed to come nearer. I felt disoriented, so squatted to steady myself on the timbers of the ceiling.

"All right, Mr Campbell!" Mrs Thrag's voice was faint now. "I'm out on the porch!"

"No, Mrs Thrag! I want another torch!"

"I can't hear you, Mr Campbell! I'm out on the porch! You'll have to speak up!"

That was when it happened. I'm not particularly phobic about rats. I'm a bit phobic about the dark, as I've said. Well, phobic is probably putting it too strongly. I just don't like it, because when it's dark I tend to have dark thoughts. But what I now felt was the touch of this dank, dying, furry thing; the tearing of its tiny claws against my hand. I screamed. I shot bolt upright, bloodied my head on one of Mrs Thrag's rafters, staggered back and plunged through Mrs Thrag's ceiling. What I came down into was another reality.

The trestle table that broke my fall was in what may otherwise have been a bedroom. The table itself appeared to have contained a myriad of matchboxes which, as I shattered the table, shot into the air, and then rained down around me. There I lay, partially stunned, and gazed around the room. The room was a shrine to matches! There were shelves devoted to books of matches, large boxes of matches, very old boxes of matches, wax matches, safety matches. The wheels of my mind were spinning, and could not gain traction. Something red appeared on the front of my shirt. I stared at it stupidly, dabbed at it, before realising it was blood. I reached a hand to my head, and it was bloody.

Suddenly Mrs Thrag was at the door.

"I appear to be injured, Mrs Thrag," I said.

"Them were Alphonse's!" she said accusingly.

"What?"

"The matches! Them were Alphonse's. 'E were a collector!"

There was a pride in her voice that I couldn't reconcile.

"A collector."

"'E loved them matchboxes, 'e did! His life's work, 'e called it!" She came over and poked at an old piece of card on the floor. "Look! That were 'is John Fendrich! Worth a bob or two, that was!"

"Yes. Well, I'm sorry."

I was more concerned with trying to staunch the flow of blood from my head.

"It's buggered now!"

"I'm sorry, Mrs Thrag!"

I struggled upright, and now Mrs Thrag turned her gaze skyward, and began to scrutinise the Campbell-shaped hole in her ceiling.

"An' what about my ceiling, eh? What about that!"

I glanced up. Pieces of lathe and plaster swung raggedly, and occasionally dropped.

"I'll... I'll fix it!" I said stupidly.

How would I fix it? I was a man with no practical skills, no tools and an often unsteady hand. But my head ached, I felt numb where my arse had met with the table, and I was still uncertain as to the state of my coccyx. I just wanted to put Mrs Thrag and her rat behind me.

I did venture back later in the day with a piece of cardboard I'd found outside the local off licence, and some scotch tape, and made a reasonable fist of patching the hole. The matchboxes, many crushed or broken, had now been gathered up, and erected in a corner, as a kind of monument to Alphonse. I've avoided Mrs Thrag since.

But the episode with the matchboxes, the whole idea of collecting, brought me back to my cell mate, Dave. Like me, Dave had been on remand. Unlike me, Dave was a recidivist, so he held out no hope of getting off. He knew how the system worked, and so the idea of hope was foreign to him. He was going down "big time".

"Well, I done it," he said in a resigned sort of way, when I asked him why he wasn't at least putting up the show of a fight. "An' even if I never done it, they'd say I done it an' no-one would believe I never done it."

What he'd done was to steal a snow globe. You know those things that have plastic scenes inside them? You shake them, and little granules of white float about, and you're supposed to believe it's snow. I could immediately identify with Dave, because I'd once stolen a snow globe myself. The difference was that I had been eight, and Dave was now forty-seven. I had stolen one, whereas Dave seemed to have stolen hundreds. My theft had been born from envy: my neighbour, Mike Gable, had one, and I didn't. In fact, Mike had many things that I didn't, but the snow globe was what really caught my eye. Snow on tap! In Freeman's Bay! I'd managed to conceal it for a couple of weeks before it was discovered in my otherwise empty underpants drawer, and the wrath of my mother, and by extension God and Jesus, fell upon me.

Cellmate Dave, though, seemed to be possessed by some sort of compulsion, and the reason he was on remand was not because of the enormity of his crime, which would normally attract a tut tut from a judge, and a trivial fine. The reason he'd been remanded was because, if released, no snow globe in the city would be safe from him. Once, he confided in me, once he'd had a substantial collection. Santa snow globes, obviously, snowman snow globes, penguin snow globes, but also more exotic examples: a Marilyn Monroe snow globe; a Henry Kissinger snow globe; a large snow globe that featured in exquisite miniature detail the town of Nome, Alaska. All gone, he lamented. Taken, when he'd been busted, and mostly returned to their rightful owners.

"But what *drives* you?" I asked him. "What makes you want to collect snow globes?"

He thought about it for some seconds, shook his head, and then said:

"I's the snow. I jus' love snow."

"Well, wouldn't it be easier to go somewhere where there's *lots* of snow. Nome, Alaska, for example?"

He shrugged, and looked downcast.

"'Ow?" he said.

And there we let it lie.

But my biggest fear in prison had been getting myself banged up with some two-hundred kilogram orang-utan, who might have a more than passing interest in the contents of my trousers. Dave, therefore, was a welcome relief. The only thing that would have given Dave cause to be interested in the contents of my trousers would have been if I'd had a snow globe stuffed down them.

At night, as I lay there willing sleep to come, I would hear Dave's gentle snore, and covet his ability to accept whatever life threw at him. The hours would tick by, and when Death came nuzzling at the door at three or four in the morning, even then he didn't stir.

Yes; I envied Dave.

Chapter 15

The reason I'm delaying this is because, I suppose, I'm concerned you'll think less of me. We're conditioned into thinking that killing is wrong. Sanctioned by the state, it goes on all around us, though, doesn't it? So before you go getting all judgemental, I think we need to agree on one thing: killing is a human dynamic! Well isn't it? It was there at the cradle of civilisation, and it's enshrined in any myth of human social evolution I can readily think of. Cain and Abel; Medea and Apsyrtus; Höðr and Baldur; the Pandavas and Karma; Cronus and Uranus; the death of Maui. People die, gods die, and they die for good reasons, frequently at the hands of other people or other gods, and often good things come from those deaths. It's easy to see death in a negative light, but as with, say, the Green Man legend, new beginnings can spring from death. That's why we humans are so ready and willing to give Death a helping hand in the name of progress.

Most of the lower predatory mammals are quite happy to follow the Darwinian way of things: they kill to eat, and those that kill best live best and longest and breed most, and sire offspring that do the same. Boring! But we humans, having the advantage of consciousness, are infinitely more efficient. We can plan. We can devise more creative excuses to kill things, than that we just want to eat them. We will rush out and kill millions just because some tinpot potentate gets it into his head that he fancies some piece of land or other. Or we'll kill because someone's a different colour, or believes in a different god. For God's sake! We'll even kill people for no better reason than that we don't like the look of them! Just consider the following as a starting tally.

Genghis Khan and Tamerlane: a little Mongolian junket that put paid to hundreds of thousands of people on the grounds of differing ethnicity or religion. But that was ages ago, so let's move ahead a bit.

Beginning in 1885, up to fifteen million Congolese die at the hands of jolly old Leopold II of Belgium. But let's not be too hard on him; similar things were going on all over Africa, in the America's, in New Zealand, in Ireland; and in Australia the British had even struck on the novel idea of spreading smallpox amongst the natives as a way of solving their problem of not having the place to themselves. It rather put the responsibility and hard work of killing onto those who were being killed. Quite innovative and novel. Still, it's going back a way, though, isn't it? We've learned a lot since then!

Well, let's skip all those shenanigans of the early twentieth century; let's leave whatever happened in Nanking or Buchenwald or Tibet unspoken. Let's not even mention Australia's stolen generation, or give a thought to the more than six million who succumbed in Europe between 1914 and 1918. And gas chambers have been done to death, haven't they? So let's get right up to date, with Rwanda's eight hundred thousand ghosts clamouring for vengeance, or the two million Cambodians who died for some idiot's ideological cause.

I've gone and got a bit loquacious, and rather lost my point? That's right! My point is, don't go getting all judgemental! I have ideologies, too!

The little accountant! Planning! Yes, now I've got that rant off my chest, let's get back to how I planned the removal of this weaselly lover of ledgers from his tedious spot in the world. Better still, let's move on to the actual doing of it!

I'd planned it for a Wednesday, knowing that it would give me an additional hour before he began to be missed, and reasoning that any reasonable person would give it another hour or two before raising any sort of alarm. I mean, surely Lena would consider the option that he'd just decided to do something interesting, maybe for the first time in his life, and if only to see what it felt like.

This was back in the days before they had those automatic security doors on underground car parks, so I was able to walk in, conceal myself behind one of the couple of dozen cars, and wait for him. I'd done a couple of practice runs previously, and on both occasions he'd been alone when he came down, grey-looking and moping sluggishly towards his Toyota. But on the Wednesday, another bloke emerged into the car park just before him, and I was thwarted. This fellow buggered about, and by the time he left, my dabbler in digits was already in his car and had initiated the warm-up procedure. I was obliged to abandon the operation until the following Wednesday, which wasn't a bad thing, because it gave me time to iron out a few technical difficulties that had hitherto not occurred to me: for example, wind erosion on a dune coastline. But we'll get to that later.

The following Wednesday went like clockwork. Down he came at one minute past five, squeaked open the heavy fire door linking the car park to the stairwell, and slumped towards his car: a picture of ennui. This had to be a finely judged thing, and that was where my planning came in. I had on my back a rucksack containing what I would need later on in proceedings, and stuffed under my jacket I held my wool hook, its wooden handle poking outwards. As he fumbled with his keys at the car door, I quickly approached from behind, thrust the protruding handle into his back and said, *sotto voce*, "This is a gun! Don't move!"

That approach had always seemed to me to work all right in the movies, but in real life things happen differently. This little squirt spun about, so that we were eye to eye, glanced down at the protuberance beneath my jacket, and said, "No it isn't!"

The last thing I'd expected was a debate as to whether I had a gun or I was just pleased to see him.

"Yes it is!" I countered, when even I could see the wooden handle of the wool hook had slipped from beneath my jacket.

"No it isn't!" he shot back.

Suddenly I was struck by inspiration, and I whirled backwards, whipped the wool hook from under my jacket with a theatrical flourish, and said, no longer *sotto voce*, "No! It's a wool hook!" and drove it into his shoulder.

Obviously there was a modicum of yelling and struggling at this point, but you'd be surprised at the degree of control an embedded wool hook gives you over a person. I discovered later that it was hitched under his clavicle (sheer serendipity – I hadn't planned it that way), so the chances of him wriggling off the hook, so to speak, were minimal.

"Get into the car!" I commanded.

"Help!" he yelled to the empty car park.

"Get into the bloody car!" I commanded again, this time hurling him around on the end of the hook. More yelling, but at least a degree of cooperation. He seemed to have already unlocked the vehicle, and now began yanking at the door handle until it opened, and he tumbled into the driver's seat, my hook still lodged in his shoulder, and half dragging me with him. This was ideal! I reached back, opened the rear door, slid onto the seat, all the while keeping my catch under control, the only difficulty being when I had to move the wool hook from a forward-facing to a rear-facing position. The yelling rose in both pitch and tempo.

"Drive!" I said, slamming the door.

He was moaning, with pain I assume, but he duly fumbled the key into the ignition and kicked the vehicle into life. And then he sat there, quietly lamenting his predicament.

"*Drive!*" I commanded again.

"Warming – up!" he groaned, through clenched teeth.

"Bugger warming up! Just drive!"

He didn't seem happy about the idea, but he depressed the clutch, and tried to reach forward to engage a gear, and then howled with pain.

"Can't!" he squeaked. This was a reasonable objection, because the wool hook was penetrating his left shoulder, and obviously partially disabling his left arm. There was no point in insisting on it. I mean, I wasn't a sadist, for goodness sake!

"All right," I said. "You operate the clutch, and I'll do the gears."

Again he depressed the clutch, and after several attempts, straining forward, I discovered reverse. He duly released the clutch, and we shot backwards.

"Careful!" I cautioned. "Any funny business and this goes through your throat!" I said, giving the wool hook a jiggle.

He nodded and yelped. I was making this up as I went along, because what I'd thought I'd be doing was calmly sitting there pretending I had a gun. In my bag I had a perfectly good knife and a razor-edged hatchet, which I'd intended to use when things got messy. I now realised that the wool hook was an unintended stroke of genius.

So in this unconventional manner, the nitpicker managing steering, clutch, brake and acceleration, with me on gears and navigation, we proceeded out of Auckland City. I'd hunched myself forward, not only so I could reach the gear stick, but also so that any observer would have thought I was having a friendly chat in my driver's ear. After we'd gone a few kilometres he seemed as happy as Larry. In fact I had to give the hook the occasional tweak, and elicit a small scream, just to reassure myself that it was still connected to him. But that had the unintended side effect of getting the blood flowing again, so I stopped, fearing he may bleed to death before we reached our destination. I imagined us puttering to a stop as we headed out west, and me having to explain why I had my driver on the end of a wool hook.

"Where – we – going?" he asked, again through gritted teeth, as we were motoring through suburban Glen Eden.

"Oh, just for a drive," I said airily.

"Why?" he groaned some time later.

"Why what?" I asked.

"Why – this?"

"Oh, this! Well, I have a little surprise for you," I said.

"What – surprise?" he asked after a few more kilometres had gone under the wheels.

"Well," I said. "It would spoil it for you if you knew, wouldn't it?"

More time passed.

"Birthday – surprise?" he asked.

"*What?*" I said.

The little bloke must be getting delirious, I thought. And anyway, I hadn't anticipated having to engage in conversation with him. I'd imagined it would be too boring.

"Today – my – birthday," he grunted.

"Oh! Is it? Well, happy birthday," I said to him.

I didn't want to know any of this. It only added an unwanted element of pathos to an already tense situation. But as we journeyed on, my curiosity was stirred.

"How old are you?" I asked after a while.

"Thirty-two," he moaned.

"Oh! Same as me! We have something in common. You're a rat, too!"

He seemed to labour over this, and a couple of minutes later he came back with:

"No – accountant."

"Yes, I know. But I mean you were *born* in the year of the rat." He obviously had no idea what I was talking about. "That makes you adorable and hard-working and intelligent. Mind you," I told him, "I'm not seeing much of that at the moment!"

He grunted.

"Did you know that Lena was a dragon?" I asked him.

Conversation seemed to take his mind off his present dilemma, but now he seemed stumped again. I could see his furrowed brow in the rear-view mirror.

"Highly regarded in Chinese culture, the dragon," I said. "Certainly a dragon girl may be a bit arrogant and impatient and impulsive – do you find that with Lena?" But he seemed to be lost down some side track of his own, so on I went. "But those negative qualities are more than offset by their generous, romantic and sensitive nature. Now that's Lena to a T, isn't it?"

"How – you – know – Lena?" he winced.

"Lena? Oh, I've known Lena for years! Didn't she tell you? We virtually grew up together. I'm the man she was always intended to marry!" I said.

This information seemed to be news to him, and he began to move about in a state of some agitation, obliging me to rein him in with the hook.

"Let's just drive on in silence," I suggested.

There's a conveniently isolated and rugged coast to the north and west of Auckland, inhabited only by sand dunes, rabbits, pine trees and the occasional fallow deer, and we were nearly there.

We pulled up a track from the main road that I'd pre-selected, and when it petered out into a desolation of marram grass and scrubby pine, I ordered him to stop. I had expected some opposition to the idea of entering a bleak and uninhabited area such as this, but he was going like a lamb to the slaughter.

"Right," I said. "End of the line! Pass me the keys, if you wouldn't mind."

And he docilely obliged. We then went through the rigmarole of getting out of the car, me restraining him on the hook, him yelling as, I suppose, it bit into him. But we managed, and I toddled him a way into the tangle of trees. I estimated we had about an hour and a half before dusk made progress difficult, so after a couple of hundred metres, I stopped him and asked him to sit. He seemed to realise that he was about to become marram fodder, because it was now that he decided to make one last, valiant attempt for life. He tried to whirl around, but again, the hook made him so easy to control. A simple tug on it, and he was on his backside on the ground, howling in agony.

"*Why?*" he moaned again, as I was restraining him with one hand, and unshouldering my bag with the other.

"Why what?"

"Why – you – do – this?"

It was a fair question.

"Look," I said, and I disengaged the wool hook, and went around to face him, holding the hatchet. His eyes now seemed unfocussed, and his head was tending to loll, probably through loss of blood. "Look!" I said more sharply, slapping his face to get his attention. His head jerked upright. "It's nothing personal. I want you to understand that. But you must realise you're the most damnably boring cretin ever to walk the face of God's earth! You simply don't deserve Lena!"

And with that I brought the hatchet down, and watched with a sense of detached fascination, as it almost cleaved his head in two. He toppled sideways, and a series of gurgles proceeded to emerge from somewhere around where his mouth must have been. There was an elaborate jerking of the extremities, which went on for long enough for me to consider delivering a second whack, and then all was still. A fantail flitted nearby, snapping up the insects stirred to life by the ruckus.

I retrieved my collapsible shovel from the backpack, and set about digging a hole large enough to comfortably contain a small accountant. It was sand; the digging was easy, and well within an hour I was down to depth. I'd been very aware that where people tend to go wrong is that they go too shallow, and wind erosion or stray dogs bring their handiwork to the attention of the authorities.

I could see the western sky turning to gold as I prepared to roll him into his final resting place. But then, I couldn't resist. I really needed to see what the inside of an accountant looked like! The wool hook unzipped him quite neatly, exposing the viscera as if they'd been carefully folded in there. Just as boring as the outside! I gave them a cursory nudge, thought of pulling them out for a closer inspection, but then a putrid smell began to waft out, and so I shoved him in the hole and filled it back in.

The drive back into the city was a quieter one. I'd left the Anglia parked on a busy street in the eastern suburbs, and now I parked the recently departed's car in a nearby, newly formed, but as yet deserted, subdivision, and walked the couple of kilometres to my Anglia, again donning my glasses and cloth cap disguise.

I felt I could sleep more easily that night, knowing that Lena would be free of this shackle on her life.

Chapter 16

And then, going into 1982, well I don't know what happened, really. I'd been a bit tied up with Rags – just checking on her, making sure her life was on track, that she wasn't involving herself with some other deadbeat. Once every few months I'd call in and see her, using the "old friend" pretext. I could see she wasn't that keen to ask me in, but after we'd been standing at the door for an awkward few minutes, she always did, and while she brewed up a pot of tea I was able to check for any signs of anyone in her life. Zilch, as far as I could see – could've been a nun. She'd obviously learned her lesson.

The son she had didn't look in the slightest like the accountant, which was fortunate. I don't think I could have tolerated that. Instead, he was almost a male replica of Rags – a tiny Russian doll that had emerged, fully-formed, from Rags's flawless belly. I could forgive him his parentage, because I felt I'd had a part in it. I'd spared him the necessity of knowing his father, as I wished somebody had spared me the necessity of knowing mine. There was still a photograph of the bean counter gathering dust on the mantelpiece, which used to piss me off.

They never found him, you know. He was like the Amelia Earhart of Green Lane: set off on a mission one day, and simply vanished into thin air. They made assumptions. The quantity of blood in his car was sufficient to confirm foul play, and to suggest that he may no longer be in the land of the living. But I'd thought there might have been "sightings". We must have made an odd couple as we headed out west, me hunched over him, gears graunching; and particularly during the final stages of our journey, when he was weaving a tad. You'll normally get some tattletale who can't keep his nose out of other peoples' business. But nothing. He might as well never have existed.

I'd tried to comfort her, of course. I'd left it for a couple of days, not wanting to appear vulture-like, and then called in to offer my condolences. But I wasn't alone. There was a policewoman there, and "friends" I hadn't even known she had. Platters of food; flowers; cards. All I'd brought was me. She thanked me for my kindness, but said she just needed some time alone. Incongruous, seeing as how the house was overflowing with people. I'd glanced at the dome of her belly, I don't think my disgust showed, but I nodded and left. It was perhaps six months before I went back, and she was a bit more hospitable then.

Rags had gone back to radiography, as soon as the boy was old enough to go into care – kindergarten, and then some old woman who lived nearby who used to manage him during the afternoons. I tried to engage myself with the child a couple of times, but he was standoffish. He would glare at me from across the room, twisting at the tails of his shirt, and looking serious. "Och! He's just shy," Lena would say, embarrassed by him. It didn't worry me particularly. I've never really clicked with children, even as a child. So I played the helper, asking if there was anything that needed doing. But there never was.

The cats for me were just a hobby. I had about thirty of them, and I'd be the first to admit that the taxidermy on the earlier ones left a bit to be desired; but they were improving! I also had a few in the freezer, because I was managing to trap more than I could mount. Even the trapping was fraught, because once caught in the gin, the cats make the most cacophonous din, and I'd be out there at all hours, subduing and then trying to kill them without causing too much damage. And on the odd occasion I didn't respond to the caterwauling, I'd go out in the morning to find that all I had was a chewed-off leg, and there wasn't much I could do with that.

Eve was always edgy about them though; she considered it an odd thing to be doing, which I thought rich coming from her. Additionally, she was always worried about the neighbours; but as I said to her, they'd just go out and get another cat.

It had started quite coincidentally, with an old moggy that had latched itself onto Rags, and which she then developed an irrational attachment to. I'd go round there, and this thing would be mooning over her, or sitting on her lap, and I got to thinking how unhealthy it must be. There was the child to consider, too! I mean, there's Cat Scratch Disease, toxoplasmosis, cryptosporidiosis, not to mention simple fleas and hook worms. It just wasn't worth the risk, but I could see there would be no point in trying to talk Rags out of the animal. It was a straightforward matter coaxing it through the noose, using some fish oil, and then once the hitch was tightened there was barely a squeak from it, as I carried it wriggling and clawing to the boot of my car, under cover of darkness.

Taxidermy is actually quite fun. You'd think it would be messy, but it isn't. Well, at least it doesn't have to be, although I must admit that, for me, part of the fun was in studying the viscera. You'd be surprised what you can learn about a creature from what it's been eating. Then there was the challenge of seeing if I could get the brain out in one piece. Often I'd preserve the organs in alcohol, in small, decorative jars, but Eve was hesitant about me displaying them round the house. She found them grotesque, she said. Personally, I found them less grotesque than her paintings.

The technique I was using was quite complex, and involved retaining the skull, and some of the skeletal structure. These, therefore had to be completely stripped of anything that might decompose. Very time consuming. I had a book on it.

Things seemed to go wrong just before Christmas, after school had broken up for the holidays. Admittedly, I'd been hitting the drugs pretty hard, having also found a reliable source of cocaine by then. Early December had been a bit of a snowstorm of cocaine, and some of the problem may have been linked to that.

Exactly what I was doing to the cats at this stage, I'm not prepared to say, because I can't entirely recall, and for much of it I have only Eve's word, and I just don't feel she's that reliable. Suffice to say she had decided it was not "normal". This from the creator of "Abortion", "Foetal Position" and "Death of a Virgin Bride".

What happened was, about a week before Christmas I kind of blacked out. Everything became a blur, and then I found myself waking up in the nut shop. No alcohol there, of course; no drugs apart from the neuroleptic "fluphenazine", and a few odds and ends to help ward off the evil effects of alcohol withdrawal.

Apart from that, there was a lot of talking: talking with people who *were* actually bonkers, which was fun, and talking with psychiatrists, which was less fun. What drugs had I been taking? they wanted to know, because they could have been a trigger for my "condition". What condition? I asked. A touch of psychosis, they suspected. *Psychosis?* I asked, stunned, while taking my own shit and smearing it over the wall of my cell. Just a hint, they thought. And the drugs? Well, nothing more than the usual. Cannabis was still my favourite, ameliorating reality, enhancing the alcohol into a nice, golden glow. I still had a small appetite for Tuinal when I could get it, but now found the effect a little heavy. I preferred to go up, rather than down, and if I was going down, then I didn't want to go too far down. LSD on special occasions (Although I *had* tried it once in class, which was an interesting experiment: you try getting through *Ode to a Grecian Urn* with half a tab of Clear Light working its transformative magic inside you, with thirty thirteen year olds, each with the face and head of a werewolf foaming at you; you try and do that without breaking down into maniacal laughter.).

And of course, the cocaine. Had I been sleeping? When? At night. Well, no, not much, although that was where the Tuinal would come in. But generally I was too busy with my cats. Even one could take weeks!

From a narrative point of view, I'd like to be able to say that this developed into some meaningful *One Flew Over the Cuckoo's Nest* scenario, ending with me as an heroic, brain-dead McMurphy, or that, like Janet Frame, I was rescued from surgical brain destruction at the final, crucial moment. But none of that happened, because whatever Weltschmerz I'd slipped into, I just seemed to slip out of. Whatever had happened, and I'm still not certain what it was, unhappened, and I was declared sane and well towards the end of January. I was able to go back to school, and hardly missed a beat.

But Eve had thrown all my cats out, all my bottled organs, all my taxidermy tools and my book, and I couldn't really summon up the energy to start over again. We were back to being stuck with her morbid paintings to look at.

I had "follow up" appointments with an excruciatingly boring bloke, a gangling type, who used to nod at me encouragingly, with his head cocked to one side, as if he'd been hanged. We both yawned through our sessions together, where we pored over my "progress". I had also been prescribed a milder neuroleptic called perphenazine, which I was supposed to take "indefinitely", but didn't. After three or four visits with the boring bloke, I simply stopped going. No one cared. I was just some harmless eccentric who liked stuffing cats, and whose wheels had spun on reality a bit. I did knock back on the cocaine, though. You need to watch that stuff. Lethal!

The only other person I ever confided in about this was Rags, because we were so close. It was during one of my visits to see if I could help. Our chat was lagging a bit, as they tended to; the kid was over next door playing, so I introduced it as a sort of conversation-filler.

"You'll laugh about this when I tell you," I said.

But she didn't. She just stared at me. And when her son rushed in, the smile dropping from his face when he saw me, she drew him into her side, and looked vaguely worried.

Chapter 17

These days I deal with social situations much better, necessity perhaps being the mother of invention. I'm quite good at bluffing my way into parties, and the reason I do it is because of the alcohol. Actually, that may be a bit simplistic. I do crave human company. I find most people distressingly boring, but I'm prepared to keep trying.

I have a little shoulder bag. These things are quite fashionable now, and although my appearance might tend towards the scruffy, I can generally get by if I affect a gay or intellectual persona. People are prepared to overlook a lot if you're considered to be harmlessly different, even the fact that you're not supposed to be there. So I can generally come away with my shoulder bag stuffed with all sorts of goodies.

I don't feel any recriminations about bluffing my way in. After all, politicians do it all the time, and they stay for three years. Generally, by the time the host has twigged to the fact that I'm uninvited, I've managed to ingratiate myself with enough people that I'm allowed to stay. And normally I have at least a nominal relationship with *someone* there. It's not just a question of walking in off the street, although I've been known to do that. I'm quite good at mingling.

I've been analysing it. Ninety-nine percent of people adopt a horizontal approach to social situations. What I mean is, they wade in from the shallow end, hoping the water doesn't get too deep because really they can't swim very well. I prefer the vertical approach: I simply dive in. Socially, I'm an Olympic class swimmer. 1500 metre distance event, 50 metre dash, freestyle, backstroke, medley; I can do anything. You see these Waders struggling along, and you really can't help but feel sorry for them. You've only got to stand around smiling vacuously, and within minutes you'll attract a Wader.

Watch, here , as a Wader tries to strike up a conversation.

Wader: Hullo.

Victim: Hi.

W: So, um, how do you know the host? [Waders learn these lame opening gambits from self help books written especially for the socially inept.]

V: She's my wife.

W. Oh. [Wader stares at feet]

V. And how do you know her?

W: Um, we work together. I'm in accounts. I've been there for thirty-nine years. Last year I got promoted to junior accounts manager. So that's good. Um. It's a really great firm to work for. Did you know they buy us lunch on the last Friday of every month?

V: Really? How interesting.

W: Yes! Pizza! Or sometimes those little bread things shaped like horse shoes...

V: Croissants.

W: Yes! That's it! With ham and cheese and lettuce, and...[At this point a little alarm sounds in the Wader's head that tells him he's breaching all the protocol recommended in the self-help book, so he tacks off towards a safe harbour]...so, um, what is it *you* do, then?

V: I'm a teacher.

W: Gosh! That's interesting!

V: Not really. I try to teach English literature to a bunch of dimwits who'd much rather be checking out their social media sites. In fact, half of them are actually doing it under their desks.

W: Oh. Well, I suppose...

V: Excuse me. I see the hummus is running a bit low.

There's nothing wrong, *per se* with the Wader's approach here, except everything. I mean, perhaps it could have worked, but he flogs it to death! If only he'd used the spring board tactic to dive deep. Here's how I would have used the same approach.

Me: Hello!!

Very Interested Person: Well, Hi!

M: So! How do you know old Jugs Jansen, then?

VIP: She's my wife!

M: Really!

VIP: Yes! And who invited you?

M: Well, Jugs did, of course!

VIP: Her name's Darlene!

M: Darlene! That's right! I always forget! Superb tits, though!

VIP: So how does she know you?

M: Well, Jugs gives the best head I've ever had! Actually we've been having an affair on and off for five or six years now.

You see how I steer the conversation into a much more interesting place? To be honest, I don't use this sort of approach much, because it can have unpredictable consequences. Here would be a more common opening play for me.

M: Hello!!

VIP: Oh! Hi!

M: Did you see that they've discovered evidence of cosmic microwave background radiation left over from the Big Bang.

VIP: What?

M: Yes! Apparently! I was surprised, too! Just think what this will mean to the average person!

VIP: Mmm. Excuse me. I see the hummus has just run out.

M: [Shouting at VIP's receding back] Just think what it will mean to microwaves!

As they say, you've got to kiss a lot of frogs before you find a prince.

I was at a party when I heard about the suicide. I'd got stuck with this Wader who'd been going on about how running a half marathon had changed her life, for God's sake.

"Really?" I said. "How interesting!" eying up an unopened bottle of Glenmorangie just looking for an owner.

But irony tends to be lost on these sorts of people, so on she blundered.

"Oh, yes! I feel so much better for it! A new woman! Do you know, I've lost thirty-seven kilos? I'm down to a size six! My heart rate has dropped to fifteen beats a minute! My menstrual cycle's all up the whack, of course, but the benefits outweigh that!"

"Did you know they cut Nijinsky's feet open after he died?"

"What?"

You can sometimes get rid of people like this by bringing up an anecdote as an antidote. Or just throw in some unusual fact that is just barely tangential to the conversation, in this case, feet. They think you're a bit strange, so they wander off to find someone of their own ilk. Waders have an aversion to odd or different people. Well, that's a bit of a generalisation. It depends on what sort of odd you're talking about. If you've got a fashionably different person there, say a person in a wheelchair, or someone with Down Syndrome, they'll have Waders climbing all over them.

"Yes. An autopsy. They wanted to discover if there was anything unusual about the bone structure of his feet – anything that might have explained his extraordinary leaps."

"And, um..."

The Wader was looking a bit uneasy. She'd gone from a full-on frontal position, where she had me hemmed into a corner, and was blocking my escape, to a lateral one. Just one more nudge, and she'd shuffle off.

"Nothing! Same feet as you or me."

"Oh!" She almost turned, and seemed prepared to put those feet to good use, and shuffle off. But then she was struck with an afterthought. "Speaking of autopsies, did you read about that poor girl – that horrible suicide?"

I dread people who start dredging through news stories, just to keep a conversation afloat – human interest stuff, or political – it's all the same. Who's invading whom, the latest famine spot in the world, was the CIA really behind nine-eleven. Or as in this case, some blood-drenched local ditty about someone topping themselves. There's nothing we can do about it, so, why, for Christ's sake, labour it to death over a plate of crudités?

"No," I said, trying to sound bored, and inching round, so that we were now standing side by side, each ready to make good our escape. The Glenmorangie was still standing there, unloved.

"That girl – the one the teacher raped. Remember. About five years ago?"

"He didn't..." I started indignantly, and then caught myself.

I'd changed my appearance, of course. Grown a beard, let my hair grow out a bit, stopped dying it. I'd gone back to wearing glasses again, almost permanently, and I'd deliberately chosen heavy-framed ones, so you wouldn't necessarily have picked me as the same chap from the photos that were being published at the time. Anyway when I'd been going in and out of the court they'd only got glimpses, because I always had a blanket over my head. They offer you those, you know. I'd always though it a bit strange, these people, these criminals walking around with blankets over their heads, but the prison blokes are decent enough to provide one. So what with the new makeover and the blanket, you'd have been hard pressed to have recognised me, unless you'd made a study of it.

"Been missing for ages, poor girl. You'd have thought she'd been through enough, wouldn't you? And then they found her! She was..."

"Mmm," I said. "Terrible! Ooo! If you'll excuse me, I'll just get some of that hummus before it's all gone!"

That's one of the problems with being largely divorced from the mainstream media – you tend not to know what's going on, and when something like this crops up that affects you, you're completely unaware of it.

But later I checked it out on-line, and sure enough, it was her. Guilt, I suppose. She must have been ravaged by it.

Chapter 18

We're hopping around in time here, I'm sorry. I'm just not a very organised sort of person and, bear in mind, what I'm doing is giving birth to memories. Some of them pop out easily; some are long and painful, and require hours of labour; some even require surgical intervention, and drugs. A few even turn out to be twins. Anyway, if you want chronology, read someone's diary!

After my five weeks as a lunatic, my life achieved a kind of tableland. From this vantage point, I could look back over the plain that I had crossed, and I could see those people in my past as insignificant lice, sluggishly trawling across the hide of endeavour. And yet I knew that ahead of me, shrouded in mystery, were mountains I was yet to climb. I think everyone reaches this plateau in mid life. Most people submit to it. They look around them, look ahead, think "bugger this!" And they either turn around and go back, or they hunker down for the long haul.

This period lasted through the rest of the eighties and well into the nineties. It was quite humdrum. Oh, I'm not saying there weren't high points, but in terms of going somewhere, I seemed to be in buffering mode. I seemed to be experiencing a loss of traction. Actually, I don't think my wheels were even spinning; I was just sitting there in neutral, occasionally revving my motor.

My mother died in eighty-nine, at the relatively tender age of sixty-seven. Perhaps as a result of all the pan scrapings she'd eaten during our years of poverty, she'd turned into a bit of a lard bucket. She'd slimmed down somewhat for old Bill, although God knows why, because he had the physique of the Michelin Man. But once Bill was up on Boot Hill she took to buying herself "treats". These "treats" were invariably of a sugary and fatty nature, and by the time she reached her early fifties she'd bloomed into a hundred kilogram blimp. Immune to the whispered ridicule that followed her, she still wore her signature rainbow of dazzling colours. She would shimmer into view from afar, and grow to blinding intensity as she neared.

Then she got diabetes, which she controlled with insulin, and to fully rein in the disease, it was intended that she curtail her treats. From what I observed on the odd occasions I'd visit her, she didn't. The weight stayed firmly put, juddering like the rings of Saturn around her midriff, and the cupboards were jam-packed with carbohydrate-laden rubbish. The result was deteriorating eye-sight, problems of a gangrenous nature in the lower extremities requiring a small amputation, and a series of minor coronary events that culminated in a massive heart attack on the morning of April 17th, 1989. I remember the date, because I had it inscribed on her headstone:

Mavis Roberts

12.2.22 – 17.4.89

Wife of Bill

That was it. Eve said it seemed a little unfeeling, a little to the point, but as I said to her, you pay for these things by the letter. Who cared, anyway? Unless you're odd or dead, you don't go hanging around cemeteries, do you?

Incidentally, Eve and my mother had never got along. These are some of the words/phrases my mother used to describe Eve: a slut; an arrogant little so and so; a gold digger [?!]; Miss Fancy

Pants; stupid; unworthy of me. These are some of the words/phrases Eve used to describe my mother: a bad-tempered old bitch; a big fat old cow; a useless fucking piece of shit; a human waste disposal unit; Shit-for-Brains; a grizzling manky old crone; a mouth on legs; Fat Guts; a stomach on legs; old and useless. As you can see, Eve probably trumped my mother's anodyne collection of insults, but she did focus on the obesity issue, which I thought was rather a cheap shot. However, she did have the decency to show up for the small funeral, swelling the mourning party to seven, and whereas you might have expected her to cheer, or dance on the freshly-filled grave, instead she duly shed a tear, which was more than I could do.

I'd been quite keen to see my mother immediately before she quit the mortal coil, thinking she may have something of interest to say. Some last words that might impart meaning to her, or my life. But nothing. She lay there, with tubes coming out of her, fluids going in and fluids coming out, huffing and puffing like a stationary steam train and occasionally grunting with what seemed like pain. She opened her eyes once and said something that sounded like "Bleh!" and closed them again. So if "Bleh!" was the sum total of what she'd learned from life, I now had it. I left her to it, and was phoned by the hospital that night to say she'd "passed away".

The good thing to come out of this was the inheritance. Bill had apparently not been short of a buck or two, so the house was freehold, there was a tidy little sum in an investment account, and the usual household odds and ends. All of which might have set an ordinary person up for a life of relative ease. I, however, am not an ordinary person.

Why didn't we just move into the house? asked naive Eve. We would save so much in rent. Quite obviously, I explained, because I'd lived in the house for a number of years, and it held bad memories for me. What memories? asked Eve. I painted a colourful picture of a Victorian house of horrors, with Bill as Edward Murdstone to my David Copperfield. Out of consideration for his memory, I stopped short of sexual molestation.

"Oh!" she said. "I never knew."

"Well, one outgrows these things. One forgives and forgets," I said magnanimously. "One doesn't like to dwell. The pain lingers, though, and one doesn't like to be reminded."

In actual fact there were two reasons I had no desire to move into my mother's old house. Firstly, I'd succeeded in navigating us to a few streets up from where Rags lived. Something more modest than the place the number cruncher had set her up in, but liveable nonetheless. And secondly, I'd counted my chickens before they'd been hatched, and had plans for myself living off the fat of the land for many years from what the house would return upon sale.

But immediately thwarting my plans was some doddering old fool of a lawyer, rambling on about something called "probate". God, lawyers have tedious lives!

"But she's left everything to me!" I pointed out to him.

"I'm sorry, Mr Campbell!" he said, shaking a head like an elderly bloodhound's at me. "But your mother has appointed me executor of her will, and I cannot authorise the sale of the property until probate has been issued."

"Why?"

"Well, Mr Campbell," he said, as if preparing to launch into a long speech.

"Just briefly," I interrupted.

"Well, the will might be contested. There are creditors to take into account..."

"There are no creditors. My mother had no debts. And who would contest it?"

"That is what we need to discover, Mr Campbell."

We were sitting in an office that *was* truly Dickensian. Dust clung to files that towered to ceiling height, romped over the old mantelpiece that framed him where he sat, skittered across the floor, and stood in two pillars on each side of his desk. This dithering old dotard, an ironically named Mr Hastie, managed to delay the disbursement of my mother's estate for almost a year, during which time I was constantly in contact with him.

"How are things progressing with the estate, Mr Hastie?"

"Good, good, Mr Campbell. I've applied for probate."

This after almost three months. And then, later.

"Good morning, Mr Hastie. Has probate been issued yet?"

"Not yet, Mr Campbell."

"Well, when do you think it *might* be issued?"

"Hard to say precisely, Mr Campbell. These things take time. Due process, etcetera."

"But I could be dead myself by the time it happens!"

"A risk we must take, I'm afraid, Mr Campbell."

And then, towards the six month mark.

"Any luck yet, Mr Hastie."

"I believe I can say that things are progressing, Mr Campbell."

"Progressing."

"Apace."

"Mr Hastie, I think it's fair to say that I'm experiencing the law's delay. Should I also then expect to experience the insolence of office?"

"Most witty, Mr Campbell, most witty!" And there was a sound as of dried leaves being crunched underfoot, that I took to be a Hastie chuckle.

The day the estate was delivered into my hands, with Mr Hastie's not inconsiderable fees deducted from it, the money was into an on-call bank account, and the house was on the market. Wouldn't the proceeds be better put towards a house for us? asked Eve. Not really. I was able to demonstrate for her how, over a period of time, with money wisely invested, a rented property can be more cost effective than one that is owned.

"So you intend to invest the money wisely?" she asked.

"Absolutely!"

And over the next few years I invested it wisely in my growing range of addictions, predilections and hobbies. By the time it was gone, Eve had either lost interest or forgotten about it.

Chapter 19

So I suppose that brings us naturally around to Vivien, and the event that brought about the end of the plateau years, and inspired, not a marching on to distant unconquered peaks, but a plummet to the depths of despair.

How should I describe myself as a teacher? Adequate perhaps sums it up best. I did the least amount of work required to get by. I was never one of those teachers who bring about life-changing moments in their students' lives, because I was more interested in my own life. I set a syllabus, tried to vary it as little as possible, and only responded positively if a student responded positively to me. I managed gymnastics as an extracurricular activity, not because I knew anything about it, but because I disliked contact sports, I found cricket both incomprehensible and boring and tennis pointless. The added bonus with gymnastics was being able to see exposed flesh, without a trace of wrinkle or cellulite; flesh finely honed to its true purpose. And this is perhaps where things started to go wrong for me.

Don't misunderstand me. I didn't rush up and molest girls on the vaulting horse, or even drool as they swivelled scissor-legged astride the beam. I was a simple admirer of form and beauty, which in the art world would go unchallenged, but in the teaching world would not. But also, to fully appreciate what was about to happen, you need to understand one other thing: teachers have sexual liaisons with their students. Male and female; it happens. You may not like it, society may not like it, but it happens, and I always considered it an occupational hazard. It's highly likely they even teach you avoidance techniques now at teachers' college. Never put yourself in a situation where you're alone with a student of the opposite (or possibly even the same) gender, for example. Never allow a student to touch you.

You will have read recently, no doubt, about the female teacher who had a relationship with a fifteen year old boy. He's been irreparably damaged, his mother claims. Scarred for life! He needs counselling, he needs support, and more importantly, he needs money. Now this is something I fail to understand. Good God! When I was fifteen I was condemned to hiding under the blankets with a torch and a dog-eared copy of one of those "health" magazines they used to publish, that showed profile black and white shots of naked women. There's nothing I'd have liked better than for Miss Gumbril to have sidled up to me, and said, "Hey, Campbell! How about a bit of hanky panky on the teacher's desk after class? You bring the apple!" But no. I had to wait a further three agonising years before I could finally unearth the joys of intercourse where two people were involved (there were four, actually, but being a beggar, I could not also be a chooser. And anyway, that's another story, and one with which you're already familiar).

The point I'm making is that teachers have relationships with their students, and that is what I did. Not frequently. In fact, there were only two before Vivien, and both of those relationships petered out, as these things do. I've seen these girls in the street since, both young women now, we've exchanged smiles, and on one occasion pleasantries and I can't see that they seem to have been harmed by the experience. Certainly, at the time, they seemed to rather enjoy it.

Vivien, though, and I should have recognised this, was needier. She was apt to cling, and that is how the whole thing came about. She would hang around after class, and if it was last period, that could stretch into half an hour or more. She was a bright enough student, and showed a keen interest in modern poetry. We would discuss things such as the parallels between poetry and rap music, street poetry, slam poetry, how it could be related to the troubadour tradition, whether classical poetry had any application to modern life. It was interesting for both of us because, believe it or not, there are few people out there who have more than a passing interest in English literature.

I think if you're young and intelligent, it's easy to become isolated. I've seen a lot of particularly bright kids simply suppress their native intelligence to be accepted by their peers. It's a kind of voluntary dumbing down. They might as well have a lobotomy, really, and it's all so they can fit in with their Facebooking, twittering mates, although, certainly the incident currently under discussion predates those distractions. There's always something though, isn't there, whether it be Barbie dolls or hula hoops? And now? Well, God forbid that they should have an opinion that hasn't already gone global and become a meme! So I was always more than happy to help out where I could.

Another possible contributing factor was that I'd begun to teach stoned. I don't mean I taught it as a subject, but I'd begun to find teaching so utterly soporific, that I used to smoke cannabis prior to going into the class. I can't say if it improved my teaching, or if it brightened things up for the students, but certainly it brightened things up for me.

I was nearly rumbled once. A young teacher, in his first year approached me in the staff room, and leaned close to make some enquiry or other. Obviously he was familiar with the smell of the stuff, because at first he drew away, then leaned in again, and I could see him sniffing subtly. He peered into my eyes to detect any glassiness, and then grinned broadly. After that I began taking it orally. The effects lasted longer like that, anyway, but I'd have to say I was never one hundred percent in control of my faculties during my last few years teaching.

Anyway, this is how it happened. Vivien approached me with some query after class one afternoon, and our little discussion dragged on longer than normal. I'd been marking essays as we talked, because it's an essentially mindless task anyway; in all my time marking essays I never encountered a single Dickens or Dostoyevsky. By the time I'd finished, it was getting on for five o'clock. I packed up, and she walked with me out to my car, where we stood awkwardly.

"Would you like me to drop you off home?" She nodded shyly, tugging at her gym frock as she did so.

My home was on the way to her home. We had to drive past it, and at the time Eve and I were having another one of her "trial separations". An early menopause had come as a shock to Eve, and she resented it bitterly. In fact, it would be fair to say that life had come as a shock to Eve. So, she had once again gone to stay with one of her woman friends, who, I'm sure, understood her better. I'd become convinced that these were, in all likelihood, lesbian dalliances, and it was never quite clear to me why she came back. We'd had several trial separations, and each one seemed to go better than the one before. Quite honestly I'd got to the point with these trials where if one of them had been a car, I'd have bought it.

Vivien and I had been talking as I drove, and from habit I pulled the car into my driveway, hit the remote on the garage door, and it wasn't until the door was coming down again, and we were sitting there in semi-darkness, that I realised my mistake. Yes, I could have apologised, raised the door again and backed out. Instead, I turned to her and said simply, "Would you like to make love?" I mean, I could have said, "Would you like to borrow my copy of *Great Expectations*", or, "Would you like my recipe for mousaka?" But I didn't.

There was no pretence or coercion, though. No etchings were suggested, and there were no promises of a cup of coffee. She was not drugged, and neither was she plied with alcohol. She stared at me for a few moments, and her eyes became moist. Then she nodded. She walked of her own free will into my living room, then up to my bedroom, she freely disrobed, and afterwards I felt her tears moist on my shoulder, as she lay in the crook of my arm. Vivien was fifteen, but I'd been surprised to discover she was a virgin.

The relationship continued for ten or twelve weeks, and I acknowledge that I became aware that Vivien had a much greater emotional investment in it than I did. I enjoyed her company, but an age difference of almost thirty-five years meant that our interests were inherently different. The two things we had in common were bits of English literature, and sex. And, of course, Vivien's need to be accepted and understood. It was a halcyon few weeks, but now both our lives were about to be irreparably damaged.

Vivien's mother must have detected some change in her daughter's behaviour. I don't know – perhaps she was happier. Certainly to me she seemed happy. I'd begun to notice a brightness to her, a sparkle in her eyes, which had previously seemed lack-lustre and lifeless. And then her mother noticed some bruising (as I've said, my lovemaking tends to be passionate), and under interrogation, the girl confessed to our relationship.

Within hours I had Detective Senior Sergeant Grant Slur, and Detective Constable Dawn Dido at my door, and within a few more hours I'd been charged with having sex with a minor. Further, more serious charges may be pending.

Rape, as it turned out.

The ideas you have about prison are not necessarily correct. For example, I always believed that a prison would have stone or concrete walls, open windows with bars on them, and a slops bucket in the corner. Nothing can prepare you for it, though. The impact is as much emotional as it is physical. There is the "this can't be happening to me" feeling. But it was.

In court I'd been portrayed as a Svengali type of character, with Vivien as my Trilby. But I had not hypnotised her. I did not control her. In fact, I wanted nothing less. But midway through the prosecution's case, as the eyes of the jurors bored malevolently into me, as Vivien's mother silently berated me with curled lip, as I realised that I'd been a condemned man the moment I walked into that courtroom, I made a decision, and changed my plea to guilty: stated reason, I did not want to put Vivien through the ordeal of having to give evidence.

It worked in my favour when it came to sentencing. Five years out of a life is not so bad.

Chapter 20

I was thinking just the other day how much I love German! I love the way that, when done properly, it can, to the English-speaking ear, resemble a choking fit.

It was Christmas of 1991, when people were of good cheer, exuding goodwill towards their fellow men and women, as well as wads of cash towards shopkeepers to ensure that the birth of their Lord and saviour was properly celebrated. I had by now updated the Anglia, and was the owner of a 1975 Toyota Celica, a fine-looking vehicle with twin headlights, in canary yellow, which Eve had christened "The Rustbucket". Cars have a tendency to rust in Auckland, because of its proximity to the sea, particularly if you drive them on the iron sand stretches of lonely West Coast beaches, looking for spots where no one is ever likely to dig. Honestly, though, once the dealer down on Mount Eden Road had got me focussed on the twin head lights, I'd rather overlooked the rust.

Wishing to join in the fun of the festive season, Eve and I had gone Christmas shopping on the Friday night, Christmas Day being on the following Monday. So had everyone else in Auckland, with the result that the city's streets were like a compacted bowel. We had inched our way up Vincent Street, with the intention of eventually reaching Karangahape Road, where the newspaper advertisement had promised that "Bargains Galore!" awaited us. At the junction of Vincent and Pitt Streets, something happened.

I had been waiting, with all the patience that a person under the serious influence of amphetamines can muster, for a break in the traffic. Minutes, or possibly seconds, passed, and none occurred. And then, suddenly, a vehicle seemed to slow. I released the clutch of the Celica, and with a screech of tyres it hurtled out into the stream of traffic. Immediately a toot occurred from the following vehicle, to which I responded in the time-honoured tradition, by making an obscene gesture out the driver's window. And there the matter might have ended.

But as we continued to inch our way up Pitt Street, I became progressively more agitated by the sheer gall of the tooter in the car behind me. Eventually, around the Grey's Avenue intersection we became enmeshed in a hopeless snarl of interlocked cars, still some distance from the promised bargains, so I decided to get out of the car and remonstrate with the driver behind. As I left my car, he left his, and we met somewhere around the halfway mark.

"Have you got a problem?" I asked, somewhat rhetorically, I suppose.

"Do you realise that you should have given way back there?" he enquired.

"I had assumed you were being polite enough to let me in," I countered.

"Well, I might have, had you given me the chance," he said.

"I thought *you* had given *me* the chance!"

Now Eve had emerged, and was standing, watching the exchange like a spectator at a table tennis match.

"Let's just go, Bruce," she suggested in the gap, while my opponent was fumbling the conversational ball. I could see him mentally matching up pronouns, trying to work out exactly what I *had* said, and who had or had not been given a chance. I licked dry lips, and glanced around at the field of stalled cars in front of us. No one was going anywhere, so I turned back to confront my tormentor, and suddenly realised that he was wearing the collar of a priest or a minister of religion. This, for some reason, infuriated me even further.

"I'm sorry, but I just thought it was rather rude," said the man of God.

"Rude! Rude, was it? And who made you the arbiter of etiquette, you trumped up little tosspot?"

"Well, no one," he said, seeming to backtrack a bit. "I was just saying, I didn't feel it showed good manners."

"Good manners! Well how's this for good manners?" I said, shoving a raised digit under his nose.

"Bruce!" said Eve.

The preacher man took a step back, and began to stutter a reply.

"Well, well," he stammered. "Why don't we just let the spirit of Christmas prevail?" he proposed, suddenly conciliatory.

"Bugger the spirit of Christmas!" I replied, feeling my whole world start to redden. "What would some bloody little Nazi like you know about the spirit of Christmas?" I said to him.

And that was when I exited, and the amphetamines took over. With my forefinger under my nose to provide a makeshift Hitler's moustache, and my arm extended in a Nazi salute, I began goose-stepping around his car, while the cleric looked on agog, and Eve ran after me, plucking at my arm. Not happy with that, I then began loudly singing that much loved German carol, "O Tannenbaum".

"O Tannenbaum, o Tannenbaum

Wie true sind deine Blätter!

Du grünst nicht nur

Zur Sommerzeit,

Nein auch im Winter, wenn es schneit.

O Tannenbaum, o Tannenbaum,

Wie treu sind deine Blätter!"

By the end of the first verse, the religious fanatic was pressed hard against the side of his car, and I had worked myself into a frenzy of guttural spitting. The second verse I proposed directly into his face, stamping my feet up and down in a stationary march, while he tried to shield himself from the rain of saliva, and Eve tried to pull me away.

"O Tannenbaum, o Tannenbaum!

Du kannst mir sehr gefallen!

Wie oft hat nicht zur Weihnachtszeit

Ein Baum von dir mich hoch erfreut!

O Tannenbaum, o Tannenbaum!

Du kannst mir sehr gefallen!"

Now people in surrounding cars had wound down windows, or opened doors, and a bit of an audience had formed. A bloke with the physique of a second row prop, or a front row flanker, or whatever it is they call them, had now come to Eve's assistance.

"Come on, mate," he was saying, "come on, quieten down."

Between the two of them they wrestled me back to the Celica, whose door still gaped ajar, pushed me into the driver's seat, and slammed the door behind me.

"Stay!" the bloke with the physique warned, wagging a warning finger at me through the window.

The priest had taken the opportunity to scuttle back into his car, but the boil of my anger had not been fully lanced. I sat there, fuming, with Eve sitting beside me, saying, "Jesus, Bruce, just fucking calm down!"

"I *am* calm!" I snapped.

And then, for no good reason, I jammed the Celica into reverse gear, revved the engine until the tachometer appeared gratifyingly in the red, released the clutch, and shot back into the ecclesiastical vehicle, which then shot back into the vehicle behind it, which then created a domino effect involving four more vehicles. At the moment of the satisfying crunch, both Eve's and my seats disengaged themselves from whatever it is that restrains them, and continued on back until they came in contact with the rear seat. Simultaneously, it seems, as the padre's car was propelled backwards, his face remained stationery, and it met with his windscreen.

I had, in that single moment of amphetamine-fuelled passion discovered what has since become a national pastime: road rage! Fire personnel emerged from the nearby Central Fire Station, and the steaming chariot of the God man was doused with an extinguisher. Soon sirens sounded and flashing lights appeared, bouncing over kerbs and circumventing trees to negotiate the traffic deadlock, and before long a peak-capped head appeared at the window of the Celica. A hairy knuckle rapped.

"Excuse me, Sir. Would you mind getting out of the vehicle?"

This was at a time when the police still exhibited the patience of Christ. Not quite like those good old days, when you could be battering a constable about the head with a leaden cosh, and he would be calmly offering the mildest of protests: "Now come along, Sir! That's not the attitude!" But still polite; still reasonable.

I was semi recumbent, my seat having tipped back, and I still held the car's steering wheel in my hands, although it was no longer attached to the car.

I fought my way forward to the driver's door, only to find it wouldn't open. In fact none of the Celica's doors would open, which only went to confirm my suspicions as to the durability of Japanese cars.

"Ow!" I said.

"Is there a problem, Sir?"

"I... I think I may be injured."

But then, having been remotely examined by the St John's ambulance people called to attend to the parson, I was declared as fit as a fiddle, hauled out of the car window, and bundled off down for a cooling-off period in the cells. It was to be my first experience with imprisonment.

The next morning I appeared in the District Court, charged with something that the mists of time have dimmed, but which involved "reckless disregard". That seemed to be the nub of the thing – the sheer recklessness of it. In the ensuing court case, I defended myself, and pleaded "Act of God".

"What do you mean, 'Act of God,' Mr Campbell?" enquired the judge, a crusty old mantis, who peered from his throne over half-moon glasses.

"Well, it was an accident, sir," I explained.

"Well, why don't you simply say so, then? I can't see that God had any hand in it."

So I changed my defence to "accident", even though I felt that "Act of God" carried more weight, particularly as it involved a man of the cloth.

"So what you are saying, Mr Campbell, if I am to understand you correctly, is that your foot slipped off the clutch..."

"Exactly!"

"Propelling your vehicle back into the complainant's."

"Precisely!" I said.

"But I understand," pursued the judge, "that you were heard to be vigorously revving your vehicle immediately prior to the incident."

"Mmm."

"Well, how do you explain that?"

"I suspect mechanical, failure, Sir."

"I see. I understand also, Mr Campbell, that you were seen to be performing some sort of dance, and behaving in a threatening manner towards the victim, and that you had to be restrained by onlookers and returned to your vehicle."

"A simple misunderstanding, Sir. I do agree that the reverend gentleman and I may have had a small difference of opinion, for which I unreservedly apologise, but in deference to his suggestion that we forget our little contretemps in the spirit of Christmas, I thought to lighten proceedings by singing a Christmas carol."

"In *German*?" asked the judge doubtfully.

"To celebrate my heritage," I said.

"Campbell doesn't sound very German to me!" said the judge.

"On my mother's side, sir."

"I see. And the dance?"

"A simple Teutonic folk dance with which my family used to usher in the solstice," I said.

In the event, it was decided that I would be given the benefit of "some doubt". Not "*the* doubt". But "*some* doubt". I would not spend time in prison, although the judge confessed to being "sorely tempted". Instead I would be fined two thousand dollars, half of which would be paid to the "victim" of the incident, the ecclesiastical muttonhead who'd caused the whole thing with his toot.

Furthermore, in the absence of insurance, which I have always thought of as a poor bet anyway, I would be required to make good the damage for all six vehicles involved, plus my own. That certainly created a sizeable hole in my inheritance, which had, in any case, been dwindling away quite nicely of its own accord.

No one got Christmas presents that year.

Chapter 21

Some time in 1992, I think it was. Still the plateau years, and I was becoming bored out of my mind. Again, it was one of those scrubby pine and marram scenes of the west coast dunes.

Her eyes were bulging, and her mouth was working furiously behind its duct tape gag. She was hyperventilating, and I was concerned that she may become unconscious.

"What's wrong? Are the bindings too tight?" I asked.

She tried to nod, but with her head bound to the tree, was finding it difficult. I walked to her, zipped back the duct tape a small amount, but all she did was try to scream again, so I was obliged to force her jaw up, and replace the tape. I checked the bindings – the one around her head, the tape binding her hands behind the tree, and those around her waist, legs and feet. They were not too tight. There was no sign of swelling or purpling of the extremities – only a mild amount of chaffing from where she fought against the restraint. So I don't know what her problem was. If they'd been any looser, she would have moved, and then the apple would have fallen off her head. As it was I'd had to hollow out the bottom of the fruit, because she had one of those pointed heads. You don't think of these things when you're planning, do you?

We'd made love earlier. She'd been passionate about it, almost to the point of violence, reminding me of Eve. She'd even bitten me. Firstly there'd been a pretence of not wanting to; said she'd just wanted to be taken home, as we'd agreed when I picked her up at the bar the night before; but there, amongst the trees, it was a completely different story. I'd had to stifle her squeals of pleasure by stuffing my handkerchief into her mouth, for fear she may attract unwanted attention.

Now I was having trouble with the crossbow, never having used one before. It was a cheap thing, because I'd only intended to use it the once. What was it for? the fellow in the shop had asked. Hunting, I'd said. Hunting what? Animals. Deer? he'd asked. Pigs, I'd said. Pigs? Something with a scope, then, he'd suggested. Something with a bit of grunt to it. They were *enormously* expensive – at least a month's drug budget. So in the end I'd settled for this little thing, which was only a quarter of the price. Lacking in range, he'd said. Lacking in power, with a cheap little scope on it, rather than the expensive Zeiss thing he'd recommended. Well, I'll just try it out and see, I'd said to him.

I'd got six arrows with it; bolts they were called. I'd have been happy with one, but he assured me I'd lose them, and sure enough, the first one zoomed off a good metre from its mark, and disappeared amongst the trees. It was a damnable thing to load: you had a sort of stirrup thing you put your foot in, and then pulled the string back. All the while this woman was uttering repressed little squawks behind her gag.

"It's all right!" I said to calm her down. "I'll be aiming for the apple!"

I'd got a nice, big red one, thinking it would be an easy target, but I'm red-green colour blind, and I was finding it was blending into the bark of the tree in the dappled light of the forest. In fact, the whites of her eyes were presenting a more obvious target. The first time, after I'd loaded up, I spent ages aiming, but I couldn't stop the business end of the bow from wobbling all over the place. So then I'd got down on the ground, like we used to do in military training at school.

We used to march around with old World War One 303's, led by prissy Eton types in the upper school; we used to pull them apart (the rifles, that is, not the prissy types), and put them back together, so that if ever the country was invaded they'd find this acne'd army ready and waiting in drill shorts and school caps, with severely outdated technology. And then, once a year, we'd get a turn on the rifle range with a small bore rifle and a couple of live rounds. Trained killers, we were, by the time we came out of secondary school.

Not in vain, though – here it was, standing me in good stead! Down on the ground I was now more steady; so I aimed again, and by the time I eventually got around to pulling the trigger, it was only to discover that the safety catch was on. Then the target fainted. I saw her eyelids just droop down, so I had to get up and go and slap her face and apply some water to bring her round. There was no point in going through this if she wasn't going to be there to savour the moment.

So we'd already been at this for half an hour by the time I got my first shot off, and that was the one that soared off into the bush. How hard was this going to be? William Burroughs had managed it in one, and apparently he hadn't even been trying!

Zing! The second bolt followed the first, and the third followed the second. I deduced from this that I must be jerking the bow sideways when I tugged on the trigger. Squeeze on the trigger, don't pull it, I remembered Puddington-Jones warning us at school. Better! The bolt skimmed the side of the tree at about ear level, and whined off after its companions. I had two bolts left, so focussed all my attention on the next shot. Squeeeeeeeeze, and...

Thunk! It entered the tree, perhaps ten centimetres above the apple, but dead-centre.

"Look at that!" I shouted. "I'm improving!" But then when I tried to retrieve the bolt, it refused to budge. And now she decided to close her eyes, and feign lack of interest.

"Come on!" I said. "Open your eyes!" No response. "Look!" I said. "I've only got one shot left. You could at least show a bit of enthusiasm!" Nothing. I might as well have been talking to myself. I tried a bit of physical coercion, but still drew a blank. So I was obliged to traipse back to the car, a good half kilometre away, and get my first aid kit. It had a needle in it, for prying thorns out I suppose, but you'll marvel at my genius here! I picked at the thread holding up the hem of her skirt, until a short length of it came away. I threaded the needle, and just a couple of stitches were all that was required to hook each eyelid up to its respective eyebrow, and ensure her full attention. Quite painless, I would have thought, although with the fuss she made you'd have thought I was murdering her.

One final shot! I primed the bow, took careful aim, fired, and again the thing took off into the forest.

"Damn!" I said, to convey my disappointment. "You stay here, and I'll see if I can find one of these things."

They're quite small, and it must have taken a good hour of searching before I turned one of them up. Almost spent, its trajectory had dropped to just about ground level, and its tip was lodged in the bole of a tree. It came out easily, so back I went with the good news. I must admit, I did cheat a bit then. I'd been shooting from thirty paces, and I now shortened that to fifteen. Load; aim; fire, and thwack! Missed the apple, but a perfect William Burroughs!

She slumped as much as she was able against her restraints, while I swallowed my disappointment. I'd really wanted to hit that apple, a few times at least, before this happened. I buried the crossbow with her. It had been all very interesting, but a lot of hard work; a lot of risk. I decided to go back to the wool hook. Tried and true!

And then I remembered. I'd never even asked her name!

Chapter 22

Boring, boring, boring!

Now began a period of intense self-loathing, brought on by the very thought of what I'd been doing to these people. It was so unimaginative! Same methodology titivated, admittedly, with the odd frill; but the same tiresome, repetitive pattern. A crossbow? An apple? For Christ's sake, Campbell! Where's your sense of inventiveness? Where's your artistry? What had happened, I began to realise, was that I'd simply fallen into a rut.

This period of loathing was brought to an abrupt end one serendipitous spring day in November. Central city; imagine one of those small cafe things that spits a few tables out onto the pavement, so that people can sit, enjoy the ambience, while they suck in the fumes of passing traffic. Imagine a slit of blue above the narrow canyon of buildings. The business end of the cafe occupied a hole in the wall at the base of one of those buildings, an ugly, squat thing of perhaps eleven or twelve floors. I was with Eve, and she had struck up her anthem to the inequities of life, so I had tuned out and had become preoccupied with the antics of a group of pubescent girls. They were cavorting about, trying to draw attention to themselves, as girls of that age do, and in doing so were displaying huge amounts of pubescent flesh. There were piercings; the odd, small tattoo was on display.

"Are you fucking listening to me!" said Eve.

"Of course I am!" I replied, when not a word of what had passed her lips during the past five minutes had even registered.

"What!" she countered. "What have I been talking about?"

I could simply have guessed, and I would have stood a high percentage chance of being right: injustice as it applied to her; the evils of "the system", particularly as it pertained to the Art World, and more particularly as it applied to her lack of success in it; men and their evergreen bastardry. But no; I was not quick-witted enough for that. Instead, I tilted my head back and cast my eyes skyward, as if appealing to the heavens for inspiration.

"Fuck you, Bruce!" she said, and began to clatter noisily amongst the items that she'd for some reason taken from her bag, and which now littered the table.

But as she said it, my attention had become riveted on a tiny figure eleven or twelve floors above us. It was perched on the railing of a small balcony, its legs dangling in space, kicking lazily, causing me to think of the diminutive Alice in her too-big world. The balcony seemed too big for this figure; the building seemed too big. As I watched, as Eve gathered her things together and continued to berate me, the figure seemed to come into tighter focus, as if I was now seeing it through a lens. The world around me ceased to exist, and Eve's bluster was the distant hum of a mosquito.

Now I could see this young woman as clearly as if she had been sitting next to me: short, blond hair; a dress of dove grey, decorated with a tiny floral print; her face was not beautiful, but neither was it plain; her arms were bare, and the dress ended above knee level, exposing slender, pale legs. She could not have been more than twenty-five, and as I watched her, her legs swinging through a lazy arc, a sandal slipped from one foot and fluttered, an alien thing, the wind catching it finally, altering its almost vertical trajectory so that it slapped to earth in the centre of the road. Some heads turned towards the source of the sound, but then quickly returned to the nothings of their own lives.

But still she sat there, this tiny, brave figure. You could see from looking at her, that nothing would ever fit her: the balcony; the building; the dove grey dress that seemed somehow wrong; the sandal, just that much too big that it had slipped from her foot. And then, as if she had realised in that one moment that the world would never accommodate her, she eased herself forward into space.

There was a Nijinsky-like moment where she seemed to hover, as if defying gravity's tug. And then, as Eve slung her bag across her shoulder and turned to go, this small, dove grey sack of humanity crashed to the pavement in front of her.

During her two second journey she had said nothing, but Eve's bellowed scream said it all. It was then taken up by others sunning themselves on the forecourt, until there was an orchestra of howling. Blood, I noticed, and probably particles of grey matter, adorned the shop front window. They adorned Eve, and many of the other patrons, some of whom were now fleeing, as if somehow fearing that they may be next.

I am not quickly driven to emotion, but my own feelings in that moment were of intense pathos. Not for the life that had been lost; not for whatever misery had driven that life to end itself; but for the fact that the dove grey dress was decorated with tiny rosebuds. The pathos in that single eventually futile gesture seemed to say everything about the pointless human stand against space and time. And as Eve turned to me, her face riven by horror, I could sense that I was smiling.

There was counselling, of course. There is always counselling. Did the children of Rwanda receive counselling? The widows of Gaza or the eternally, universally displaced? Probably not. But we bloated burghers of Auckland who had had our mornings ruffled in this untimely manner were counselled.

"What are your feelings, Bruce?" asked the earnest woman who sat across from me in the small, stuffy office. Her drawn face, the grey roots to a head of hair compelled to nut brown, spoke of disillusionment with her trade.

"Feelings?"

We sat in silence while a lone cicada struck up a cacophony in the bushes outside, muted by double glazing. Time passed, while the cicada faltered and lost its rhythm, as she waited for my answer.

"I have no feelings," I said eventually. We allowed a decent period to elapse, digesting that information, while the cicada stuttered and stammered.

"What did you feel when it happened?" she asked.

I racked my brain for feelings. "Admiration," I said.

She seemed to be composing herself, fitting this into her view of the world. "And why do you think you felt admiration, Bruce?" I shrugged, and the cicada lapsed into silence. Perhaps it had found a mate, or perhaps it had simply given up. "What did you admire?" she persisted.

"The act."

"The *act*?"

"Its artistry; its symmetry, its originality; its beauty."

"I'm not sure I follow you, Bruce."

"Well, as a piece of performance art it was consummate," I said.

She seemed to inspect me for a while. "Is that why you applauded – afterwards?" she asked.

"It deserved applause," I said.

But I was not being entirely honest. If I'd been honest, I'd have listed my feelings at that moment as annoyance, shame, envy, jealousy, remorse and anger. Annoyance at having been upstaged; envy of the courage of this young woman who had been able to mount such a performance; jealousy that I had not thought of something equally impressive; remorse that I hadn't; and finally anger that my life seemed to have petered out into this trite, tedious, repetitive cycle. But also, in some way, anger that this whisper of a girl had had the temerity to act beyond my control.

And then, as December wore on into January, I began to realise that, like the young woman in the grey dress, I held my future in my hands.

One counselling session had been enough for me to reconcile my emotions, but once Eve had her snout in the trough, she was as happy as a Freemason with a silk-trimmed apron. Her counselling went on for more than a year. I would have thought that, for a counsellor, Eve would have presented a *tabula rasa*. A clean slate on which, if they chose, they could have written their personality of choice, after wiping it clean of the small, bitter thing that Eve had instead of one. But no; rather, they chose to support Eve's view of herself as a victim, and in doing so to vilify me.

It didn't worry me. I had bigger fish to fry.

Chapter 23

The falling woman had inspired in me the realisation that I held my life in the palm of my hand. And when I witnessed her sublime performance, I understood that what I had come to think of as my métier, my trade or calling, had become stale. Where was the flare? Where was the artistry? I was no better than some codger who trudges off daily to perform the same demeaning job every day for forty years and then retires to a life of daytime television.

The problem of spontaneous combustion, as it relates to the human body, had preoccupied me for a quite lengthy period of my childhood. I was around twelve, I suppose, when I came across it somewhere, in some magazine, where someone had spontaneously combusted, and the idea filled me with a dreadful excitement: that a human being could suddenly combust! It reeked of mysticism; you could clearly see the hand of God in it. And as a child you yearn for transcendental meaning, don't you? Anything that might supplant the banality of the day to day reality you're confronted with: a birth which you don't remember; an existence that is intolerable, and a death that will in all likelihood be worse. You need something more. Alien life forms, for example: Bigfoot; flying saucers; fairies; the spirit world; and people erupting into flames for no good reason. These things suggest that we live in a world that is only half-known, and that if we could only understand these things, we would discover we lived in a world with meaning.

Later, of course, some scientist poured cold water on a billion young hopes and dreams by proving that, rather than being ignited by the fire of the holy spirit, it was more likely that some obese bonehead, lying in bed with a half dozen empty family size pizza boxes, had simply ignited himself with his own cigarette butt. The premise was simple: fat burns. And he'd proven it, using a pig carcass and a smouldering butt. The flaw in his methodology, however, was obvious: a pig is not a human being, although in some cases the resemblance is uncanny.

I'd set up outside the local Weightwatcher's headquarters, and was keeping my eye peeled for a real porker. Strangely, though, most people who go to these things do not exceed the pale. Well, to me, at least, they seemed to mostly inhabit the normal range. A bit of overhang here and there perhaps, but nothing a bout of liposuction and a few gym workouts couldn't resolve. Women do tend to become fixated on their weights, though, don't they?

I'd been hanging around for a couple of days with nothing more to show for my trouble than a few wobbly bottoms, and then along came Jenny. She hove into view like a galleon. A magnificent woman; the wisps of taffeta and lace with which she embellished herself carried her forward like a spinnaker. She was an ode to adipose tissue; a song to suet; a tower of tallow.

I'd acquired some wire-framed spectacles with which to complement my growing wardrobe of disguises, and dressed in those and a simple grey suit with an open-necked shirt, I contrived to bump into Jenny when she exited the building. It wasn't difficult; Jenny was a target that was hard to miss, and as I cannoned off her she began a profuse string of apologies. No, I insisted. It had been my fault, pre-occupied as I was with my wife's recent passing.

Women are drawn to tragedy, because it is in their nature to want to apply a balm to it. Jenny was no exception. Her ample face clouded with concern and her jowls see-sawed back and forth as she shook her head sadly. There was an oily gulp as she fought back tears, inhaled an atmosphere of air, and a tremor as that same air whiffled back out through pulpy lips.

Soon we were sitting in Blasé, I on one of their recycled, retro, chromed, tubular steel chairs with its genuine fifties red plastic seat, Jenny occupying a church pew opposite me. Blasé is nothing, if not eclectic. Before me a short black steamed, while Jenny battled her way to the bottom of a cream-laden iced chocolate. A family of profiteroles stood on a nearby platter, waiting their turn to join the iced chocolate, and a brace of giant sausage rolls were on standby. Crash dieting doesn't work, Jenny was to tell me during our brief association. It pays to ease into these things, and it seems I'd struck Jenny during the easing phase.

There was no pretence of sexual dalliance during the time I knew her, and I'm not entirely sure it would have been possible without an investment in special lifting or climbing equipment. And in the event, the matter never raised its head, because any carnal desire that Jenny had was channelled into eating. We were friends; chums; eating buddies. On the two intimate occasions of my planning phase of Operation Jenny, we did nothing more than lie on her king sized water bed, useful, she explained, because they distribute weight more evenly, thereby limiting ulceration. We would surround ourselves with food, and she would talk soothingly to me of loss, not weight loss, but loss of a partner, and how to recover from it. I would come away from these encounters bored and speckled with partially masticated food.

As I have been at pains to point out, I am not a sadist, and I therefore had no intention of incinerating Jenny whilst she was in a waking state. Anyway, the noise she would inevitably have set up while smouldering would have precluded it. But because she was easily coaxed into ingesting anything of a sweet or fatty nature, and in any quantity, it was a straightforward matter to slip her a knock-out dose of pethidine, an opioid I had been enjoying myself on an occasional recreational basis, although in somewhat smaller quantities.

"I'm feeling a little sleepy," she announced, as she tucked the final spoonful of her seventh parfait inside her. "I think I may have a little nap."

"Why don't you?" I agreed. "I'll whip up a batch of cup cakes."

Soon a lusty snoring filled the room, as Jenny lay supine, her arms flung from her sides as if she'd been crucified. Although neither of us smoked, for the experiment to be authentic, ignition must be by butt. My gloved hand pulled at the tab on the celluloid that sheathed the golden packet, flipped it open, produced one of the white sticks of death, inserted its filtered tip between Jenny's flapping lips and held it there. Coordinating the lighter strike with an inhaled breath proved to be somewhat of a problem, particularly as I was manipulating Jenny's hand to do the lighting. It was like operating a giant puppet. The arm alone would have weighed as much as any average woman. But perseverance won out, and soon the cigarette's tip was glowing red with each rattling intake of breath.

I allowed the arm to fall back, the lighter now lost somewhere in the meat and sweat of the palm. I watched, fascinated, to see what would happen. Slowly the cigarette sagged between the lips, until finally it dropped and rolled into the yawning cavity of a cleavage. I waited. Minutes passed, before acrid fumes began to emerge, suggestive of burning fabric. Smoke started to waft from the funnel of the cleavage, and almost immediately a heinous shrieking began to sound.

Isn't it amazing how, despite the best planning, you can overlook the simplest of details? The smoke alarm was now making a noise sufficient to wake the dead. It didn't wake the dead, but it did rouse the interest of some crone who lived next door. A knocking began.

"Are you all right, Jenny?" came a creaking voice through the door.

"Yes," I answered in my best falsetto. "I just burned the toast."

There was a moment's silence, and then, "Are you sure you're all right? You sound funny. Do you want me to send Alan over?"

"No," I answered, the falsetto quavering as I struggled on a chair to remove the alarm from the ceiling, and then the battery from the alarm. "I'm – I'm not decent at the moment." I left the neighbour to wrestle with the image of Jenny making toast in a state of indecency, and I could hear her milling around outside the door while doing so. "See!" I squeaked, as I ripped the battery from the alarm. "It's stopped now!"

"All right, dear. But we're here if you need us."

Small puffs, like smoke signals, were now spurting from Jenny's bodice with each heave of her chest, and it was auguring well for full combustion. I allowed myself to become carried away by the scientific enquiry of the moment, and edged forward for a closer inspection. Peering down the cleft between the two massive hummocks, I could detect a flicker of flame, and the disturbed snorts that now punctuated Jenny's breathing confirmed that the fire was indeed taking hold. The tantalising aroma of roast pork began to permeate the room.

Two things now went wrong, both of which, had my planning been adequate, would have been accounted for. For a start, I had known that Jenny was given to flatulence. Intestinal gas, I imagine, is directly proportional to food consumption, and a person whose daily food intake is measured in truckloads would harbour a small methane plant inside them. With a thunder-like roll, Jenny now passed a huge cloud of flatus. The result was instantaneous. The vast, flimsy, carnation pink shift that concealed her rose around her form, and she was lit up like a gigantic sky lantern. Within seconds, the carnation pink shift, the bed and Jenny were engulfed in a conflagration, while I was left standing agog.

It was at this point that the second wrong thing about this situation occurred to me: I was standing, holding the smoke alarm. While I had empirically proven my theory beyond doubt, I was now at risk of becoming a victim of the experiment. I dropped the alarm and headed for window, catapulted myself into the hydrangeas, and fled.

The flat Jenny occupied was contained in one of those grand old mansions that has fallen on hard times, and she shared that mansion with several other people in other flats, mostly loners, I gathered, whose passing would cause barely a ripple upon the face of decent humanity.

I watched from some distance as the glow from the fire increased. A tongue of flame lapped from the window I had left open, and crept hungrily up the wall. Minutes passed before an elderly woman, presumably the owner of the creaky voice, emerged onto the veranda, and croaked, "Help!" before collapsing. Some more time passed before a head poked itself from an upper level window and began bellowing something incomprehensible, but suggesting that the owner of the head thought assistance may be in order.

Soon a siren's ululation began in the distance, and minutes later several fire appliances arrived, dispersing firepersons like ants from a nest. The bellowing head was now draped over the sill of the upper window, from which a glory of flames was sprouting. Explosions came from deep within the belly of the house, windows erupted, and finally, as the fire crews began to aim jets of water at the inferno, the grand old building shuddered, seemed to cry out in pain, and finally caved in upon itself.

The morning news revealed that the property had been inhabited by no less than seven persons, whose identities were being withheld pending positive identification.

"Tragic!" commented Eve, as she passed me at the breakfast table, where I was sipping coffee and perusing the story in the *Herald*. "Horrible!"

"Isn't it?" I sympathised. "It says here that the fire seems to have started in a downstairs bedroom. It says that, once the blaze got a foothold the fire fighters were powerless to stop it." I shook my head and tut-tutted. "No doubt someone smoking in bed. You do have to be so careful with fire!"

And Eve nodded at the wisdom of this observation.

Chapter 24

In the spring of 2002 I came out of the slammer and into a world that didn't exactly welcome me with open arms. As I've said, while I was prepared to let bygones be bygones, my former profession was not.

I have no intention of detailing my time in prison. It was not a pleasant time, and I can imagine few people choosing incarceration as a lifestyle. But I must be fair about this: they don't simply turn you loose, and expect you to cope. There is a degree of preparation. And, of course, I was on parole. I'd made a pretty good fist of hamming it up for the parole board, approaching them cap in hand. Yes, of course I accepted full responsibility for my actions. Remorseful? Good God! I was more remorseful than a penitent monk flagellating himself while wearing horsehair underpants. I'd also completed the sex offender's programme, so while we all agreed that I was a potential risk to society, that risk was considered "minimal".

Don't try to over-reach yourself, my probation officer had said. I would need to re-establish myself in society, and win its trust. I should start thinking about a new career. She was a dumpy little woman for whom over-reaching was never an option. Wonderful woman! Everyone agreed on that: caring; giving; dedicated to her job. I loathed her. I fantasised about what I could do to her with my wool hook, and all the while I smiled and nodded.

Unfair as it may seem, the child rapist label tends to stick. People are invariably hesitant about renting to recently released child rapists, and of course I had to find somewhere that was not near where children might be, in case I raped one. The dumpy woman helped me find a small unit in the central city, from where it was intended I should "fan out" across the city in search of gainful employment.

I didn't fan, but I looked about me and, yes the world had changed somewhat, but not much. Human nature was as crass as ever. People were as self-serving as they'd always been. Greed and narcissism were still society's predominant driving forces, so I fitted in pretty well.

I'd decided to stay in Christchurch; I felt it boded better for my future to make a new beginning in a city where I was unknown. Lena was still foremost in my mind, but it made sense to put her on the back burner for now. I called Eve to see how things stood there. They didn't stand very well.

"You've got a fucking cheek calling here!" was the response I got after introducing myself.

"I just thought I'd call and see how you are."

"Well how the fuck do you think I am, with a child rapist for a husband?" Do you see what I mean – that label again?

"Ex husband," I reminded her. She'd divorced me some time during my second year in prison. It had been a simple matter. We hadn't owned much, and she was welcome to all the old L.P.'s.

"Look, Bruce!" she said finally. "What the fuck do you want?"

It was a fair question. Kindness? Understanding? A little warmth and affection? Isn't that what all human beings crave? In the end I settled for a box of what she described as my "shit", that she'd found while cleaning out our flat.

The small box arrived a week or so later, delivered by one of those courier people who live their whole lives at a gallop. I pried it open eagerly, and out spilled a censored version of my past. A few books, although less than I'd expected. In fact, some of my most prized titles were missing: "Build Your Own Gas Chamber", translated from the original German by Oskar von Werner. "Onanism, Masochism, Sadism: Your Choice", by G. Trouter. Early copies of de Sade's "Justine" and "La Philosophie dans le Boudoir". Eve must have sold them, and no doubt made a pretty penny, although an accompanying note suggested there was more shit, but that it "wouldn't fit in".

Some of my better clothes had been stuffed into a couple of supermarket bags – a suit, a sport jacket, dress pants and two ties. And there was an envelope containing a cheque for nine hundred and seventy-three dollars and twenty-nine cents, with a note attached to it explaining that this represented half the proceeds from the sale of the car, and the entire proceeds from the sale of "various personal items": my books, in other words. And there, nestled amongst everything, was my wool hook, its needle-sharp beak gleaming at me like an old friend. It must have held almost as many memories for Eve as it did for me!

So I took the proceeds from the sale of my former life, and I went out and I got mind-numbingly drunk, and the world suddenly seemed a little more rosy. Particularly when the bloke sitting next to me at the cheap bar in Sydenham was able to connect me to a reliable source of illicit drugs.

Finding what my probation officer described as "a new purpose in life" was not quite the easy task you might imagine. Granted, I had my own case manager at the Social Welfare place, a Ms Worth, who was fanatical in her desire that I become employed.

"What are your skills?" she asked at our first meeting.

"Well, I'm a teacher," I said.

"Yes, Mr Campbell, but as we both realise, that is no longer an option for you. What else can you do?"

It was an interesting question, and one to which I gave serious consideration, before realising that there was very little else.

I was a one trick pony. Sure, I could dispose of the odd body or two, and I could do that very successfully. And while there may even be a demand for such skills, I doubted if it was what Ms Worth wanted to hear.

"Well," I said, "I've had very little experience at anything else. I have a master's in English Literature, and have done a PhD thesis on..."

"Can you labour?" she interrupted.

"I *beg* your pardon?"

"Is there any reason why you cannot do manual work?"

"My back..." I suggested vaguely, and let it hang there in a silence that she allowed to stretch more than was strictly necessary.

"What's wrong with your back?"

"It's weak."

"Do you have a doctor's certificate attesting to the weakness of your back?"

"No."

"Well, then perhaps a little hard work will strengthen it." My casein-loading experience had forever extinguished in me a willingness to earn my way by means of physical labour, and it must have shown on my face. "Look, Mr Campbell!" she said crossly. "You cannot expect the New Zealand taxpayer to continue to support you! They have been doing so for the last several years!"

So appointments were made for me to attend interviews for jobs that involved digging (and certainly I was experienced at that), or carrying, or loading, all of which I managed to bat away by the simple expedient of appearing over-qualified and under-skilled. I would arrive in my suit and tie for a job digging drains.

"'Sperience!" the boss would demand, standing there in his shorts and black singlet, arms like legs of mutton folded across his chest.

"None," I would say.

"C'n y' use a shovel?"

"A what?"

"Look, mate. I don't think we c'n use ya."

And I'd appear crestfallen and move on to the next job interview, and at the end of the week I'd report back to Ms Worth. After some months of this, we both agreed it wasn't working. By now I was no happier with the situation than she was; it had been difficult trying to sustain a respectable level of substance abuse on what the government was prepared to pay me, supplemented by the odd wallet I could pick up. How did I feel about re-training? asked Worth. Did she mean, how did I feel about it objectively?

"I mean, how do you feel about it for *you* Mr Campbell?!" She'd been becoming increasingly short with me of late. Quite unnecessary, I felt, given that my taxes contributed to the nice little racket she was running.

"Well, what would I re-train for?"

We looked into what she described as "opportunities": hospital orderly, which had a certain morbid appeal to it, particularly if I could have wangled the morgue run; car park attendant, which had no appeal, and for which I was surprised you had to train; surveyor's chainman, of which I'd never heard, but which involved holding one end of something called Gunter's chain, and which all sounded very open air and boring.

And then she came up with it. Insurance! It was obvious! No particular skills needed! Train on the job! Remuneration less than I'd been earning as a teacher, but scope for advancement! I was already picturing it: Bruce Campbell: Senior Accounts Manager! I could imagine it was the sort of thing that would appeal to Rags. But what appealed to *me* most was the voyeuristic aspect of it. I'd be Johnny-on-the-spot for people whose lives had fallen apart! I'd be there to help them pick up the pieces, and surely some of those pieces of lives could find their way into my pocket. Perhaps even a *whole* life!

A few days later I was perched on the edge of an uncomfortable plastic chair in a bland office. On a wall hung a bad water colour of a small rowing boat on a placid lake. In front of me was the classic middle management desk of that era: cheap, imitation timber; in basket on one side, out basket on the other; blotter pad containing jottings and squiggles. A cream coloured telephone with a blinking red light; a desk calendar; a bulging filofax, implying that the person who owned it was indeed an important and busy man. And a further artistic touch: a little container with pens and paper clips carelessly spilling from it, to suggest a slightly impish side to their owner's character. And then, on the L-shaped return, a keyboard connected to one of those monstrous screens they had back then, that glowed information and radiation at its owner. Everything the busy executive might need was contained in this one "work station".

On the other side of the desk was the busy executive: one Sid Heath, although he did prefer to be known as Sidney, thank you very much! And now that he thought of it, until I was somewhat more established in the firm, perhaps I should err on the side of caution, and refer to him as Mr Heath. Quite obviously he was some brainless cretin, who had inadvertently managed to percolate to this level of seniority in the general ferment of the insurance industry. And if Sid could do it, it certainly boded well for me! Sid was the human resources face for the international insurance giant, Torr.

He was thumbing through my rather thin curriculum vitae, while I was entertaining him by detailing the etymology of those words. Did Sid, sorry, Mr Heath, know, for example, that the plural of curriculum vitae was curricula vitae, and not, as most people insisted on saying, curriculum vita; or worse, curriculum vitas, or worse still, as I'd once heard, curriculums vitae? His blank stare suggested he didn't.

"Teacher, eh?" he said. I was switched on to full charm mode, with a boyish grin and boundless enthusiasm.

"Yes!" I said. "Great career! Loved it!"

"So, why'd you give it up then?"

"My wife..." I said. "She's been..." I moved a hand to flick at a tear. "...unwell. Recently passed..." I pulled a handkerchief to staunch a further flow of tears. The fellow looked away, embarrassed.

"Oh! Oh, I'm sorry to hear that, Bruce."

"I'm... I'm learning to cope. I just don't feel I could go back teaching, though. Not... not the way things are."

"Of course."

"Clean break," I said.

"I quite understand," said Sid.

The possibility of Sid understanding much was limited, I thought, by the sheer banal nature of his existence. I doubt if Sid understood more than rising at seven thirty in the morning, sitting on his expanding backside behind his faux-timber desk all day, drawing his weekly pittance, and then going home to his mortgage, his wife and his two point three kids and his television dramas. He might as well have been a hamster on a running wheel.

Nevertheless, he'd pulled me aboard. Here I was, a deck hand on the good ship Torr.

Chapter 25

I have come to believe that free will is an illusion. Hindsight is an excellent vantage point, and from it I now see my destiny as a skein unravelling before me. For example, I have grown to realise that, with Rags, I have no power of choice. As if one does have choice with destiny! I thought, I always thought that the unravelling skein would lead me to Lena, and that she would be mine. A hollow victory, perhaps, after thirty or forty or fifty years, but a victory nonetheless. I have now come to suspect that it may never happen. And in this realisation was born my decision to see her yet again.

It had been more than seven years, and yet each hour of each day of each of those seven years had been lived for her. While in prison, I could not see her, except in my mind's eye. I'd thought she might visit, at least while I was on remand, and accessible, but as the days stretched into weeks, I came to understand that it would not happen. I came to understand that she now saw me as blemished, as perhaps unworthy of her. And then, once convicted, branded, and removed to the limbo of Paparoa, I was no longer accessible.

And then, when I emerged from prison, even I could sense that taint, that branding, and I still felt unworthy of her. Because Rags deserved nothing short of perfection. I know I said that when I came out of prison I decided to put Rags on the back burner, but honestly, I'd been out less than a week, when I knew I had to see her, and I decided to do so, juggling it between visits to my probation officer and her nagging demands that I find employment.

I began my journey to Auckland by hitch-hiking, a slightly post-middle-aged man incognito in tramp's clothes. It was hardly a triumphant return, but was nevertheless an interesting journey in and of itself.

Out of Christchurch, there was the wealthy old gentleman farmer, on his way home to Cheviot, a pair of prize rams bouncing along in a trailer behind us, his clipped vowels ringing about the interior of the new Mercedes he'd just bought. Took pity on me, no doubt. He was decent enough, though, to shell out for a pie and a latte at some roadside dive near Greta Valley, and he bade me goodbye and good luck as we pulled into Cheviot and a thunderstorm around midday.

From there to Picton my driver was a deranged individual, who claimed to hear the voice of God, and it seemed to distract him considerably from his driving. The conversation inclined more and more to the bizarre, as I became increasingly uncertain whether he was addressing me or his maker. We'd crossed from Canterbury into Marlborough, and were about to head inland, when he began to shout hysterically out the window, now apparently addressing a third, also invisible party. This unseen entity continued to pursue us as we wound our way past the salt piles of Grassmere, through Ward and Seddon, and was still with us as we sped into Blenheim.

On the ferry crossing, a rough and windy few hours, the three (or possibly four) of us found ourselves alone on the aft deck, where I was able to separate this lunatic from his wallet, his car keys and his fraught existence by tipping him over the railing. The last I saw of him, he was now fulminating against the injustice of his situation, still, I imagine speaking with God. But at least he was now doing so from the creamy wake of the "Aratuna".

So I drove into a darkened Auckland, the new owner of an aging Toyota Camry, and passed the night in a quiet backstreet not far from Rags's last known place of residence. Dawn found me in Corbin Crescent, a couple of hundred metres downstream from the urbane suburban villa that the accountant had bequeathed to her. I was unsure whether she even still lived there. But sure enough, around seven, as I chomped on the last crust of possibly the tenth pie I'd eaten in the last two days, she appeared, scurried quickly down the path, retrieved a newspaper, and returned, glancing up and down the street, as if she sensed my presence, before closing the door. Even from this distance, I could see that she'd aged terribly. Perhaps it was the beginnings of osteoporosis that were causing her back to hunch slightly; her gait was now less graceful and less certain, and her once platinum hair was now cheapened to silver. Even so, my heart bounded at the sight of her.

But my bounding heart plummeted when, minutes later, a hulking fellow emerged from the same door and stomped in workman's boots across the street to where one of those meaty-looking utility vehicles waited. He raised his head to the sky, seeming to survey the weather, the cut of his jaw harder than stone, his look more bitter than wood. Apparently satisfied with the weather outlook, he climbed in and drove away. I'd been intending to pick up some decent clothes, using the God botherer's money, and to call in to see her later in the morning. But this new development cast a pall over all my plans.

I drove around aimlessly for a while, then called into one of those Salvation Army shops, and picked up a quite reasonable suit, a couple of dress shirts and a pair of shoes for less than twenty dollars. And then I thought, while I'm in town, I might as well check on Eve.

When I knocked on the door of where we'd lived, a po-faced woman answered, and turned me away with the information that she'd never heard of anyone of that name. There are not many Ruigen's gracing the streets of Auckland, though, and the white pages soon revealed that she'd moved to Parnell. A half hour later, and I was ringing the bell of one of those tawdry flats on level three of a seven level building. There was no response, so I parked outside, gnawing at the problem of the large bloke with the meaty utility vehicle, and waited.

Around five-thirty, I saw her plodding up the street. Eve had also aged, but even more unfortunately. It was as if her entire insides had dropped down and accumulated around her hips. Her hair, obviously dyed, was somewhat darker than it had been, and the way she walked suggested perfect defeat. As she got nearer, I opened the car door, got out, and waited. Her gaze was riveted on the pavement, and it wasn't until she saw my legs that she raised her eyes. There was still no expectation, no hope in them, during a few seconds when nothing registered, and then a look of utter shock came over her.

"What the fuck are you doing here!" she shouted. "Get out! Get out! Get out!"

It was obvious time had not mellowed Eve. I raised my hands in a gesture of submission, and smiled.

"I was just in the area, Eve. I thought I'd call in and see how you're doing. It's been so long!"

Her outburst seemed to have calmed her, and she spoke more quietly. The heads that had popped from windows to discover the source of the discord, satisfied that it had little entertainment value, withdrew.

"Well I'm fine! Now you can fuck off!"

"Can't we be friends?"

A humourless laugh escaped her, and she glanced skywards, as if for inspiration.

"Friends! You were never my *friend*! You're a filthy fucking child rapist!"

"It wasn't quite like that, Eve."

"Wasn't it? Well, I seem to recall you agreed it *was* like that in court!"

"Whatever. Can't we let bygones be bygones?"

"Just fuck off, Bruce!"

And she pushed past me, her huge hips swaying from side to side, as she made to enter the building. She turned at the door.

"You can come up and get the rest of your shit, and then I never want to see you again! You're dead to me, Bruce!"

The rest of my "shit" consisted of a plastic supermarket bag stuffed with a few oddments. I was made to wait at the door, while she retrieved it, and when she came back a minute or two later, she said:

"Everything else, I sold or was in the box I sent you. Take it and go!"

"How's your art?" I asked, still striving for some sort of connection with her.

"What the fuck do you care?"

"I always cared, Eve. Perhaps I could have shown it more..."

Again the mirthless laugh.

"Fuck off, Bruce. The only thing you ever cared about was Bruce Fucking Campbell!"

She was right, of course. I'd never cared about her art. I'd never particularly cared about her. I could see now that she'd been a convenience of sorts; something to plug a gap that I'm not even sure ever existed. Perhaps more of a stage prop.

"Well, goodbye, then," I said.

She sneered in response. And when I turned at the end of the passageway and looked back, she was still standing there. Her look reminded me of those nights I had watched her through our living room window, the immense and inconsolable sadness etched onto her face. Lives are so hard, and really so unnecessary, but I left her to hers.

Plans were fomenting in my mind, and given the nature of those plans, I preferred not to register my presence in Auckland. I became Oscar S. Lehmann, once chatterer with God, now fish food, because Oscar's absence from the world had not seemed to raise a ripple. My beard had grown out somewhat, so I bought a razor and trimmed it. I donned my glasses, and I registered in a reasonable motel. Mr Lehmann would be staying several nights, and would pay on departure. An impression of Mr Lehmann's credit card was taken as a precaution against him scarpering.

Why is life never easy? It had begun to seem as if Rags was determined to make things difficult for herself. Now I was confronted with the problem of tracking down the owner of the meaty utility vehicle, and ascertaining whether or not he was suitable company for her to be keeping. The result of that investigation was rather a foregone conclusion.

He proved to be a builder of sorts. A builder, for Christ's sake! Admittedly in some sort of semi-management role, but nonetheless, a glorified banger of nails into wood. I followed him round for a couple of days, as he hopped from one building site to another, like a large, frenzied flea. There he'd be, lugging pieces of timber around and banging them in place. A hard worker, admittedly. But no! On the whole, it just wouldn't do! Rags deserved much better. Rags deserved me.

It was quite apparent that I could never take on this bloke in a head to head confrontation. He was a good centimetre taller than me, probably younger, had limbs packed with surplus muscle and was the owner of one of those heads that, having abandoned all hope of ever growing an adequate supply of hair, had been shaven, and now shone like a bowling ball. A more oblique approach would be needed, and time was of the essence, because Ms Dumpy, my probation officer, was expecting a visit from me in four days' time. The more I thought about it, the more I thought back to the immolation of Jenny, and the more I thought about that the more I realised that fire was my friend.

There is a great deal of misinformation surrounding the combustibility of petrol, and much of it can be sheeted back to these Hollywood movies, were you see petrol being poured around buildings with gay abandon, and then a match being carelessly tossed after it. The result, in most cases, is a gradually expanding fire that sniffs carefully along the course of where the petrol has been poured.

Wrong! Petrol is a volatile substance, but when contained you can rest assured that it will not auto-ignite, provided it is kept below two hundred and eighty degrees Celsius, and unless you happen to live on the surface of the sun, that is not difficult. The vapour from petrol, however, is a different matter, and its flash point can be as low as minus forty-three degrees Celsius. So if you were to pour petrol around the interior of a house, and then toss a match after it, assuming an average ambient interior temperature of around twenty degrees, much of the petrol would have vaporised before the match had been struck, and the result would be a great WOOF! of an explosion.

I invested some of Oscar's money into a pinch bar, a length of high tension lead, a spark plug and some insulating tape. There would be damage to the meaty utility vehicle, caused by the pinch bar, but that could not be helped.

The wee hours of Wednesday morning saw me, black-clad, inching in Salvation Army cushion soles down Corbin Crescent, until I was adjacent to the meaty vehicle. A dog barked distantly. A cat mewed, hissed, spat, and then raced across the road, startling me. I crouched lower, my pinch bar held like a weapon, surveying the area for insomniacs. None. I lowered the bar, and crept on, finally reaching the sleek shadow of my target. Gingerly I raised the pinch bar, and noiselessly offered it up to the gap between the driver's door and its frame. And then a thought occurred – what if the vehicle was alarmed? The vehicles I drove, being of generally a veteran vintage, invariably lacked such protection. But fortune, it seems, had favoured the nail banger, and his vehicle was newer. I surveyed the interior, looking for some flashing light that might indicate an alarm. Nothing. And then a second thought occurred, and I gently lifted the handle on the door. It gave, and I gradually eased the door open. So confident was this meathead in the protective power of his muscles and his bowling ball head that he'd not even thought to lock the thing!

After that, it all became a simple matter. Flip open the fuel tank cover; unscrew the cap; drop in the spark plug that I'd already connected to the high tension lead, ensuring that the spark plug hung clear of the fuel; route the lead so that it ran inconspicuously, and then under the vehicle, until I could poke it up into the engine cavity. Easing the bonnet up, and by the light of a small torch, I removed one of the high tension leads from a spark plug, and into its terminal I jammed the exposed wire of the high tension lead I had run from the fuel tank. Inspect that all is well, gently close the bonnet, leave the fuel cap loose, so that sufficient air will mix with the vapour to create a combustible mixture, close the cover on the fuel tank, and I'm done.

At seven in the morning Mr Lehman's car was parked some distance up the road, when the owner of the bowling ball head opened the front door, glanced skyward as if checking the weather, and then stomped his work boots down the front path. No peck on the cheek for Rags, as had been the custom of the accountant, but she did appear behind him, and seemed to stand, waiting to farewell him as he shot off to – well, in this case, I hoped to eternity.

He slung a bag into the front seat, hopped in after it, and I could see the vehicle visibly sag beneath the weight of his bulk. An age seemed to pass, but he must have started the vehicle, because a puff of steam began to stream from its exhaust. I imagined the spark plug dangling there in the fuel tank, and imagined it sparking away furiously. Rags was waving, but nothing was happening. Perhaps I'd done something wrong. Perhaps my assumptions had been incorrect. Perhaps some vital part had slipped off, or come undone, and there was no spark in the fuel tank. The vehicle began to move away. Rags turned to go inside, and as she did so, as she closed her front door, there was a titanic explosion that must have rattled windows in surrounding suburbs. The meaty vehicle was hoist metres into the air, and when it returned to earth it was engulfed in a ball of flame.

Rags scuttled from her front door, ran down the path, and as she did so I could see her mouth working at what I took to be a scream. My heart went out to her, but this was necessary. As she stood helplessly beside the inferno, flapping her arms uselessly at her sides, the other residents of Corbin Crescent began to creep from their dens, some in pyjamas, some holding cups of coffee, one with shaving cream on his face, and together they stood and surveyed what remained of Rags's second failed attempt at a relationship.

And while they did so, the Camry belonging to Oscar S. Lehman pulled quietly away from the kerb and accelerated up Corbin Close, and for the moment, out of Rags's life.

Chapter 26

Now that I was aboard the good ship Torr, there followed some boom years for me. Of course, as Sydney (yes – it was a matter of no more than a few weeks before I was invited to call him that) pointed out to me, I would need to start out on the bottom rung. No problem! I was a good climber! I'd scamper up that corporate ladder in no time!

Day one: Did I know that insurance "as we know it" began in the coffee houses of London in the seventeenth century? Well, no, I didn't! Good Heavens! How interesting! Yes, in the afterglow of the Great Fire of 1666, there emerged a desire amongst property owners to protect themselves against loss, and blah, blah, blah...

What it all boiled down to was that the history of insurance is a three hundred year yawn. And what it could all be boiled down to was that the insurance industry came into being to assist its customers in times of loss. Until now, that was.

I was some way up the ladder before it suddenly clicked that what I was being told was that the insurance industry was no longer in the business of insuring its clients against loss. Of course, that was the facade behind which it operated. But in fact, the insurance industry was now in the business of making large profits. And it certainly wasn't going to make large profits if it kept paying out on its clients' losses. Put like that, it was obvious. Each claim needed to be thoroughly scrutinised; loopholes needed to be explored and exploited; claimants needed to be discredited, and wherever possible, claims needed to be denied. Suddenly the whole business was looking far more attractive.

When I began to appreciate the system in its simplistic beauty, I then understood where my future lay: investigations. The idea of poking my nose around in the muck of other peoples' lives held huge appeal for me!

Meanwhile, Sydney and I had gone from being colleagues, to buddies, to almost soul mates. We confided in each other over the sticky lunchroom table, while swilling vile instant coffee; we discussed insurance in all its depth, as if it mattered, and we considered both its future and ours. And then the day arrived! He invited me to dinner, where I was introduced to his wife and their two point three kids as Bruce-He-Sadly-Lost-His-Wife. Mrs Heath, Donna, was a wellspring of sympathy.

She darted about the open plan on short legs, a gay, floral apron barely concealing the point three of the new Heath-in-the-making, watermelons of breasts poking out either side of its bib, until finally the roasted chicken was produced. A size eighteen, Sydney was quick to point out, to show that no expense had been spared. It sat there mid-table, like an offering, Donna's special olive and walnut stuffing spewing from its arse, while little Timmy or Tommy or Tony or whatever his name was offered up our collective thanks to our Father in Heaven, that he had seen fit to feed us for yet another day.

"Good boy!" enthused Sydney as the lengthy invocation eventually petered out to its inevitable "amen".

"Yes!" I said. "Well done!" The poor little chap became quite suffused with pride, and began to flush. And as Sydney lifted the knife, pressed it against the glazed breast and began to cut, I imagined that breast as belonging to Donna, and raising my eyes to catch hers, I smiled.

"Lovely! I said. "I'm so grateful!" And she beamed.

The chief problem with climbing the corporate ladder is that you're not the only one on it. If you look up, there can be a host of other people above you, all waiting to shit on you. In my chosen area of investigations the rungs were less crowded, and I gather that was because people were not keen on being seen as confrontational. They preferred to cast themselves in the role of do-gooders, always helping others, rather than being seen as trying to manufacture reasons not to help them. I, on the other hand, quite enjoyed that role.

I had begun in investigations in a subordinate position. Jim Toast was above me. I was the Tonto to his Lone Ranger; the Luke Skywalker to his Obi wan. Jim was there to show me the ropes! He would teach me everything he knew, which fortunately seemed to be very little.

"We're here to catch crooks, Campbell!" he said to me on that first, proud day that I occupied my investigator's chair.

Jim Toast was one of those blokes who circumvent the whole problem of the, do I call him by his first name or his second name issue by diving straight to the heart of the matter. Ex Army! I was Campbell and he was Toast. Campbell and Toast! Campbell on Toast! Toasted Campbell! We were the A Team of Torr. In our Toyota Starlet, armed with our files and our cameras with long-range lenses, and our tenacious manner and our menacing attitudes, we zoomed about in pursuit of the villains. And if they weren't villains, then by God, we'd do our best to make them appear as such!

Toast was a giant of a man – a good two metres tall, with a neck like a bull's and a chest like a barrel. When he squeezed behind the wheel and into the seat of the Starlet, bits of him oozed out. He seemed to be driving a pedal car. The seams of his cheap off-the-rack suits bulged with ominous muscle, and his feet were of such a size that the toes of his shoes appeared through doorways some seconds before he did. His mouth was an open sewer, and his vocabulary contained a basic thousand words, all designed to intimidate. Great man for the job, and he was determined that I should become just like him. Well, perhaps not *just* like him, because Toast was Toast – the nonpareil!

Much of the work of an insurance investigator can be mundane, and this tended to be the area to which I was fobbed off. Someone claims a stolen car trailer, but in reality they've sold it a couple of months before. To prove that involved dredging through old newspaper classifieds, or the specialist magazines that sold these things, and comparing telephone numbers. People are surprisingly stupid in this regard. Of course, you look for warning signs: perhaps a person has made a number of previous claims, or perhaps they just seem too smooth and professional in their approach. People provide hand-written invoices, claiming that things they never owned have been broken. The range of human duplicity is endless, but always it was brought up short by the crack team of Toast and Campbell.

And then people would claim that their wallets had been stolen, and I found it interesting to be on the other side of *that* particular equation.

My first really interesting case involved an Indian couple, or as Toast described them, "a pair of fucking curry munchers". Mr and Mrs Wazir had owned a small restaurant, specialising in Kashmiri cuisine, and it had burned down, taking with it much of what the Wazirs had owned, including the Wazirs three month old baby.

"Arson!" announced Toast as soon as the file crossed his desk.

"How do you know?" I asked.

"Just look at them!" he said.

I did, and saw nothing that immediately proclaimed them as arsonists. And why, I wondered aloud, would they incinerate their child along with their restaurant.

"It's obvious!" said Toast. But to me it wasn't. "Use y' fuckin' head, Campbell!" he said. "Makes it look more like an accident, dunnit? Who'd think anyone'd kill their own kid? Eh?

But these bastards! Huh!" He spat the word. "These bastards'll do anything!"

Toast already had one of his specialists investigating the scene, and the specialist had deduced that, although the fire appeared to originate from faulty wiring to a tandoor, that fault could "easily have been manufactured". Furthermore, the books pertaining to the enterprise had also gone up in smoke, having been kept in a small office at the eatery.

Soon Toast had me on the job, prying, poking, muckraking. I discovered that the tandoor had been installed by a relative of Wazir. I discovered that the national credit data base contained a debt default by the restaurant, although admittedly the amount was small, and was being disputed. I discovered an error in the claim the Wazirs had filed, where the numbers of the street address of the restaurant had been transposed, and the street name had been incorrectly spelled.

"Mr WHIZZER!" said Toast in a booming voice at our first meeting with the claimants. He had a manner when interviewing clients, where he would accentuate certain words, almost shouting them.

"Ah, you say that 'Wazir'," said Mr Wazir, a smile trying to lighten the sadness of his face. His wife sat beside him in a gold and blue sari, her demeanour calm, but with an all-embracing melancholy to her.

"YES!" boomed Toast again. "Mr WHIZZER! You must understand that your claim has been passed to me for investigation because of certain IRREGULARITIES!"

Wazir looked uncomprehending.

"I don't understand," he said.

"DON'T you Mr Whizzer?! It has been suggested to me, by an EXPERT in these things that the fire started in some sort of OVEN!"

"Yes, the tandoor," said Wazir.

"Yes! And that the WIRING had been TAMPERED with!"

Again, Wazir looked nonplussed.

"But..." he stammered. "I don't understand."

"Mr Whizzer, I've been led to believe that your little BUSINESS had not been doing very WELL lately!"

"No!" said Wazir. "That is not true. We are working very very hard, and business is good!"

"Do you have RECORDS to PROVE your claim?"

"No. They are being burnt in the fire."

Toast smirked. "And how did that fire START, Mr WHIZZER?"

"I am telling you! It is starting in the tandoor!"

"And who installed that tanda, Mr Whizzer?" said Toast, dramatically lowering his voice to a hoarse whisper.

"My... my brother," said Wazir.

"Your brother! And is your BROTHER a qualified electrician, Mr WHIZZER?"

The Wazirs looked at each other, before Wazir shrugged.

"He is being qualified in India."

"In INDIA! INDIA is not New ZEALAND, Mr Whizzer! Was your brother licensed to carry out this work in New ZEALAND?"

Wazir shrugged, and looked flustered. "He... he is working for a man."

"Your claim, here, Mr WHIZZER!" said Toast, tacking off in a new direction. It contains a false address!" And he slapped the document down on the table.

Now Wazir looked flummoxed.

"I...I...I..."

Toast lurched back in his seat and glared at the couple.

"You CLAIM, Mr Whizzer," and Toast thumped his finger up and down on the offending portion of the document, "you CLAIM that your curry house was at 220 Kakatea Street!"

"My... my wife is filling out the claim. She is making many mistakes. She is very much hurt because our son... he... he..."

And now the Wazirs burst into a concerted display of tears that could not have been better orchestrated had they rehearsed it.

"Thank you Mr and Mrs Whizzer! I'll prepare my report, and you'll hear from our claims department."

And so Toast and I produced a report that suggested the Wazirs had been complicit in the destruction of their own restaurant. Evidence to support this was the "probability that the wiring to an oven had been tampered with"; the fact that the Wazirs had filed "two previous claims during the last five years, one being for damage to a vehicle and the second being for a lost pair of spectacles"; that the tandoor had been installed by a relative whose qualifications were "doubtful", and that this had been done without Torr being informed; that a false document had been created – namely the claim that cited the address as 220 Kakatea Street, whereas its actual location was 202 Kahikatea Street; and finally that, "the accounts for the business had been 'conveniently' lost in the fire".

The claim was subsequently declined, and the Wazirs' policy was cancelled, as were the policies held by the company on the Wazirs' house and vehicle. A declined claim and a cancelled policy meant that the couple were unable to buy insurance elsewhere, and an uninsured home meant that the bank called in their loan, and they were obliged to sell their house.

But the Wazir's were made of surprisingly stern stuff, and with the proceeds from the sale of their sold house, they fought back. They brought a court case against Torr, which they won. Torr, of course, appealed, and with the Wazirs' finances and resilience now exhausted, as the date of the court hearing for the appeal drew near, Torr proposed a settlement. Torr would acknowledge that it had been wrong in declining the claim. However it would not accept the claim, and neither would it agree to insure any other assets the Wazirs might own, although these were now minimal.

It was high octane stuff. I was loving it! You could sense the will to resist ebbing from the Wazir's with each court appearance. And then finally, emotionally and financially drained, their lack of will to resist was translated into a lack of will to live.

"'Member those fuckin' curry munchers?" asked Toast, during one of our Monday morning meetings. I nodded. "Beat the fuckers!" he said, and slammed the note he'd been reading down in front of me. It was from the Wazirs' solicitor. It announced their deaths by suicide, and advised that their claim against Torr was being withdrawn.

I began to realise the full potential in my position. Until now I'd been a solitary operator. Now I had the weight of an international corporation behind me, and they had the same cavalier attitude to human life as I did.

We were a perfect match.

Chapter 27

I had begun copulating with Donna Heath soon after my dinner invitation. I use the word "copulating" in full knowledge of its mechanical connotations, because for me the act was an impersonal one, akin to being blown by a street whore. She was not an attractive woman, poor Donna. Spherical would best describe her. Her legs were so short as to give her an almost dwarfish appearance, and what those legs bore about could have best been represented by drawing two circles – a large one depicting her body, and a smaller one for her head. On the larger circle you would then superimpose a further pair of circles, suggesting two enormous breasts. I should note, too, that at his stage she was in a reasonably advanced stage of pregnancy. How advanced, I am uncertain, but sufficiently advanced that the enormous breasts were prone to lactate a clear fluid during coition.

She was one of those simple women, who desire nothing more than to be liked. Her face glowed like candles on a cake whenever the slightest praise came her way. It wasn't a pretty face. It was moon-like, as if it had been forged from a gob of clay, and then decorated with short, stringy hair. Something a child might make at playschool.

I had noticed her smile playing over me during dinner, and so, about a month later, I called in on the pretext of "being in the area". The smile ignited itself as soon as she opened the door, and the moka pot was soon rumbling a brew of coffee on the stove, while we talked about HER. She was unused to talking about HER, and was at first reluctant to do so. But by our third cup, she had opened up, and from the kitchen table we had moved to the comfort of the lounge. We covered Donna, the early years, and then moved on to marriage and children, and then – well, that was it, really, for Donna. And then, from the comfort of being vertical we moved to the comfort of being horizontal.

While Sydney laboured away at his faux-timber desk, this act of fornication with his wife became a regular event. She confided in me that Sydney's bedside manner was erratic and slipshod, and that he had declined to continue pleasuring his wife after her third month of pregnancy, fearing that his doughty organ might harm the unborn Heath. Campbell, on the other hand, was able to assure her that such gentle stimulation was good for the foetus, and would then pound away like a jackhammer, hoping to skewer the little blighter. No such luck.

After several weeks, Donna began to have misgivings. She'd consulted God on the matter, and God had told her that what she was doing took her out of the virtuous woman category. In other words, her price was no longer above rubies, and Sidney, God bless him, deserved nothing less than rubies. I surveyed her vaulted stomach with disgust, and agreed. Together we knelt, and we prayed for forgiveness, and then one last time I seduced her, and was able at last to penetrate her both orally and anally.

When I left her in a flood of tears and recriminations, I felt my victory over Heath was, if not complete, at least adequate.

Chapter 28

Okay. You can accuse me of being cavalier if you like, but the thing was, I *had* the benzodiazepine, and it's not just a simple matter of walking into a shop and asking for a hypnotic in injectable form. Sure – I had no real idea of an appropriate dose for a galoot the size of Toast, and too much could have killed him. Still, it was a risk I thought worth taking

He'd become a problem. I'd always known he would, because he was the one obstacle to my ascent of the corporate ladder. When I looked up, there he was, clinging like a limpet to his rung, and casting an ominously long shadow. The possibility of climbing over him was remote in the extreme. I could proceed up the ladder only if Toast voluntarily relinquished his hold, or if he fell. He appeared hale and hearty and to be a nimble climber, so either prospect was remote in the extreme. He would need to be nudged. And the means by which I could dislodge Toast from his perch had begun to preoccupy me.

These big, physical types present a special challenge. Take Rags's second failed attempt at marital bliss as a typical example. You can't rely on physical supremacy. You've got to outwit them. And Toast was a trained professional! At least, I assumed that the New Zealand Armed Forces trained its personnel in some sort of unarmed combat, tai chi or something. I could only hope he hadn't picked up an AK47 while serving in some foreign field, which he now carried stuffed down his sock.

But certainly, an oblique approach would be needed, and again fire seemed like the most plausible option. Great stuff, fire: when you're dealing with a bigger or stronger adversary, it creates a more level playing field. You can't argue with fire. And as an added bonus, it can destroy much of the evidence. I'd considered the spark plug in the fuel tank trick again, but then, I do hate to repeat myself. Did da Vinci paint the Mona Lisa twice? Did Beethoven write his fifth symphony twice? Of course not; and neither did Campbell intend to duplicate one of his previously created masterpieces.

Add to that the fact that Toast was one of the more odious examples of humanity I'd ever encountered, and I felt a rising need to see him suffer.

Do you think you'd notice a small prick in your bum? Well, I can tell you right now, you wouldn't. Believe it or not, most people will remain oblivious to the discomfort of a small prick, and I have empirical evidence to support that claim. I went to some trouble, placing myself in crowded situations – at a football match, which was stultifyingly boring, even at a rock concert. And then I thought, well, perhaps people at football matches and rock concerts are too numbed by drugs or alcohol to notice, so I tried busy checkout queues at the supermarket. I would carry a syringe full of distilled water concealed in my palm, and I would bump into people. Bumping into people is an art form, and it was an art form I'd perfected over the years, because it can be useful when trying to relieve people of their cash. But now, as I was bumping into them, I was giving them a jab of H2O in the gluteus maximus.

The result? Most people would bounce off, accept my heartfelt apology, and off they'd go. A few would make a show of rubbing their buttocks, but suspect nothing, and the odd one would become abusive. But not once did anyone complain of having been pricked in the bum. Which all goes to show that it's not the pain of the needle, but the thought of it, the sight of it, that makes people squeamish.

Toast would always become progressively more glum as the week passed. I believe it was linked to the fact that people in the office invariably talked about how much fun they were going to have on the weekend, whereas all Toast had to look forward to was two days in the company of his cat, Todger. This particular Friday afternoon rolled around, and Toast and I were inspecting premises to the north of the city that had been damaged by flood. A nearby creek had become obstructed by logs or something, causing it to burst its banks, directing a swathe of water through this couple's house, and our job was to try and concoct some excuse for Torr to wriggle out of its contractual responsibilities. Flooding's difficult, because you can hardly accuse people of contriving to have their homes flooded, and so the nit-picking more commonly comes down to how they might have submitted their claim, or whether they have failed to declare something in their past that might have meant Torr would have declined to insure them. After all, most people have something murky in their past that they don't want shouted from the rooftops. But these people were proving intractably and squeakily clean. It was looking as if Torr might be saddled with fronting up to its responsibilities, and that never made Toast happy.

But what was concerning me right then was less Toast's level of happiness, but how I might transport him once he'd been reduced to a state of unconsciousness. Given the bulk of this lout, I didn't fancy my chances of carrying him a great distance. Even dragging would have been problematic.

I had my syringe at the ready in my pocket, primed with benzodiazepine, and I'd been wondering how I could transfer the drug from the syringe into Toast. The opportunity presented itself as we waded in galoshes back to the car. It was muddy. I was following in Toast's wake, and I was making a pretence of slipping and sliding. Finally I tumbled into Toast, propelling him forward, so that he fell face-down into the sludge. Even worse, from Toast's strictly homophobic point of view, I was now on top of him, administering a little prick to his bum.

"Fuck you, Campbell!" he bellowed. He surged from the bog, casting me off, and with his entire front coated in mud, he stormed off towards the car, where he folded himself into the front seat. There was a final burst of profanity, after which he promptly fell asleep.

Things could not have been more simple. Because Toast had decided he liked to be chauffeur-driven, he now always occupied the passenger's seat; so there he was, quietly nodding away next to me. I re-loaded my syringe with a half-dose, in case the sleeping giant should show signs of awakening, and then drove him off to his final resting place. Well, I was not planning on too much resting, because I felt that Toast needed to experience his demise, and to experience it keenly.

North of Christchurch is a lonely, sandy, wooded area that, apart from the occasional walker or mountain-biker, remains desolate, and it was here that Toast and I headed, he slumbering loudly next to me.

Spring was coming in, and as we pulled onto one of the secondary roads leading into the trees, as dusk fell, we could have been any eccentric couple out for an unseasonal sunset drive – a pair of friends, perhaps, seduced by the allure of nature. As the light faded, and as Toast snored on, I gathered armfuls of dry wood until I had the makings of a generous bonfire. My work was nearing completion when I detected a stirring from the Starlet. Again, this could work in my favour, because lugging Toast about was simply not an option. I opened the passenger's door, to be confronted by a muddy spectre, struggling valiantly against the residual effects of benzodiazepine.

"Wha'..." he mumbled. His head lolled about on his shoulders as he gazed blearily about him. "Wha' the fug?"

"You nodded off," I said. He eyed me uncomprehendingly. "Come on," I said. "I'll give you some help." The car lights cast a yellow glow onto the pile of branches. I mobilised Toast, and propelled him towards it on shaky legs, my half dose at the ready, should there be a show of resistance.

"Where the fug are we?" he enquired, in an almost conversational tone.

"Don't you remember?" I asked, playing for time. He shook his head, and we slowly pressed on.

"What the fug?" he said again, as we arrived at our destination. He seemed to be coming around, and to be registering a degree of suspicion, so I quickly administered his half dose. It was awkwardly done, and even I felt the needle strike the bone and break off. Toast looked around at his arse in shock, so I gave him a sharp shove onto the pile. He lay there, still shocked, but sufficient of the drug had got into him, that his eyes began to cloud, and then close, and his mouth dangled open. But he hadn't fallen squarely, and so I had to tug at him to re-arrange him, so that he lay face-up, central to the pyre, where he would receive the full benefit of the flames once they started.

A stake driven into the ground would have been ideal, of course. But I had no stake, and I had no means of driving it into the ground. Instead I heaved four of the heaviest branches I could manage into place, and with twine I had brought, fastened each of Toast's limbs to them.

And then I waited. I waited in darkness, trying not to doze in the Starlet's front seat until, at around four in the morning the vehicle began to rock in the most peculiar manner. Quite obviously, someone was shaking it, and doing so quite violently. Either Toast had come around and freed himself, or we had interlopers. Suspecting the latter, I flicked on the headlights, and carrying the small torch I had, tumbled out of the wildly pitching vehicle, prepared to confront them. Once outside, and staggering against an impossibly yawing ground, I saw no one. But the Starlet still continued to buck like a frisky horse, and now an ominous rumbling sound was coming from the ground. It was seconds before I managed to piece all this information together and to arrive at the unlikely verdict of, "Earthquake!"

The trees thrashed about in the darkness, and branches now broke from them, and fell about me. After perhaps half a minute the shaking subsided. I shone my torch on Toast. Not a flicker. I resumed my watch, troubled by intermittent after-shocks, until the sky above began to show signs of lightening, and I could wait no more.

It was possibly the smell of the diesel that roused him, as I poured five litres of the stuff over and around his cruciform shape, and again he started mumbling.

"Back with us again?" I enquired.

But all he did was revert to his "What the fug? What the fug?"

"Look!" I said, feeling a need to get on with things. I indicated the pile of branches on which he lay. "This is a fire! You are on it! I now intend to light the fire!"

His eyes widened. "Fug off!" he said.

"No!" I said. "I will not fug off!" And lighting a match, I squatted and held it towards the diesel-soaked timber. A playful dawn breeze rushed in and extinguished it, as another aftershock rolled beneath us.

A howl of obscenities was now coming from the pile, as I applied a second match, with the same result. I retreated to the car, and in its shelter I tore a page from a road map and lit it. Hastening back, I applied the burning page to the pile, and was rewarded with a flicker that gradually crept over the timber, and began lapping at one of Toast's legs. The howling now changed from simple obscenities, to a genuine, heart-felt fury, all of which seemed to be directed at me. He now seemed fully conscious, and it was gratifying to see the extent to which he was participating in proceedings. His limbs were a flurry of activity, as he vainly tugged at his bonds.

But then, again, the unexpected. The twine began to burn through, and one by one Toast's limbs came free. First a leg; then an arm; finally another leg, at which point he reared up, dragging his final constraint with him. A walking, cursing ball of flame, he rushed at me, but then seemed to falter. With the stick I had retained to tend the fire, I hurled myself upon him, battering him about the head. He began to fall back, back towards the fire, and it was obvious from his lack of resistance that he was succumbing to the effects of the heat. As I drove him back to the edge of the inferno, one final thrust sent him tumbling backwards, performing a graceful pirouette as he did so. It was truly artistic, and having done that he fell face down into the flames, his arms outstretched, seeming to embrace his fate.

But still he was not done for. There was a final surge of energy from him, as his body raised itself up, like a cat arching its back, before falling forward with what seemed like a final, thankful moan. Toast was toast.

Fearing that the conflagration may attract attention, I set about beating a hasty retreat, and as the sun breasted the eastern horizon, delivered the car back to its customary park, outside Toast's house, wiping my prints from the wheel while being bothered by Todger. But the seismic disaster that had struck the city had worked in my favour. Only Todger was interested in me. People were far more concerned with their own small crises, than they were with me.

So I arrived in time for my customary Saturday morning all day breakfast at Gustave's, only to find Gustave seated amidst a sea of shattered crockery, spilled food and condiments, seemingly in a state of shock. An assistant drove a lazy broom around the floor, and whined unnecessarily each time the earth shook.

Eventually I gave up and left. There would be no Eggs Benedict, no mochaccino that morning.

Chapter 29

Of course, post-earthquake, I was a shoo-in to fill Toast's shoes. Torr, suddenly in the firing line for billions in payouts, and therefore not flavour of the month with its reinsurers, was chomping at the bit to decline claims wherever possible. I suddenly found myself not only head honcho in the investigations department, but also with a considerable swag of offsiders. My salary blossomed into something highly respectable, and I was able to invest a considerable sum each week into a variety of recreational drugs, and also to develop a taste for the rarer single malts.

My predecessor got largely overlooked, given the strain placed upon emergency services at the time. In fact, it was more than two weeks before Toast finally popped up, when a recreational walker stumbled over what was left him, a few more days before he was positively identified, and even longer before foul play was mooted as a possibility. While it was eventually established that he'd been murdered, well the man just had so many enemies, where would an already over-worked constabulary begin? Certainly they didn't begin with me.

A collective shiver ran through Torr, that one of our number had been so cruelly felled, and it was cheer-led by me. And then I got down to the serious business of poking about in people's private lives, and discrediting them and their claims wherever possible. And I did so happily for the next few months, saving Torr millions in the process. But was this relationship to prove reciprocal? No, it wasn't. As soon as the going got even a little rocky, Torr cut me adrift.

It all began with one Jason Crump, no relation, he was keen to point out, to the well-known author. Nevertheless, while he was after gold and greenstone, I was all for seeing him up Bullock Creek without a paddle. I suggested to him that his claim amounted to little more than forty yarns and a song, as the saying goes – no more than a cobbled together collection of bedtime yarns. And to strengthen my case, I indulged in a little artistic licence, and altered some documents that Mr Crump had submitted in support of his claim.

Most people, confronted with the might of an organisation like Torr, will simply crumple, but Mr Crump was made of sterner stuff. Even worse, he seemed to have the weight of a considerable family fortune behind him, and he proceeded to bring a well-drafted case against Torr, citing "constructive declinature" of his claim. The judge agreed with him, and Torr's lawyers, normally like ferrets when it came to pursuing these things to the bitterest of ends, examined the evidence and decided that such a pursuit would only involve extra and unnecessary expense to Torr, and that they were unlikely to enjoy a happy result.

So once again I found myself perched on the edge of an uncomfortable plastic chair in a bland office. On a wall there still hung a bad water colour of a small rowing boat on a placid lake. In front of me was still the classic middle management desk of a now former era: cheap, imitation timber; in basket on one side, out basket on the other; blotter pad containing jottings and squiggles. A cream coloured telephone with a blinking red light was still in attendance, as was a desk calendar and a bulging filofax, all intended to imply that the person who owned them was indeed an important and busy man. And the further artistic touch – that little container with pens and paper clips carelessly spilling from it, to suggest a slightly impish side to their owner's character – that was still there. The one difference was that the monstrous screen that had glowed radiation at its owner was no longer glowing, having been superseded by an LCD screen of smaller proportions. But still, everything the busy executive might need was contained in this one "work station".

And on the other side of the desk sat that same busy executive: Sid Heath, although now a little rounder, a little ruddier of face.

"I'm sorry, Bruce," Sid was saying, waving his head around dolefully, as if he meant it. "We're going to have to let you go."

I hate whiners, but I now began to whine. I'd come to quite enjoy my life of relative ease, and I enjoyed the fact that it gave me power over people, and legitimate access to their private lives.

"It was an accident!" I threw in by way of an opening gambit.

"Well, Bruce," countered Sid, "you can hardly say it was an accident, when you forged documents."

"But I did it for *you*!" I whined.

"For *me*?"

"For Torr! They wanted me to do it!"

"I don't recall anything in your employment contract that specified you forging documents on behalf of Torr, Bruce."

"But..." It was going nowhere. I looked at this smug little dimwit, wrapped up in his own self importance, and I said, "Did you know I screwed your wife, Sid?"

His face blanched. "I'm *sorry*?"

"I'm not! Screwed her on the sofa, screwed her in the bedroom, on the kitchen table. She was eight months pregnant at the time, too! Lapped it up!"

Now his mouth hung open. "Noooo....," he managed.

"'Fraid so," I said. "Buggered her, too. She loved that! Although I'd have to say her attempts at giving a half decent blow job were pitiable. You should get her to brush up on that side of things, Sid."

And with that I excused myself, and left Torr behind me forever.

I did hear that Sid and Donna had parted company, and felt a surge of pleasure at having been complicit in it.

Chapter 30

Strange, how forgetful I'm becoming. I seemed to have forgotten entirely about Ava, and then suddenly, I was sitting here staring at the holes in the wall, when it all came back to me.

I'd been giving serious thought to the idea of contributing to a sperm bank, before it was too late. It seemed somehow unthinkable that I should allow my genetic material to just die out. I'm convinced that, in general, the sorts of men who donate to these things are intellectually inferior specimens. I'd been puzzling. How would I go about it? Are these places advertised? And another point – would they pay me, and if so, on what basis? Are you paid per sperm, or is it simply based on volume.

And then, what would happen to my sperm? Would I retain some control over them? Would I be able to determine what ovum they might meet? And where do these ova come from? Do they have a similar facility for women, I wondered – an ova bank, perhaps? It got complicated, as these things do, but I was finally deterred, in large part, by the repugnant idea of masturbating into a specimen jar. It's not something I've ever done and, I don't know, it just didn't seem right to start now. So weighing everything up, I decided against it. Surely a human life should be conceived in a hot lava of rapture – not in a Petri dish.

But it got me thinking along these general lines again – sex, I mean – and when I came into a few dollars from a wallet that seemed to lack an owner, I decided to splash out on what I old-fashionedly thought of as a call girl. It was one of those home delivery services, designed, I suppose, to avoid the embarrassment of queuing at a brothel door.

A fleshy woman was delivered to me, peering out from the inside of an Avon Kab. I'd seen her arrival, and watched with interest as she waddled up the path, cautiously glancing this way and that, as if danger lurked, before timidly tapping on my door. The Avon Kab remained, its turbaned driver craning over to the passenger's side to follow proceedings. It was the area, I decided. We don't have a lot of deliveries of this, or any, kind around here, and he was perhaps concerned for her safety.

"Yeah," she introduced herself. "I'm from Haul-a Honey!" She had the coarsest of voices, like a nutmeg grater.

"Hello!" I was my most effusive self, setting her at her ease. "Ira!" I said. "Ira Wigans!"

"Ava Bonk." A *nom de jeu*, I imagined, like mine. "Hunnerd bucks! Up front!" she said.

"Oh." I felt a little taken aback that I was expected to pay before having taken ownership of the goods. I rummaged in my pocket and produced a sad crumple of notes, counting out a hundred dollars worth of them into a small, chubby palm that was awash with perspiration.

"Ta. 'Ang on!"

She turned and trundled off back down the path, a little soccer ball of a woman. She wore ridiculously high heels, which she had yet to master, and a skirt that exposed far too much of a pair of ham-like legs. Having reached the taxi, there was some discussion with the driver, a mutual waving of arms, and an exchange of money. After which she turned, and again lumbered up the path.

"Please," I said to her, "come in! Can I offer you coffee? Tea?"

"No!" she said, her face turning acidic. She had become brusque, and appeared to want to get down to business.

I'd gone for the budget option – half an hour, no optional extras, so I suppose time *was* at rather a premium. But perhaps her confidence in my ability to last the distance was greater than mine. To be honest, though, it had been so long since I'd performed anything of an intimate nature that I was uncertain if everything was still in good working order; whether I would be able, as it were, to rise to the occasion. Prison rather gets you out of the habit of regular sex; there'd been Donna Heath, of course, and the odd encounter on street corners, but over the last few years I'd moved more and more towards a life of the mind, assisted by an assortment of drugs and alcohol.

I looked her over, and I wasn't entirely happy. I'd expected someone younger – that hoary old aphorism about all whores being eighteen, I suppose. Ava looked every inch of forty. Now that I was confronted by her, I could see creases and wrinkles that covered her vast canvas of exposed flesh; giant lips that slithered across her face like a bivalve, and spoke of Botox. Her nose formed a bony prominence that cast a shadow across her face, like a sundial. I was imagining saline-filled breasts sagging to knee level, and body parts stretched beyond usability. Worse, she looked sallow and sickly, hinting at disease, and I now believed I could detect a rank odour coming from her. I was beginning to feel I may have made a mistake. If she'd been younger, it may have been different, or if she'd looked better. For a hundred dollars I didn't expect the earth, but I did feel justified in expecting less fat and more cleanliness and hygiene.

"Perhaps we could just talk a little first," I suggested.

"It's your bucks!" said Ava. She flopped herself into a seat at my dining table, harrumphing as the weight was taken from her legs, and emitting a small amount of flatulence.

"Well!" I said. "What shall we talk about, Ava?"

"Your bucks," she reminded me, turning her pudgy palms skyward, as if lost for an answer.

"Yes, yes. I understand that," I said. "I just thought you might have something you'd like to talk about." I realised I was sounding like a therapist. "You know: a hobby or something? Your job?"

She shrugged, and began rooting about in her bag, finally producing a crumpled-up packet of cigarettes.

"Mind if I smoke?"

"No, go ahead."

"Just, some people are funny."

I did mind, but we needed something to defuse the tension that was developing between us. She appeared to be elaborately counting her remaining cigarettes, seemed to do a quick calculation, then chose one, placed it in her mouth, took it out, reconsidered, replaced it, rooted in her bag again, found a cheap plastic lighter, plucked the cigarette from the packet, lit it, inhaled deeply, and began staring out the window.

To be fair to Ava, she'd made no pretence of being a skilled conversationalist, so I could hardly claim misrepresentation on those grounds. If I'd wanted to hire a conversationalist, I should probably have called Toastmasters.

"So, um, where do you come from then?"

She shrugged, puffed on the cigarette.

"Why d'ya wanna know?"

"Oh, well, just making conversation."

She narrowed her eyes suspiciously, and her fleshy lips took on as hard a line as they could.

"Y're not one o' these bloody nutters, are ya?"

"No! No, of course I'm not!"

"Get all sorts!"

"Yes, I'm sure. As I was saying, I was just making..."

"Tuma-roh!"

"Sorry?"

"Tuma-roh. Swear I come from! Down past Eshburdon!"

"Oh!" I said. "Timaru!"

She glared at me, her suspicion seeming to heighten, her eyes now tiny gashes amidst a greasy sea of shadow.

"Look!" she said. "'Ow 'bout I give y' a wank an' we call it quits?"

Put as bluntly as that, I no longer felt like a wank. In fact, I no longer felt like anything. And I certainly didn't feel like having Ava cluttering up my kitchen any longer, exuding her stale smell.

"Ava," I started, and she reared back.

"Don't touch me!"

Well, this was novel. What was the point, I wondered, in hiring a whore you can't touch?

"I wasn't going to touch you," I said, but she remained cringing back in her chair. "I was just about to say, I think there's been a bit of a mistake."

"There's been a bloody mistake, all right!" she agreed, and with that she surged forward, stuffed her cigarettes and her lighter back into her bag, struggled upright, and hauled herself towards the exit.

"Bloody ol' pervert!" she said, as she slammed the door behind her.

I watched her short legs carry her wobbling buttocks down the path. She hauled a cell phone from her bag, tapped in a number, and soon the Avon Kab reappeared.

And now I felt a stirring of anger. I had definitely *not* got value for money!

Ava Bonk, Ava Bonk,
Short of stature, large of conk!
Your frame will never win awards,
With piles for legs and tits like gourds!
It is my sadly reached perception,
> *You are a mistress of deception!*
> *But remember, when a snook is cocked –*
> *Both God and Campbell are not mocked!*

Chapter 31

The Avon River is a thrombotic vein that plods through Christchurch. It begins its life somewhere to the west of the city centre, wends a weary, meandering passage generally east, describes a question mark, and then makes a bolt for the sea. It is named to remind the occupants of that city, the city that is more English than the English, of Stratford and Shakespeare and all that is right and good in our colonial past.

As it chugs resolutely along its serpentine course it carries with it all the waste and residue sloughed off by our genteel city and on one brittle spring morning part of that residue was Mrs Thrag.

You'd think, being such a small piece of flotsam, that she might have just bobbed off out to sea; but no. She got herself hitched up on a willow branch that had fallen into the river, and there she stayed, wafting to the whim of the current, for some time.

The body was reported to be in a state of "advanced decomposition" when found by a couple walking their bichon frise. Shock was the result for the couple, although how the bichon frise had fared was never reported. But it goes without saying that counselling had been ordered, for the couple, if not for their flea bag. "Foul play" had not been ruled out. In fact, police were conducting a scene examination, and there was a second site that was also "of interest". Meanwhile, the whereabouts of Mrs Thrag's "loyal canine companion, Trevor", had yet to be ascertained.

There were comings and goings at the Thrag household. Police cars buzzed about like angry hornets, and enquiries were made of neighbours. A Detective Stuart Piddick raised the long arm of the law, the calloused knuckles of which rapped on my door several days after the news had broken.

Was I aware of the situation regarding my neighbour? Unfortunately, I was. Tragic! Most tragic!

When was the last time I had seen Mrs Thrag? Let me think; let me think. Was it two weeks ago last Tuesday? Or was it three? Anyway, she asked me to assist her with the elimination of a rat.

A rat? Yes. She'd poisoned it or something, but it refused to die, and was in her cupboard, and then it was up in the ceiling. Ha ha. Long story.

Had she seemed in good spirits? *Very* cheerful, I'd thought, considering her age and condition.

Her condition? Well she was arthritic. She used a pair of sticks to get around, and was constantly in pain. She bore it very bravely, I thought. I used to assist wherever I could, of course, as one does.

Was she in the habit of walking off alone? Oh, you could never tell with Mrs Thrag. A hardy old soul! So independent! Lovely woman!

Had I seen any unusual goings-on at the house? Goings-on?

Well, anything out of the ordinary. Hmmm. Not that I could think of. A quiet neighbourhood and I do tend to keep to myself.

Had I happened to see her dog, Trevor, about? No! I hadn't! And I had thought it a bit strange. He often comes over and says hello when I'm hanging out my washing.

Hadn't I thought to check? Check? When?

Well, when I hadn't seen Trevor about. Hadn't I thought to check on Mrs Thrag? Foolishly, no. As I say, we tend to keep to ourselves.

Well, if I happened to think of anything that might throw further light on their investigation, would I mind contacting Mr Piddick? Of course I wouldn't! Pleased to oblige!

Finally the foul play theory was confirmed, and the police verified that the case was being treated as a homicide. And then the gutter press began to circulate rumours that the poor woman had been horribly mutilated. Why can't they let these things lie? Don't these hyenas give a moment's thought to us – the bereaved?

The funeral was at the local Anglican franchise, and was followed by a quick puff of smoke up at the crematorium. There was a surprisingly good turnout, which there often is at these celebrity funerals. You can live a pointless, anonymous life, characterised only by viciousness, and then by virtue of ending up in the river, become a luminary overnight. I attended, of course, as a friend and neighbour. Bowed my head during the assurances from the minister that, though she had left us, yet Mrs Thrag lived on. I mouthed the hymns; agreed that the Lord was my Shepherd, and that he did make me to lie down in green pastures, albeit that those pastures were conspicuous only by their absence in the greater Aranui area. There was even a loan lone piper at the crematorium, piping her off as she descended to the depths. Quite moving, really.

I'd sent along a little card, anonymously, of course. One doesn't want to hog the limelight. It showed a simple bouquet of violets (I'd been unable to find hemlock), and I'd inscribed it with a short, heartfelt verse:

Mrs Thrag you might have been a pain,
But your passing has not have been in vain,
For it will stand as admonition
To those of vengeful disposition.

<u>Chapter 32</u>

Yes, yes, yes, yes!

I killed Ava Bonk! There! Are you happy? *Why*? Well, she was an affront to humanity, to all that is decent! To my Rags, and therefore to me! She was a squamous blot on the face of society! She was a cancer, and needed to be excised!

It wasn't difficult. Killing isn't, once you get the hang of it. Ask anyone in the business. Ask the fellow who daily slaughters your meat and goes home to smiling wife and frolicking kids and puts up his feet and cannibalistically gobbles down the sacrifice of the day, breast or thigh or brain or liver, while watching cops on reality TV to make life real. Ask Bush. Ask Bin Laden. Ask Clinton or Putin or Rasputin, or any other -in. Ask that basher, Bashar al-Assad.

God! I feel my mind wandering sometimes now, and I feel the need to rein it in. It's just... there's a great sadness at the core of human kind, don't you think?

A mouse will yield up its life for a smidgeon of cheese, a smear of the taste of peanut, the merest smell of it. A hint. A promise. Ava would not sell herself so cheaply. With Ava it took a pair of crisp, newish, although slightly soiled (as Ava) hundred dollar bills, that old hair-splitter, Sir Ernest ogling her earnestly from above walrus.

We met down by the river side. An anonymous cab this time, the turban vanishing in profile quickly into the dusty distance of post-apocalyptic Christchurch. I, dressed to the nines: old suit, rumpled, admittedly, from banana box storage, but white-now-creamish shirt, soiled at collar and cuffs; conservative polka tie, glasses, of course, and, you'll like this – trilby. If I say so myself, I was dapper. I could have fallen for myself, had I not already done so.

Ava was, well, Ava. A disco ball on heels, sinking into soft ground like quicksand, her life already slipping from her. Her odour preceded her like a herald, trumpeting her presence: "Here cometh Lady Ava Bonk! Make way! Make way!" Her complexion: well, what can one say? She had excelled! Blackheads upon blackheads now, erupting through caked years of foundation. A stagnant pimple dead centre, like Cyclops.

What was in the bag I carried? Well, a picnic!

I had gone overboard this time; splashed out on the full two hours. Champagne, I promised; a smorgasbord of delights to ignite our night of love. Down by the riverside.

Her arms windmilling now, as she falters on heels, and becomes, finally, bogged.

"Let me! Let me!"

Cavalier Sir Bruce kneels and gently eases the whore-red shoes from wearied, bunioned feet, to be rewarded with a groan of satisfaction and a malodorous waft. And idly swinging those noxious prizes from a hooked, carefree finger, moves on, his companion, now a good half-head shorter, at his side.

Sir Bruce charges into the glade first, prepared to purge the place of evil-doers, then, finding none, plights his troth.

"This looks like a nice spot."

Gonna lay down my tartan blanket,
Down by the river side,
Down by the river side...

Ava edges in. A heraldic thrush chirrups welcome, bows to a worm; a gaggle of goggling starlings stand stunned: Lady Smellyfeet and Sir Drinkalot. And one fat, lucky, ponderously pregnant blowfly.

Ava, tired, exhausted, aging, life-weary, on hams of legs, collapses.

"Ta. Mind if I smoke?"

"Not at all! Have one of mine."

The golden evening creeps crepuscular on towards purple.

"Champagne?"

"Oh! Yeah! Thanks!"

Gonna lay down my small enticement,
Down by the river side,
Down by the river side...

Acrylic flutes clunk rather than clink. To our futures! Although she has none. Beneath respectable spectacles and now-trimmed barber-ous beard and cunning trilby, Sir Bruce rides incognito.

"Caviar?"

"Wassat? Bloody fish eggs, is it?"

"Mmm. A treat!"

"Dunno."

The lip, one half of a crustacean, curls as Sir Bruce lovingly, temptingly, enticingly places a tantalisingly crackered morsel on the pink slug that emerges, retreats crackered and egged.

"Ugh! Jesus! Tastes like shit!"

A spurt of salivated eggs and cracker spouts across the blanket.

Gonna lay down poor Ava's life,
Down by the river side,
Down by the river side...

"Sorry, matey! Can't eat that shit!"

Sir Bruce briefly considers a tactical withdrawal to the Golden Arches to bolster his arsenal; then reconsiders; regroups; reforms.

"More champagne?"

"Yeah! That'd be beauty!"

She's a bourbon girl, though, Ava, you know? Way back, eh? Mother's milk to her! Jack's milk, ha ha. Sir Bruce nods an assenting nod. A knowing nod. A nod that accedes to the fact that he has missed his target by a country mile. Next time, perhaps, and flutters comely lashes behind thick lenses.

"Can youse see through them things?"

"Perfectly! All the better to... admire you with!"

The bivalve lips part on small, dun teeth. The pink slug darts forward in pleasure, sucking back a small silence.

"So how come we're here?"

"Here?" Here in this world, Ava? Not for long.

"Down by the river. Most times I go to, you know, homes, like?"

"My wife..." A memorial hand flutters into the dusk air. "We used to..." The hand swoops down to snatch away a tear that refuses to be born.

Now the lips perform a small fandango; the eyes somehow soften magically within their sticky pools of black. Ava is experiencing an emotion. Perhaps her first. Certainly her last.

"Yeah. I do a lotta jokers lost their wives. Sorry, matey."

Choked Sir Bruce waves away condolences.

"It's... It's been a while now. I should be over it."

"Yeah, well..."

A whorish hand flaps towards the knightly arm, settles, sinks cosmetic claws, lingers for the briefest of seconds, and departs.

"I... I have a surprise for you."

"A s'prise? Wod is it?"

"If I told you, it wouldn't be a surprise. Close your eyes, now."

Hesitation. The magic softness in the eyes fades to black.

"No funny shit!"

Sir Bruce conjures up boyish charm he never had.

"Of course not!"

"Okay, then."

The lids flop down, twin shutters on simplicity, to form black-rimmed, quivering mud pools.

Gonna lay down my trusty wool hook,

Down by the river side,

Down by the river side...

"All right! You can open them now!"

The lids hesitate, then flicker open, as if on a dream or a nightmare, but in the fading light even dilated pupils fail to detect the threat. The corners of the lips cock themselves in what might be the beginnings of a smile. We'll never know.

"What is it?"

"This, my dear Ava, is a wool hook," and I begin flourishing it in a Ninja-like fashion.

"What the fuck...?"

The eyes have gone vacant, the lids trembling, the groping, hoping, prehensile lips now downturned, and partnering the lids in a tremble. The throat works itself into a spasm, as if to eject something, but there is nothing to eject. A satisfying picture of abject terror.

"Useful," I continue, "for teaching bad-mannered little whores a lesson!"

A paralysis has overcome her. We are poised, each of us savouring this moment, the wool hook raised against the last rays of a dying sun, and the last moments of a dying daughter. The lips splattered like offal in her face begin to slowly part, the jaw dropping creakily, as if needing oil, a clotted squeal still-born in the pulsing throat.

The wool hook catches her at where I imagine the junction of the frontal and the parietal lobes to be, and elicits a jet of sputum .

that will necessitate the dry cleaning of my suit pants. She struggles like a hooked piranha, the mean crevice of her mouth working at curses, I suppose. She tries to rise, for God's sake, and I am compelled to force her back down, the hook pushing itself far down into the cranial cavity, and she squelches back onto *gluteus maximus* maximus.

And now I am waltzing around her in a celebration, a frantic Morris dance of lust and joy and ecstasy, the handle of my weapon firm in my hand, its faithful hook swirling the contents of her head into a sumptuous, meaty cocktail.

Here we go round poor Ava Bonk,
Ava Bonk,
Ava Bonk...

It's eight-thirty, and I realise suddenly that I'm starving!

Do you think it ironic that Ava's last word was "fuck"? Or am I reading too much into this?

Chapter 33

Several days later you might have fetched your cling-wrap wrapped copy of your local morning gutter snipe from its puddle in your front garden, and been belted across your intelligence with this headline:

Body

Found!

Helvitica, possibly. Or is it Bureau Grotesque? Whatever! It's size that matters here! Sans serif! Bold! 200 point font! Only the sad demise of Rugby legend, Frank Scrum (127 point) and an impending state visit by the Duke and Duchess of Wormelow Tump (a mere 72) merit further front page mention.

Perhaps, then, inured to simple human drama, you yawned, buttered your toast, and turned to the funnies. Or flicked to the births and deaths to see if you, too, were dead, or had been born. But had you read on, you would have discovered that:

"The body of a woman has been discovered in a secluded area by the Avon River. Detective Sergeant Dirk Stickybeak of the Christchurch CIB confirmed that the find was made by a young couple out exercising in the early hours of yesterday morning.

"'A pair of teenagers performing aerobic exercise down by the river at around 2:30 A.M. on the morning of the twentieth happened upon a body in the early stages of decomposition,' said Stickybeak.

"The couple are understood to be traumatised, and are undergoing counselling.

"Stickybeak said that the death is being treated as 'suspicious'. Our reporter understands that a scene examination has revealed that the woman died violently. When asked if the body was that of missing Christchurch woman, Maria Hat, Stickybeak commented that he could not comment.

"'The police treat all violent death seriously,' said Stickybeak. When asked if the injuries could have been self-inflicted, he said, 'Due to the fact that the victim died as a result of a sharp object penetrating her cranium, it would seem unlikely. However, the police are keeping an open mind.'

"When asked if the police were seeking anyone else in connection with their inquiries, Stickybeak said that the police were keeping an open mind.

"When asked if he had any further comment, Stickybeak said that he could not comment, but that if anyone had any further information, they should contact the police immediately. 'Any information will be treated in the strictest confidence,' he said.

"Sources have suggested that the body may, in fact, be that of local identity, Maria Hat. Hat was well known in the city for many years for her exotic dance routine, performed at Club E-Z with the aid of a Pole, or if a Pole was unavailable, a Swede or a Fin. She danced under the stage name of 'Ava Bonk'. Sources say that Hat began to suffer from early-onset arthritis some years ago. Because of that, and because of a general public trend away from exotic dance into more aggressive forms of erotic titillation, she was forced to give up her stage career.

"'Maria was such a hard worker,' said a close friend, who preferred to remain anonymous. 'A lot of people would have just chucked in the f.....g towel at that point. But Maria thought, nah, f..k it, and she done this retraining, and then she up and went and got her own, like, business.'

"We can reveal that Hat has been working in the city for some years as a prostitute, still using her stage name, and operating a Haul-a-Honey franchise.

"When we contacted Mr Ivan Allcock, New Zealand operations manager for Haul-a-Honey International, Allcock said that he had no comment. When asked for further comment, he cited privacy law, saying, 'We have been advised by our legal team not to comment on dead people, because it might infringe on their right to privacy.'"

It took a little more than a week before the big, flat feet of Stickybeak and his team of one intrepid investigator were pounding up my front path.

"Mr Wigans?" asked the freshly shaven face of Stickybeak, eying me from two steps down.

"Yes."

"Mr Ira Wigans?"

"That's right."

"Mr Wigans, I'm Dectective Sergeant Stickybeak of the Christchuch CIB, and this is Detective Constable Nosy-Parker."

"Yes."

"Mr Wigans, we're investigating a missing person, and we have reason to believe that you may be able to assist us with our enquiries."

"I see."

There followed a brief lull in the conversation, while Stickybeak ran a thirsty eye over my whisky bottle collection, took in my other collection of rubbish on what might otherwise have been my front lawn, and craned to peer around me into the dim interior of what remained of my home.

"Do you mind if we come in, Mr Wigans."

"Not at all, please. Would you like tea, Inspector...?"

"Sergeant."

"Sergeant. Would you like tea, sergeant? Coffee? A cold beverage, perhaps?"

"Very kind, Mr Wigans, but Constable Nosy-Parker and I have just had a bite."

We wrestled our way around my small dining table, Nosy-Parker, as the lightweight among us, electing to take the seat with the rickety leg. A small notebook was produced.

"Now, Mr Wigans!" said Stickybeak. "If you wouldn't mind just clearing a couple of things up for us."

"I'm certainly happy to help where I can, Inspector."

"Sergeant."

"Sergeant."

"Well, first off, Mr Wigans, can I just confirm that you are the legal occupant of these premises."

"Yes, I am."

"And yet, we are advised, sir, that the property is rented in the name of one Bruce Campbell."

"That's right."

Stickybeak looked confused. He glanced over at the constable, who was scribbling furiously in her notebook.

"So what you are telling us, Mr Wigans, is that you're also Mr Campbell."

"Indeed!" I said.

"Well, how is that possible, sir?"

"I write, Inspector."

"Sergeant."

"Sergeant."

"You write?"

"Yes. The odd thing. Trite stuff mostly. Nothing of any great literary merit, unfortunately." I could have disclosed the true nature of my scribbling, but I saw no point in casting pearls before swine.

"I'm sure, sir. But how does that have any bearing on the fact that you appear to be two people."

"Well, Ira Wigans is a *nom de plume*, Inspector."

"Sergeant."

"Sergeant."

"I see. Well, if you could just clarify for us, sir, who are you now?"

"Well, for all intents and purposes, I'm Bruce Campbell."

Stickybeak seemed to struggle with this concept of dual identity, seemed inclined to pursue it, and then decided to head off on a tangent.

"Is it correct, sir, that your alter ego, this Ira Wigans, on the morning of September fourteenth last, did contact, by telephone, the Haul-a-Honey dating agency?"

"Yes, that is correct."

"And is it true, sir, that you booked one 'half hour delight', delivered to your home, that being, 18A Camelot Terrace?"

"Yes. Also correct."

"And can you tell us, in your own words, sir, what exactly then transpired?"

"Well, about mid afternoon, my honey arrived."

I felt it fitting to drop a cloak of decency over what then happened, but Stickybeak did not.

"And what happened then, sir?"

"She came inside."

"And did she introduce herself?"

"Yes, she did. She said her name was Ava Bonk."

"And who were you, sir?"

"Who was I? I'm afraid I don't quite follow, Inspector."

"Sergeant."

"Sergeant."

"Well, what I mean, sir, is, were you being Mr Campbell or Mr Wigans?"

"Oh! I see! Well, I'd booked the service under the name 'Wigans', suspecting it might be a business-related expense, and therefore tax-deductible."

"I see. And what happened then, sir."

"Well, you'll laugh at this, Inspector, but..."

"Sergeant."

"Sergeant. You'll laugh at this, sergeant, but absolutely nothing happened."

"Nothing?"

"Nothing."

"So, if I'm understanding you correctly, sir, you paid Miss Bonk the sum of one hundred dollars, inclusive of goods and services tax, and you got nothing in return."

"Oh, no, no no! When I say 'nothing', I mean nothing of a salacious or carnal nature occurred. No! Quite the contrary! I found Miss Bonk to be a woman of such unplumbed depths, and extraordinary conversational skills, that all we did was talk."

"You talked, sir?"

"Yes! The half hour simply *rushed* past! Did you know, Inspector, th...."

"Sergeant."

"Sergeant. Did you know, sergeant that Miss Bonk came from Timaru?"

"Yes, we did, sir."

"Extraordinary!"

"All right, then, Mr Campbell, or Wigans as you then were. You and Miss Bonk talked for half an hour, you paid her a hundred dollars for the privilege, and she left."

"That pretty much sums it up! The last I saw of Miss Bonk, she was tripping down my garden path."

"You mean she fell, sir? Tripped on the rubbish?"

"No, no! I mean tripping gaily. She seemed as happy as a puppy with two tails! The last I saw of her she was heading off up the street in a taxi driven by some fellow with a turban."

"Yes, we've spoken with Mr Singh, sir."

"Well, there you go, then. I'm sure he verified events as I've outlined them."

"Not quite, sir. Mr Singh suggested that Miss Bonk seemed agitated when he collected her."

"Did she really? Well, there you go: hidden depths."

"So nothing, shall we say, untoward, happened between you and Miss Bonk that may have caused her to become agitated?"

"Nothing."

"If you don't mind my asking, sir, where were you on the night of the fifteenth?"

"Of October, Inspector?"

"Sergeant."

"Sergeant."

"Of September, sir. The night Miss Bonk died."

"*She's dead!* Oh, good heavens! Oh, my God! Oh! That's terrible!"

My hands flew to my face, and I collapsed forward, the table forming a support to prevent my complete physical disintegration.

"I'm sorry, sir. I assumed you knew. It's been on the news; in all the papers."

My knuckles were probing my eyes for tears, urging them to come.

"Well, I live the life of an aesthete, Inspector, uns..."

"Sergeant."

"Sergeant. I live the life of an aesthete, Sergeant, preferring it to remain unsullied by the events of the world."

"Do you, sir?"

"I find it helps with the creative juices."

"I see." He looked me over, seemed to be about to say something more, but then seemed to decide against it. "Well, I think that about wraps it up, Mr Campbell. Can you think of anything you can add, that may help us with our investigation?"

I made a pretence of deep thought.

"No, nothing, Inspector."

"Sergeant."

"Sergeant. But if I have any flashes of inspiration, I'll certainly get in touch."

"I'd appreciate that, sir. Here's my card."

At the door, Stickybeak again ran his eye over my empties.

"I see you have a bit of a hobby, sir!"

"Oh! My collection! Yes, I keep meaning to catalogue them, but just can't seem to find the time. Quite rare, some of these," I added.

"Empty whisky bottles, aren't they, sir?"

"To the untrained eye, maybe. To a collector, a potential fortune! Take this one, for example," I said, picking a bottle at random. "A Caperdonich '68." A fortuitous choice, and God knows where I'd picked that up from. "A superb example of a Speyside whisky, sherry hogshead matured. It has a clarity and freshness to the nose, with subtle peat and soft smoke. But countering that you have estery fruit and cereal notes, and a certain dryness. The finish is warm, with gentle smoke, of course, and a good length."

"But it's empty, sir," Stickybeak pointed out.

"Well, it is *now*," I said. "But, you see, it's generally unavailable, so even the bottle, the label, has value."

"Unavailable, is it sir?"

"I'd be surprised if you came across one."

"Much like Miss Bonk, then, isn't it sir?"

And with that the pair of them turned and picked their way up the path. At the gate, Stickybeak turned: "Would you have any objection, sir, to us searching your property?"

"Don't you need some sort of warrant for that, Inspector?"

"Sergeant."

"Sergeant. Don't you need a, what is it? A search warrant?"

"Do we, sir?"

And with that the pair of them plodded out to their waiting car.

Chapter 34

Quite honestly, I haven't been feeling myself lately; a bit poorly. Moody. I've been having dark thoughts – premonitions, seeing significance in things when perhaps there is none. My life has become besieged by omens, harbingers and portents, and I have been dwelling on the past more than I probably should. I was just sitting there the other day, pondering things, when the whole business about Mrs Thrag came crashing down around me. It was almost as if I'd put it out of my mind.

In my defence, I can honestly say I improved her condition. And Trevor's! He wasn't a well dog, as it turned out. The poor wee fellow even had a hint of mange about him! Can you believe it? I was shocked to discover this as I ripped his skin off, because she'd always made such an issue of giving him the best of everything.

I'd had this idea of making a small throw rug out of him – something decorative to brighten up the couch. The skin came away so easily, as it does when the flesh is still warm; but once I discovered the mange, well, of course, the throw rug was out of the question. And then, when I looked him over without a skin, the poor little blighter was nothing more than... hah! I was going to say "skin and bones"! But honestly! I found it hard to get a decent meal out of him!

And that wool hook of mine! I know I keep harking back to it, but such a great invention! Civilisation certainly took a giant leap forward with the invention of the wool hook. It does seem to be taking on a mind of its own, though, and before I knew it, there was Trevor's intestine stretched out along the river bank, glistening under the light of a harvest moon.

Are you familiar with haruspicy, the ancient art of divination from entrails? Well, I can't see how they can make that work. Do you know, Trevor's bowel stretched almost six metres! That's without the stomach sac, too! I paced it out. And Trevor such a little thing, it was hard to see how he could have contained it all. But that was when I discovered that the poor little devil had intestinal worms! No wonder he was so fidgety and listless, and inclined to nip at peoples' ankles! Frankly, I'm surprised at Mrs Thrag. I'd expected better things of her when it came to caring for a poor, helpless animal. Particularly as she'd always made such a fuss about what he should eat and what he shouldn't.

He used to peer through the slats in our low boundary fence, his little head cocked to one side, and once I tossed him an old chop bone. He was on it in a flash, worrying at it like a... well, like a dog with a bone. The next thing I knew old Thrag was onto *me*.

"'Oo gave Trevor this bone?" I heard her bellowing.

I poked my head out the door to see what the uproar was about, and she pinged me with one of her sticks.

"It was you, wasn't it!" she yelled, zooming over the knee-high fence with surprising agility for a woman on two sticks. "You'll bugger up 'is teeth. An' anyway, y' can't give cooked bones t' dogs! Didn' y' learn nothin' at that fancy school o' yours?"

"Well, I'm sorry, Mrs Thrag."

"Sorry! Sorry!" She was screeching like a harpy by this stage, shaking both her sticks and the bone at me. "Sorry won't bring poor Trevor back, will it?"

The animal sat on the other side of the fence, eyeing the two of us, I'm sure enjoying my discomfort. The berating persisted for at least fifteen minutes, until the postman arrived, who had to pause for his daily helping of a lashing from the Thragian tongue. Missorted letter, or something. He rode off on his bike, Thrag waving her sticks after him. But I'd made good my escape by then.

She was apt to explode at the slightest provocation, and I gradually formed the view that she was unhappy in life.

The Thrag case was experimental for me. Normally I'm in, wham, bam, it's all over and I'm out. Nice and clean. Everyone's happy. I was thinking about this one day, and it occurred to me that there's not a lot of respect for the client in that approach. Okay; some people just don't deserve respect. The bean counter, for example, and there have been others – rude and insensitive people who are not even worth mentioning. But I did feel that Mrs Thrag had earned herself a more fitting exit – something with a bit of flair to it. I'd spent most of our relationship apologising to her, and I certainly didn't want to be apologising to her about this.

I realise now, hindsight being twenty-twenty, etcetera, etcetera, that there was one consideration I should always have factored into any of my plans, and that is the propensity for something to go wrong. I'm no stranger to things going wrong, after all, but if you do your homework, dot your i's and cross you t's, then I think it's reasonable to believe that it will all turn out hunky dory. Not always so, unfortunately, and I had a lifetime's experience to attest to that. So, yes, I should have made some provision in my planning for factor X.

I'd been ruminating on Mrs Thrag's predicament for some time, and I'd decided to make it into a special occasion. I popped over nice and early, my kit under my arm, thinking we could make a day of it. I'd conjured up a nice chocolate sponge for her. Something you probably don't know about me, I'm quite handy in the kitchen! Baking's my strong suit. It's the most creative of the culinary arts, I feel. I mean, a stew's a stew, whether you call it a ragout, a slumgullion or a hoosh; and it's hard to apply any panache to a chop or a schnitzel or a pile of mashed potatoes. But give me some self-raising flour, a few eggs, a bottle of milk and a dollop of my special ingredients, and I'll have your taste buds tingling in no time! You'll be begging for more!

This particular sponge, the Thrag sponge, was incidentally suffused with a *crème fraîche* filling, and topped with a sumptuous, butter-rich frosting, dotted with fresh strawberries. You can pick these up quite easily down at the local fruiterer when no one's watching. And a little aside here, for those with a culinary bent, there is a popular misconception that *crème fraîche* refers to fresh cream, when in fact it is slightly soured, and thickens naturally during its fermentation process. Superb! Once you've tried it, you'll never go back to the stuff you whip up in a bowl with a shake of icing sugar and a splash of vanilla. Oh! I forgot to mention that the Thrag sponge also contained a dash of an opiate that I'd had hanging around for God knows how long. No use-by date on it, so I put the lot in, just to play safe.

Well, there I was, on her doorstep bright and early, sponge cake in hand, and do you think she was pleased to see me? Not a bit of it! She appeared, standing in a nightgown whose front was soiled with tea stains, with something that looked like a flour bag fastened to her head, and two of her front teeth missing.

"Bugger off!" she bellowed.

"Oh. I just..." I held up the sponge as a peace offering, but she poked at it with her stick, marring its chocolate-strawberry perfection.

"It's six o'clock in the bloody morning!" she howled.

"It's nine o'clock, Mrs. Thrag!"

"Five o'clock! That's even bloody worse!" And she slammed the door on me.

One of Mrs Thrag's problems has always been time. At first she didn't believe in daylight saving, and then she did, and then she just got all out of kilter.

I repaired the sponge, then spent a nervous few hours at my kitchen window, until I saw her head bobbing about, indicating that she was abroad, and now relatively synchronised with the rest of the world. So, armed with my work bag and the sponge, I again headed off in the direction of the dragon's lair.

"Good morning Mrs Thrag! I've brought you a..."

"Ooooo!" she cooed, zeroing in on the sponge; and she grabbed it, turned and closed the door.

Persistent knocking brought about her return. She peeked out from behind the door, chocolate smearing her face.

"I thought we could share it," I said.

"Mmmm?" She cupped a hand to her ear.

"SHARE IT." I shouted.

"Oooo! Sherry! What a lovely idea! Do you have some?"

And while I stood there, scratching my head, she again shut the door and was gone. Back home I ransacked my own personal indoor landfill to discover a bottle of pale sherry that I'd mistakenly come by, because under cover of darkness it had looked like whisky.

Back *chez* Thrag, I pounded on the door for some time before its inhabitant materialised, now almost entirely chocolate coated, and I waved the sherry at her.

"Oooo!" she said, and made a grab for it. But this time I was ready for her, and snatched it away.

"Why don't we have a drink together?" I suggested.

"Mmmm?" she asked, still clawing at the bottle.

"A DRINK!" I said. "TOGETHER!"

"Ooo, yes," she said. "Stinking weather!"

"MRS THRAG! I'D LIKE TO HAVE A DRINK WITH YOU!" I roared, while simultaneously acting out pouring liquid from the bottle she was trying to seize, into an imaginary glass, and drinking it. Eventually, deciding I was too quick for her, she stood slump-shouldered, a picture of abject disappointment.

"MRS THRAG! YOU DON'T HAVE YOUR HEARING AID IN, DO YOU?" I shrieked in her ear.

She looked at me sadly, and then, as if struck by inspiration, she raised a finger, turned and trotted back into her grotto; her sticks pounding at the floor in front of her. Fortunately, this time the door was left ajar, so in I went. There was the sponge on the table, already half gone. By the time she returned with the small, beeping gadget in the palm of her hand, she was beginning to exhibit the early stages of narcolepsy. She was trying to screw the device into where she thought her ear was, but wasn't, and eventually gave up and handed it to me.

Her head was weaving about like one of those toy dogs that people used to think it amusing to have on the rear window shelves of their cars, to annoy following motorists, and the grubby hole she presented to me was a difficult target. I eventually had to restrain her head under my arm, and force the gadget in, where it emitted a final, prolonged shriek, which brought a satisfied grin to the face of Mrs Thrag.

"Tha's better!" she slurred. "I can 'ear!"

Whereupon she collapsed on the floor and began to snore, and whereupon Trevor mooched over and began licking the chocolate from her face.

This was absolutely not as I'd planned it! And all because of a hearing aid! I pondered what to do next, and as I pondered, Trevor began to perform a little dance routine, and then collapsed on the floor beside his mistress. I'm unsure as to canine tolerance to narcotics, but apparently Trevor had ingested sufficient from Mrs Thrag's face to induce unconsciousness. I now had a pair of problems on my hands.

I glanced at my watch. Three twenty. All I could do was wait and see.

As dusk settled over Sleepy Hollow, and the sounds of alcohol-fuelled rage and the clatter of thrown crockery and the wailing of beaten children began to echo around our little dell, I'd decided on my course of action. I would convert Mrs Thrag's wheelbarrow to my own use. Folded into a foetal position, she fitted it perfectly, and with a blanket over her I could have been just any man walking down the road with a wheelbarrow, with something in it covered by a blanket. And Trevor was just as snug and invisible in my rucksack. The three of us set off towards one of my favourite haunts down by the river.

We were halfway there when my rucksack began to emit a low, mournful wailing sound. Trevor had woken from his slumber, and was making his presence known. Whilst I'd as yet encountered no one, all normal people in my neighbourhood being at this hour engaged in either spousal conflict or criminal activity of their own, it was apparent I couldn't go on. A man wheeling a wheelbarrow containing something covered by a blanket is one thing. A man with a howling rucksack is quite another.

I took the bag off my back, and out popped Trevor, staggered about a bit, and then cocked his leg against mine. His bladder emptied, he then began sniffing about the wheelbarrow, and it was while he was doing this that I dealt him a sharp rap to the head with the handle of the wool hook, again proving its versatility. Back he went to the land of Nod, and then back into the rucksack.

A few minutes later we were at a nice little treed area down by the river, the moon pouring its argentine light down on us, at which point it was Mrs Thrag's turn to make her presence known.

"Ooooooh!" An onlooker might have thought the wheelbarrow haunted.

"Oooooooh!" It came again. I whipped back the blanket to reveal Mrs Thrag attempting to sit up.

"Hello, Mrs Thrag!" I said, full of cheer. She eyed me groggily.

"Ooooooh!" she said for a third time.

"Yes, yes, all right Mrs Thrag! Enough of that!" Sometimes you just have to be firm. She was gazing about her now, seemingly at a loss.

"Where... where am I?"

"We're down by the river. I thought I'd take you for a nice walk, Mrs Thrag." She looked down at what she was sitting in.

"I's... i's a wheelbarrow!" she said.

"Quite right, Mrs Thrag. Well, you didn't seem up to making the journey under your own steam."

The whole thing was ruined now, of course. I'd intended for it to be so special for her, but now there seemed to be nothing for it but to just get it over with.

"See this, Mrs Thrag?" I said, pulling the wool hook from my bag. She peered at it.

"I's... i's a bale 'ook," she said.

"Well, where I come from we call them wool hooks," I said, and swatted her around the temple with it.

It was disappointing. I'd had such high hopes for the day – plans that together Mrs Thrag and I could boldly push back the frontiers of human knowledge, or at least my knowledge. That we could finally explore, and perhaps even answer those questions that always nag at you, like, how long can a person survive with a severed femoral artery, or is it *really* true that the average human female contains a little over five litres of blood? Not that I'm suggesting that Mrs Thrag was average, or even necessarily human, except in the broadest sense of the word. But sadly, it wasn't to be.

Incidentally, you know what I was saying about my intention to turn Trevor into a throw rug, but not being able to because of the mange? Well, as it turns out, Mrs Thrag looks every bit as good on the sofa. And the tanning has brought out all the wrinkles.

Chapter 35

Now, with the passing of Ava, the whole Thrag thing seemed to gain a new currency, and that currency seemed to have the head of Bruce Campbell stamped upon it.

There was a knock at the door. There were two of them, neither of which was a Piddick. This time there was a Detective Inspector Derek Frapley, a basset hound of a man, and his offsider, a Detective Constable Yogel. Frapley remained dominant in the relationship, while Yogel still seemed to be still wearing his L plates.

"Is that Yodel?" I asked, failing at first to catch Yogel's name. Onomastics interests me intensely. I believe you can tell a lot about a person from his name. "What's in a name?" asked Juliet, naively. A lot, in fact, as Romeo would soon discover.

"Yo-gill!" he said. "With a 'G'." Yogel, I mused; probably belongs in there with the Vogels and Fogels and Fowles's and Fuggles I decided. Probably had something to do with birds. He probably came from a long line of fowlers.

"Unusual name," I responded, opening an avenue for polite conversation, which was to go unexplored.

"Isn't it!" he said, and abruptly plumped himself down onto a chair and readied himself to say nothing more.

What is it about policemen that makes them comical? With Frapley it was obvious – his appearance. He was a slab of a man, whose features hung off him at angles of forty-five degrees. His shoulders sloped; his eyes were slashed onto his face in angular dashes, as if with an impatient paint brush; his feet splayed in duck-like fashion. His whole physique and demeanour suggested a massive landslip. He drooped. He was Forty-five Degree Man.

The thing is, I am not equipped for entertaining. My living room is sparsely furnished, with a small, square, steel-framed table, and four steel-framed chairs, none of which matches its partners. This, I suppose, is the lot of the poor; invariably we are cash-strapped, and once such necessities of life as drugs and alcohol are paid for, we have little money to throw about on fripperies like furniture.

Frapley and I joined Yogel at the table, Yogel teetering gamely on the chair with the dodgy leg.

"Now, Mr Campbell," said Frapley, rubbing his coarse hands together, and emitting a sound as of two pieces of sandpaper coming into contact. "We're given to understand that you were an acquaintance of the late Mrs Velma Thrag."

"Well, she was my neighbour." I gestured aimlessly towards the old Thrag place.

"And, did you know her well?"

"We talked, as you do with neighbours. Jason and Bozo live on the other side. And at the back is old Mr Tupley. Two doors down..."

"Thank you, Mr Campbell. We're more interested in Mrs Thrag at the present point in time. I'm sure you'll understand..."

But now I was watching his lips move. It was as if they were having trouble synchronising with whatever he was using for a brain. The words coming out of his mouth were so simple, and yet so laboured. I sometimes imagine people as having no lips; we rely on so little to make people palatable to us, don't we? We humans are face-obsessed! Take away our lips and we'd be repulsed. These Frapley lips were tissue-thin things, hung like fleshless curtains over a rocky palisade of teeth. The sort of lips, I was thinking, that would form such words as, "I was moving down Teed Street in a south easterly direction when I observed a man I now identify as the defendant approaching on foot from the direction of Gazelle Terrace. It struck me as unusual that he was carrying a grenade launcher, and that he was trying to conceal it in the pocket of his trousers." Or, "Anything you say, can and will be used..." Or, "Now, Mr Campbell, can you tell us where you were on the night of..."

"I beg your pardon, Mr Frapley! I'd drifted off for a moment there. What was it you were saying?"

"Not a problem, sir. Man in your condition. What I was saying was, we have reason to believe that Mrs Thrag met her end on or about the seventeenth of March."

"I see."

"Can you tell us, sir, where were you on the night of the seventeenth?"

"The seventeenth, the seventeenth..." I drummed my fingers on the table, noticing the many rings formed in the shape of the bottoms of bottles, and suddenly ruing the waste. "March?" I confirmed.

"That is correct, sir. The seventeenth of March."

But that was ages ago! How is one supposed to keep track of one's movements months in arrears?

"Honestly, Inspector, I have no idea. Typically, though, I would have been at home. Around five-thirty or six; I'd have prepared a light meal – some beans on toast perhaps; maybe an egg. I tend towards light meals at night now. I find I sleep better. I might have had a glass of wine. Possibly even two. I might then have sat and listened to some music. Rachmaninoff would have been a likely choice. I've been going through a bit of a Rachmaninoff phase. I seem to have given Bach a bit of a thrashing over the years – you know how it is. But I still say, and I don't know how you feel about it, Inspector, but I still say you can't beat baroque if you want to just put your feet up and relax!"

"More of a disco man, myself, sir. DC Yogel, here, he's a bit of a fan of that ACDC, aren't you, Yogel?" Yogel gave an assenting nod. "But, musical tastes apart, sir, what you're telling us is that you were at home on the night of the seventeenth, that you in all likelihood had baked beans on toast for tea..."

"Or an egg!"

"Or an egg, sir. An' that you then had a quiet night in, listening to a bit of this Rackswotsits on the radio."

"Rachmaninoff. Yes. That pretty well sums up a typical night for me, Inspector. But as I said, whether that is *exactly* what I did on the night of the seventeenth of March, I couldn't be *absolutely* certain."

Really, I had no idea what I'd been doing, didn't even know what day the seventeenth was, and I thought it unreasonable of them to be asking. In all likelihood, what I'd have been doing would have been getting absolutely pissed after which I would have collapsed, either onto my bed, or onto the old rolled-arm sofa that I'd salvaged from the dump. I couldn't very well go telling Frapley and Yogel that, though, could I?

"So you heard nothing strange, then?"

"Strange, Inspector?"

"Yes, sir. Strange."

"And what would you consider strange, Inspector?"

"Well, for example, sir, one neighbour has reported he heard what might have been a woman's scream at a little after sundown."

"Oh!" I said, comprehension dawning. "Nothing strange about that! You must consider the circumstances under which we are forced to live, Inspector. It's not exactly Fendalton or Merivale, is it? Women's screams are pretty much par for the course in our neck of the woods!"

Frapley exchanged a meaningful look with Yogel, who produced a pen and notebook from his pocket and began writing something in it.

"So you hear a lot of women's screams then, do you, Mr Campbell?"

"Well, a few. I mean, I don't want to overplay it, but it would be a rare night that *someone* isn't screaming."

"An' you never think of doing something about it?"

"Like, what?"

"Like calling the police, sir!"

"Well, as I say, it's so commonplace..."

Frapley sat and stared at me for a full minute, while I tried to meet his gaze. Yogel joined him.

"I mean, I'd be dialling 111 every five minutes," I added, but still they continued to stare.

"Look, Inspector," I finally said, "am I under suspicion here?"

"What on earth would give you that idea?" said Frapley, and Yogel shook his head in apparent amazement at the thought.

"Well... your questions seem a little, well, pointed," I said.

"Just trying to establish witnesses, alibis, that sort of thing, sir. Just typical police legwork." And he continued to stare at me. "How 'bout Trevor, then?" he said at last.

"What do you mean, 'how about Trevor?'?"

"Well, Trevor was killed, too, you know."

"Yes, I heard. Terrible!"

"Indeed, sir, it was! Not a lot left of the poor wee chap just between you and me, sir. But what I mean is, what sort of relationship did you have with Trevor?"

"*Relationship?*" I was suddenly appalled that he may have thought I'd struck up some kind of bestial arrangement with the animal.

"Yes sir. How did you get on with him?" I still couldn't fathom his intention, so we continued to eye each other. "Any trouble, was he, sir?"

"Trouble?"

"Barking, sir?"

"Oh! I see! No, Trevor was fine!"

"Yappy little beggar, was he?"

"No, no! He seemed to sleep most of the time."

"Keep you up nights with his yapping, did he?"

"No, as I said..."

"Bother you, then, did he?"

"No. As I said, Inspector, Trevor seemed to sleep most of the time."

There was another studied silence, then:

"So when was the last time you saw Mrs Thrag sir? Alive, I mean."

"Well, I haven't seen her *dead*, Inspector," I laughed.

"'*Haven't* you, sir?"

"Well, no, of course I haven't!"

"So, if you wouldn't mind just telling us, sir, when was the last time you laid eyes on Mrs Thrag?"

"Well, it would be a few months ago now. I helped her out with a rat."

"A rat, sir?"

"Yes. She had a large rat running amok in her house, and I helped her get rid of it."

"I see. 'Amok' was it, sir?"

"Yes. It was terrorising her a bit, into her dried goods and that. I chased it up into the ceiling and, well, you'll laugh at this, Inspector, but I ended up falling through the ceiling onto her late husband's matchbox collection!"

They didn't laugh, but Yogel made a note of it in his little book.

"So that was the last time you saw Mrs. Thrag, then, sir? When you fell through her ceiling onto her husband's matchbox collection."

"Yes."

"Alive."

"Yes. Well, as I said, Inspector, obviously I haven't seen her dead. But I did glimpse her around after that. We just never got to pass the time of day." His basset hound eyes were drooped all over me again. "Both too busy, I suppose," I added, to fill in the silence.

"Busy, sir?"

"Yes, well, you know..."

"And what is it you do, sir that keeps you so busy?"

"I, um, I help out. And there's my research."

"Research, sir?"

"Yes. I'm a writer."

"A writer, sir! And what sort of thing do you write?"

"Literary musings, mostly, inspector."

"What, like that, um, that Cat woman."

"Catton, inspector. But, no. In fact, to be quite honest with you, I loathe these self-congratulating literary tours de force, with their sad nod towards lost causes and outraged minorities. No, my work tends more towards the scholarly. Are you familiar with Malory, inspector?"

"Would that be DC Mellory, sir? Young chap over in dogs?"

"No, inspector. This would be Sir Thomas Malory, fifteenth century knight of the realm and chronicler of the Arthurian cycle."

"Well, in that case, sir, no, I'm unfamiliar with him."

"Yes, well. I do a lot of work on Malory."

"And that pays, does it, sir? Make a living at it, do you?" asked Frapley, looking around him.

"Well, it's a labour of love mostly. There simply isn't the appetite for good literary criticism that there once was."

"Pity. So how is it you earn a crust, then, sir?"

"Well, I'm, um, I'm on a small government stipend."

"A *stipend*, sir?"

"Mmm. A small one."

"Isn't it in fact true, sir, that you are on the unemployment benefit?"

"Mmm, yes, well... A stipend."

"And you've been on that 'stipend' since you parted company with your last employer, one..."

"Torr Insurance!" supplied Yogel promptly.

"Thank you, constable. One Torr Insurance under, shall we say, 'a cloud of suspicion', sir?"

"Well, 'cloud' would be putting it a little strongly. I mean, there was no proof. No charges were brought."

"And prior to that you were where, Mr Campbell?"

"Well, um..."

"You were in prison, weren't you, Mr Campbell?"

"Mmm."

"From where you were released in, when was it, Mr Yogel?"

And again Yogel rose supremely to the occasion.

"Two thousand an' seven, sir! August twenty-third!"

"Two thousand an' seven! Is that correct, Mr Campbell?"

"Yes, well..."

"And what were you in prison for on that particular occasion, Mr Campbell?"

"Well, it was, a, um..."

"Rape, wasn't it sir? An unprovoked sexual assault on an innocent young girl?"

"Yes, well..."

"A girl who had, in fact, been entrusted to your care."

"Yes, well, it wasn't quite like that!"

"*Wasn't* it, sir? But I understand you pleaded guilty as charged. Changed your plea at the eleventh hour. Isn't that what happened, Mr Yogel?"

Yogel wagged his big head up and down, and threw me a disgusted look.

"Yes, but there were circumstances!" I said. "Extenuating!"

"Were there, sir?"

"Yes! And I changed my plea to save the girl!"

"Saved the girl, did you sir?" Frapley's basset eyes flared. "'How noble of you, Mr Campbell! What a pity you didn't think of *saving* the girl before you raped her!"

They were just being pernickety, and this was all quite obviously going nowhere. The whole thing eventually petered out. Not, of course, before Frapley had reminded me that Vivien had disappeared in early 2010, and I had reminded him that the police had already interviewed me to see if I could assist with that matter, and that Vivien had left a note to say that she could no longer deal with her life in the aftermath of what she called "everything that had happened", and that the disappearance had eventually been put down to suicide. Tragic; unfortunate; but hardly *my* fault, was it? People kill themselves every day of the week! And certainly, I failed to see what it had to do with the deaths of Mrs Thrag, and poor Trevor.

So they left, trotting up the path with their tails between their legs.

And then I thought, what had Frapley meant by that comment, "man in your condition"?

Chapter 36

In my dream I was the world's most hated man, hunted and driven from pillar to post, and – well here I must pause to explain for those less well endowed with etymological expertise than I, the meaning of that expression.

Theories abound. The phrase first appeared in English sometime around the early fifteenth century, and has been attributed, wrongly I believe, to John Lydgate. Scholars have suggested that it refers to the practice of tying a felon to a post, flogging him, and then placing him in a pillory, or stocks, for target practice and public ridicule. Others say it is connected to tennis, as it was played in mediaeval times, apparently involving pillars and posts, but which was no doubt rendered it just as boring to watch as it is now.

You may be aware, however, that similar expressions exist in other languages; German, for example, contains the quaint adage, *von Pontius zu Pilatus*. In other words, from Pontius to Pilate; and here we have the nub of the thing. Pontius and Pilate were, quite obviously, the same person. So what this tired old bromide is telling us is that someone driven from pillar to post is being driven from one unpalatable thing to something equally unpalatable, with no hiding place between.

So, as I was saying, in my dream I was reviled, and was being driven from pillar to post, mostly around a rocky seashore. I would find refuge behind some boulder, or an old wharf pile, and then, as the leader of this ravening pack of pursuers approached, the Huntsman perhaps, his face merged into plain flesh, to become a featureless thing, so he remained unknown to me. The reason for my persecution was never understood, beyond the knowledge that I was the world's most hated man.

Eventually I found my solace in a small cave of the sea. Well, "cave" is to paint it too grandly. Its walls were concrete and slime-covered; it was a man-made thing; a sewer outlet, perhaps, but in it I skulked, and pulled seaweed over my head to conceal myself. Large crabs snapped their claws at me, and whelks clung, and dug their vicious, saw-like teeth into me, while outside the waves crashed and roared. I knew I was done for – that this was my final refuge, and that I would soon be discovered.

As I lay there I could hear the hootings and hollerings of the hunt, as my persecutors closed in. My heart beat a tattoo in my chest. Soon a shadow fell across the low entrance to my hideout, and my gorge rose with the fear at the expectation of imminent death. But then a child of about six appeared. I spied him through the thin web of weed with which I tried to conceal myself. Instantly I knew him to be my grandson, although I have none, unless something unknown has sprouted from the assumed barren ground onto which I have scattered my seed. With him was an even younger child, of no more than three, and in my dream I knew this, in that incomprehensible, time-muddled way of dreams, to be my infant self. This young figure held a prophetic finger aloft, and with all the drama of a ham actor playing Lear, said, "This is the world's most hated man!"

I awoke in a sweat, and lay rigidly awake, pondering the meaning of those words, and fell asleep only as gray dawn waffled in, to be rudely wakened around ten by the insistent yapping of Trevor, Mrs Thrag's indeterminate, dead terrier.

Chapter 37

There are people who live on for no better reason than that they forget to die. It quite simply seems to slip their minds, and their being tails off into a trite nothingness. I would hate to ever be considered one of those.

It is now the beginning of the winter of 2014. The year of the horse and perhaps, I had been thinking, the winter of my greatest discontent. Oracles had proposed that it would be a volatile year, but then what year isn't? But this one – well, it's a yang wood year, see, when people will stand firm on their principles, leading to conflict. Compromise or negotiation will be difficult.

Businesses involving wood or fire will do well, and therefore firewood merchants will do extremely well; but if you're in the business of property, forget it. The horse is a galloper, causing property prices to gallop downwards during the first half of the year, and then to gallop back up again in the second half, ending roughly where they started.

Down here in the south we can expect volcanoes and gunfire, because the fire energies are so strong. These disasters have yet to emerge, but what *has* emerged is a welter of harassment from police.

I have decided that I need to see Rags again. God! I am sixty-five, in fairly rude health, admittedly. But if this relationship is ever going to flourish, then I need to push my case, and I need to do so urgently! I cannot die without her. I simply cannot! She has been my life!

It is a Monday in mid April when I close the door to Camelot Close behind me in the thick light of pre-dawn, borrow my neighbour's bicycle, and scanning the horizon for spies, head north towards the motorway. An hour's riding proves that I'm less fit than I'd thought, but has taken me sufficiently far that I am able to hitch a ride with a passing shingle truck that takes me as far as the Waipara Junction. Truck drivers of the shingle ilk, in my limited experience, are pithy individuals, whose conversation extends to pebble size and load weight and little more.

"Deliverin' twenny-two tonnes of AP40 up t' Waikari," he tells me, before conversation lags, and we slip into silence.

Fine. I'm happy to remain anonymous. Happy not to impress myself too much on anyone's memory, lest that memory stir up a hornet's nest amongst my police persecutors. They seem to have allied the Thrag and Bonk cases, and decided that my proximity to both may suggest complicity. I can imagine them working diligently to come up with motive, cause, in fact a murder weapon, or any other evidence, perhaps even fabricating it, because they have none which links me.

They have found traces of the narcotic, oxycodone, in Mrs Thrag's remains. Her last meal, they have deduced, was "a chocolate cake", and that traces of that same "chocolate cake" discovered at her residence contained the same synthetic opioid. It had been a sponge, for God's sake; not a cake. But I did not correct them. You cannot expect a bunch of dim-witted plodders in some laboratory to be acquainted with the finer points of cookery. But I had been cautious in ensuring that none of the ingredients contained in the sponge remained in my pantry. I am, after all, a professional.

The rain of Christchurch has given way to a damp sun, and my spirits lift, as I feel my problems recede southward. I'm in Kaikoura by ten, delivered by some sort of travelling salesman, whose death I had considered initiating, for the simple elliptical beauty of it. But once seated on the foreshore, a cartoned coffee in hand, and the blue, sperm whale infested, sparkling waters of the Pacific before me, these dark thoughts quickly fade. Life was not so bad!

I take the five thirty ferry, being able to pick up a few wallets at the crowded Picton terminal, and am in Wellington some three hours later, cash-flush, but this time not being so fortunate as to be able to commandeer the vehicle of my ride. In fact, the gentleman had been a quite amiable sort; a real estate agent with the thickset build of a garden gnome and a ready supply of jokes at which we both laughed uproariously.

We separate in Wellington, I prepay a room in a cheap hotel, using cash, and the *nom de guerre*, "Jack Russell". I doubt people actually give much consideration to these registers in hotels. The young woman looks at it, says, "Thank you Mr Russell," and apart from a "Thanks" to the harassed looking Indian man in the Night 'n' Day store, when we trade five dollars seventy five for a bag of pre-packaged junk food, that is the limit of my engagement with Wellington. I am always conscious now, however, of these CCTV things, so am garbed in cap and goggles. It's incredible the degree to which the state now noses around in peoples' lives!

Sitting here alone, munching on empty carbohydrates, I am reminded of my mother. I find a remote control, and begin watching some drivel on a small television set that can muster insufficient volume to mask the ruckus of the fornicating couple in the room next door. But so happy am I, or so numbed by the couple of Tuinal, ably assisted by the better part of a bottle of Johnny Walker, that I sleep until the cleaning lady taps on my door, and yoohoo's, at eleven the next morning.

A quick breakfast, and I am butting into the teeth of a dry, gusty wind, as I stand down on Aotea Quay with a futile thumb stuck out to the world. I am considering the possibility of a second night in Wellington, when a carload of drunken young hooligans pulls up, and off we go on a circus ride as far as Paraparaumu. I am squished against a rear door, the fifth person in a car that was surely intended only ever to take four, and am subjected to vile mockery and innuendo pertaining to my age. This is only slightly ameliorated when a bottle of cheap vodka is passed around, and I am able to swig what is considerably more than my fair share. Even more happily, a joint then circulates, which I bogart, an expression that is foreign to my companions, and on which I attempt to educate them.

"Hey! Lookit the ol' fucker!" says one. They chortle as I suck deeply, and smile. But their humour fades as I continue to suck and smile more deeply.

"Hey, don't hog it, granddad!" yells the driver, glaring at me in the rear view mirror, while weaving violently from lane to lane as we zoom under the Titahi Bay overbridge.

"It's called 'bogarting'," I say.

"Wot?"

"It's not called 'hogging'. It's an art form, and it's called 'bogarting'," I say, sucking deeply again. This news seems to briefly silence them. "After Humphrey Bogart." More sucking and more silence. "Because, you know, he always had a cigarette hanging out of his mouth."

"But tha's nodda fuggin cigarette," objects the front seat passenger, turning an acne-ravaged face on me.

"*Isn't it?*" I ask, amazed as I deeply inhale again.

"Giz the spliff 'ere," says my backseat neighbour, snatching if from my lips, fracturing the educational moment of magic I'd been conjuring up. I'd been briefly taken back to my classroom days.

I arrive in Paraparaumu with a reasonable glow on. Then, Paraparaumu to Levin in one final leap, as night settles, and I am again obliged to seek out the hospitality of a kindly innkeeper. I am now fortunate enough to have with me the wallet of the rude and drunken young sod whose unwashed body was pressed next to mine during my earlier journey. It contains an extraordinary ten hundred dollar bills, and some lower denominations. I celebrate with a bar meal and some bar whisky, and then continue celebrating with a bottle of single malt, which refuses to be left alone until it is empty. That, combined with another brace of Tuinal, means I am again late to hit the road the next morning.

But it doesn't matter. I feel a welling joy in life that has been lacking for years. As I head out of Foxton, in little flea hops to Otaki, and Bulls and Mangaweka, and a final jump across the Volcanic Plateau, that gets me to Turangi by early afternoon, I feel happy enough that I want to tell the world about Rags. But I don't.

A further wallet enters my possession at a cafe, when I carelessly bump into a dodderer who has just partially inserted it into his back pocket. I'd seen him laboriously tapping in his PIN – 1942; his year of birth, no doubt. They all do it, as memory fails them, and it's the one four digit number that remains accessible to them. So I arrive in Auckland flush with cash at a little after seven.

I am moderate that night. A half of whisky suffices me. A solitary Tuinal gets me off to sleep. I am determined to remain clear-headed for the morrow.

It dawns superbly, I imagine, because I am not up to see it. I do see nine o'clock, however, and the day is resplendent in gold and blue. Hibiscus flowers border the gravelled car park, yellow, pink, purple. Rose of Sharon, a worn stake beside them says, and I think of that useless, pregnant trollop of Steinbeck's. Where the flowers have fallen to the ground, they form a stodgy brown porridge.

A croissant and a coffee, and I'm set to reinvigorate my life. And Rags's. There are people, you know, who think that older people don't have feelings; that as we age, we become devoid of emotion. People who feel that we seniors are not entitled to share in the reciprocal joys of love and giving. But we are human. We feel. If you cut us we bleed, and I have ample proof of that. I feel suddenly confident that she will welcome me into her life with open arms.

I decide to risk it, and plonk the old duffer's credit card down against a rental car, and sure enough, it's accepted. My reasoning had been that one big day out a week is enough for an old timer like him, and the chances are he won't miss the wallet until the following Wednesday rolls around, bowls day or whatever it is, after which he and the missus will hobble down for a bit of a kai-up at the local spittoon. And when he finds the wallet missing, he'll think he's just lost it round the house somewhere. I could probably dine out on this card for weeks, and may in fact do so.

The driver's licence does cause a bit of concern. I present it to the woman behind the counter, a dreary thing wishing her life away with a game of solitaire. She holds it up, looks at it, looks at me, looks at the licence again.

"I've grown the beard since then," I say, and stand dramatically in profile.

She nods. Doesn't care really. Asians, blacks, old people: all us minorities look the same to her. She goes back to her solitaire.

A haircut follows, not that there's much to cut, and then a visit to Van Gogh, the menswear shop, for a dollop of sartorial elegance. By the time I leave Van Gogh's, the old codger's card has clocked up in excess of a thousand dollars, and I make a mental note to send him a thank you. I'll compose one of my rhymes for him. A nice pair of dress shoes equals another one ninety-nine ninety-nine, and I'm really looking the part!

At five fifteen I draw the little red Mazda up to the kerb outside the Corbin Crescent villa, straighten my tie, brush back my wisps of hair, and stroll up the path. I've mapped the evening out: she'll join me for dinner; it'll be somewhere small and intimate. We'll talk; we'll be open with each other, as we've never been able to be, because of the things that stood between us – Eve, the accountant; prison, and more latterly, the builder.

I tap lightly on the door, and sure enough, she answers, casual in jeans and a loose sweat shirt. Her face has lost some of its sparkle, but it's recognisably her. The hair is cropped shorter, to about shoulder length, and is now completely silvered. Shallow lines fan her forehead, and her cheeks are slightly reddened, as if rouged. But I can see that she doesn't recognise me. A smile of friendliness lights her up, as she surveys this handsome, lightly bearded stranger on her stoop; and then slowly it fades.

"Och!" she says. "My God!" And her hands fly to her face as if in horror.

"I *thought* you'd be surprised!" I say, grinning broadly.

"But...," she says. "You...." she says. "It...." she says.

She's making no sense. She's obviously overwhelmed by the occasion, so I decide to help her out.

"It's *me*, Lena!" I say. "Bruce Campbell! Don't you recognise me?"

She nods her head up and down vigorously, her hands still clenched to her face, a look of worry or terror seeming to invade her eyes. And then, she opens her mouth, and bawls, "Hellllp!"

This is not going at all as planned. There's every chance her surprise will draw the attention of neighbours, and things will be ruined. I move towards her, and sort of dance her back into the house, our feet mingling and tripping over each other. It is the first time I've ever touched her, and she is soft and yielding. I almost press my lips to hers. But I don't. There'll be plenty of time for that later. Once inside, I take my hands off her, hold them up to show I mean her no harm, and nudge the door closed.

"What's the matter, Lena?" I ask. "What is it?"

"It's... it's you!" she says.

"Yes I know it's me. I *told* you it was me!"

"You *killed* that woman!"

"*What?*"

"That woman in Christchurch! You *killed* her!"

"Nonsense, Lena. I don't know what you're talking about!"

"It's on the television! On the radio! They're looking for you! You raped a young girl! Hellllp!"

Again, the problems of not remaining connected to mainstream media! I hadn't realised I'd become front page news. But she's becoming hysterical now, so I move to quiet her down.

"Shhh!" I say. She stops her prattling, but looks uncertain; backs away from me. "I didn't rape any girl, Lena. It was consensual! Okay! I know it was wrong, but if anything, *she* seduced *me*!" She's looking at me as if I'm some sort of mad man. "Have you read 'Lolita'?" I ask. She shakes her head, her eyes still fixed on me, terrified. "Well, it was like that," I say. "Except I didn't do anything wrong. Not like Humbert. I mean, like where he meant to drug Lolita. Well it was nothing like that. There were no drugs."

And then I realise that if she hasn't read the book, the comparison is meaningless. I can see another "Hellllp!" welling up inside her, so I move to thwart it.

"Look, Lena, *you* know *me*!" Her head nods up and down like a jackhammer. "Good heavens! We've known each other for what? more than fifty years!" More nodding. "Do you really think I'd *kill* someone?" She nods again, and then, guessing that this may not be the right answer, begins to rotate her head uncertainly. "There's nothing to be afraid of, Lena!"

She seems to be calming down. She has backed away from me until she's reached the arm of a large sofa and, unable to back any further, has semi-seated herself on it, one leg raised from the floor. Backing away from me, she has stepped out of the scuffs she was wearing, and she is now barefooted.

"Wh-why are you here?" she asks. Still the faintest of burrs to her voice, and I'm in love all over again.

"For you!" I say, and see the fear start in her eyes again, as she lurches upright. "No! No! I mean, I'm here to *see* you." A slight relaxing. She edges back onto the arm of the sofa.

"But – but the woman in Christchurch..."

"She was my neighbour, Lena. A coincidence! I don't know how she died! I didn't even know the police were looking for me until you mentioned it!"

"They – they said there was another woman. A prostitute or something."

"Honestly, I've no idea! Do I look like the sort of man who'd have dealings with a prostitute?" She shakes her head. "How's your little boy?" I ask, trying to get her off the subject.

"He – he's not little any more. He's thirty-five now. He's a doctor."

"Good heavens! Tempus fugit! Doesn't time fly?" She nods. I move slowly towards her, and she tenses again, so I stop. "You know, I never had any children. One of my great regrets, I suppose. It just never seemed to work between Eve and me. Temperamentally unsuited, you might say. I envy you though, having the comfort of a child as you age. It must be a wonderful thing!"

Her eyes soften at the thought of the child.

"Tell me about him," I say, sitting on the arm at the other end, so that we are separated by a sofa. "What sort of doctor is he?"

"A surgeon. Cardio-thoracic."

"Wonderful! Does he have any children of his own?" She nods.

"Two."

"So, you're a grandmother!" A simple inclination of the head. "How wonderful! How old are they?"

"A girl of six and a boy of two. They don't live near here!" she bursts out defensively, as if I may wish to harm them.

"How sad. So you don't get to see them much?" She seems disinclined to answer, so I go on. "You know, Lena, you know how old *you* were when I first saw you?" A shake of the head. "You were thirteen! Do you remember that day?" Another shake. "I do. It was the day I fell in love with you." I'm beaming at her, but I can see the primal fear rising again. "It's nothing to be afraid of, Lena.

I've always loved you, and I suspect perhaps, if things had been different, you might have loved me, too."

No response. We brood awkwardly on that memory, that possibility for a moment. A grandfather clock slowly ticks its seconds away in a corner of the room where time is moving more slowly, and then suddenly erupts into a startling chime. Five-thirty.

"Do you remember what you were wearing that day?" The shake of the head again. "A shawl. A white shawl. It was patched. I remember, you shrugged, and it fell from your shoulder." Her thoughts have turned inward, searching for that moment. "You made that patched shawl seem like the cloths of heaven!"

She muses on this, now seemingly lost in the memory, then suddenly:

"Why are you *here*?"

"I've said, Lena: because I love you! And I honestly believe you can love me too. If you'll just open yourself up to me, Lena!" She shakes her head violently.

"I'm on my own now," she says. "I've made my own life since... since..."

"Yes," I say, "Yes, I know your life has not been easy. But honestly, Lena, I can help."

"I'm happy on my own," she says resolutely.

"If you could just give this a try. I'd thought we could have a meal together. Get to know each other. I mean, we've never really got to know each other, have we?"

"No," she says, definite again. "I don't want to get to know you, Bruce. You need to go!" She stands, and goes to move towards the door.

"I can't do that, Lena," I say. "I'm committed to this. I'm committed to you! Honestly, if you'll just give this a chance!"

I've moved between her and the front door, and we're standing eye to eye. We stand like that for several seconds, and then suddenly she turns and bolts through the kitchen, towards a side door. She has a head start on me, and by the time I reach her, clutch at the sweat shirt she's wearing, we tumble onto the island bench in the kitchen. She's had the kitchen remodelled since I was last there. It's been done out in timber, a marble bench top, with stainless steel appliances. Too pretentious for Rags, I feel. Something more cottagey would have suited her.

As we fall towards the bench, she turns to confront me, and I tumble on top of her. She's arched back over the bench, and a savageness comes into her eyes that I would have thought her incapable of.

"Lena..." I say, and then I can resist no longer. I press my lips to hers with the pent-up passion of half a century.

She rips her head sideways, and begins to struggle against my weight. I press her shoulders against the bench, and go to kiss her again, to persuade her. It is only from the corner of my eye that I see her hand flail towards the knife block, grope, and seize a handle. What she produces is a smallish utility knife, with a blade of perhaps no more than fifteen centimetres: hardly a weapon. I hold her arm to the bench, and try to reason with her.

"Lena; this is silly! It doesn't have to be like this!"

Her knee to my groin catches me unawares, and the pain is a perfect thing that spreads through my body. I sag to the floor, and she stands above me, the knife still in her hand.

"Lena..." I groan from the floor.

She spins on one bare foot and makes for the door. I seize her ankle, and she turns again, kicking at me with her free foot. Slowly I pull myself up on her, still weakened by the pain. She turns in my grip, and again tries to bolt for the door. I throw myself at her in a desperate tackle, and we tumble forward to the tiled floor, again, me on top of her, she face-down. We both remain motionless, as I pin her with my weight.

"Lena," I try again. "Let's just talk!" She is silent, no longer struggling against me. "Lena," I start, and take my weight from her. The grandfather clock begins its slow, solemn chime. Six o'clock. Somewhere we missed five forty-five. "Lena..."

And lying there, I begin to softly talk to her; and now she listens. I know I've been inattentive to her, I say, over all these years. It's like Heathcliff and Cathy, I say. My love for her had made me bitter. But that's all in the past. I am Dante, I say, and she is my Beatrice. I draw her into my arms, kiss her face, and she no longer objects.

The light from outside turns to gold, and the old clock chimes away the hours, and still we lie there, and in my heart I feel a welling of goodness, and I know I have done right.

Chapter 38

Are we happy, Lena and I? Define "happy". We are not ecstatic; we are not elated. But we are contented. Fulfilled, I would say. I can sense it in the new serenity to Rags. She was never one of those boisterous girls; but now there is a calmness, a centre to her, and I know I have given her that. We hardly need to venture out. We are happy to stay in, eat alone. We talk, and she likes to watch the odd programme on the television, and although I've never liked the blasted thing, I do it for her sake.

"See how lucky we were!" I said to her recently.

There'd been a news item about this woman named Jones. There'd been an intruder, apparently. The neighbours reported that they hadn't seen her for several days, and when the police broke in they found this bloke, this intruder, cradling her body. There'd been some sort of struggle, and she'd fallen on a knife; terrible tragedy. She'd been dead for several days by that stage, but this fellow, he was determined she was alive. Refused to give her up. Threatened the police – it took several of them to pull him away from her.

It takes all sorts, doesn't it? And as I said to Lena, it could so easily have been her, living alone like that.

But now – now she was safe with me.

<u>Acknowledgments</u>

As always, family and friends bear the brunt of any creative enterprise, and I am deeply indebted to my wife, Marie, for her careful reading of early drafts of the text, and for reining Bruce Campbell in when he threatened to exceed all reasonable boundaries of good taste.

And as with my previous works, Chris Winstanley has again produced an excellent, and this time provocative, cover design.

My friend and mentor Kaite Hansen passed away before this work could be published, but did provide encouragement in its formative stages, for which I am grateful.

I have not made an in-depth study of psychopathy in researching this work, because it is intended as a work of fiction. Apart from what may have stuck from Psychology 101, and information freely available on the internet, I have made reference only to Robert Hare's *Without Conscience: the Disturbing World of the Psychopaths Among Us*, and a now somewhat dated work, Hervey M. Cleckley's *The Mask of Sanity*.

Apart from that, I must acknowledge the rich tradition of evil in English literature, from *Beowulf* on. Indeed, so compelling is it that it is impossible to imagine that, without evil, art in any form would exist. Even in its absence, its very shadow emphasises its opposite.

<u>About the Author</u>

Rob McFarland lives on Banks Peninsula, with his wife, their Labrador, and other assorted wildlife. They are currently working on rebuilding an earthquake-damaged home.

His other published works are *Salt of the Earth*, which was also adapted as a ten-part radio production by Radio New Zealand, and produced by Prue Langbein, and *The Rime of the Venal Insurer*, a satirical narrative poem based on Coleridge's *Rime of the Ancient Mariner*.

He is currently working on a soon-to-be-published novel, *Money to Burn*.

Made in the USA
Lexington, KY
28 November 2014